"I've been warned what will happen if I step over the line. I could lose my job over this, Teddi, but I have no choice."

I pull off my sweater silently. If Drew wants to forget about his partner's arrest—for now—I know how to help him.

"But that's not what this weekend's about," he says, waving the conversation away like so many cobwebs. "I'm trying to set a mood here, if you haven't noticed."

I toss the sweater in his direction. "I've noticed."

The fire catches, he turns around and there's a moment, just a moment, with the fire flickering wildly behind him, the wind howling outside, the depth of feeling shining in his eyes, that I want to freeze everything, stay in this place in time a bit longer, long enough to keep it with me always.

But Drew has other things in mind, and his name is _____ sed the room and I'm

D1052337

Stevi Mittman

Stevi Mittman has always been a decorator at heart. When she was little, she cut the butterflies from her wallpaper and let them fly off the walls onto her ceiling and across her window shades. She remembers doing an entire bathroom in black-and-white houndstooth patent-leather contact paper and putting strips of trim on her cupboards. The Teddi Bayer murder mysteries have allowed her to combine her love of writing and her passion for decorating, and she couldn't be happier. As a fictional decorator she doles out advice on Teddi's Web site, TipsFromTeddi.com, and receives and responds to e-mails on behalf of Teddi. Decorating is a third career for the prolific Mittman, who is also a stained-glass artist with work in the Museum of the City of New York and private commissions around the country and, of course, an award-winning author.

In her spare time (you must be kidding) she also makes jewelry and indulges in gourmet cooking. Visit her at www.stevimittman.com.

For those of you who are putting any TipsFromTeddi.com advice to use, please e-mail her your successes and failures at Teddi@TipsFromTeddi.com, and be sure to visit Teddi's Web site, www.TipsFromTeddi.com, for more murder, mayhem and sage advice on decorating!

THE Next NOVEL™

WHO CREAMED
PEACHES,
ANYWAY?

Stevi Mittman

WHO CREAMED PEACHES, ANYWAY?

copyright © 2008 by Stephanie Mittman

isbn-13:978-0-373-88150-5

isbn-10:   0-373-88150-9

All rights reserved. Except for use in any review, the reproduction
or utilization of this work in whole or in part in any form by any
electronic, mechanical or other means, now known or hereafter
invented, including xerography, photocopying and recording, or in
any information storage or retrieval system, is forbidden without the
written permission of the publisher, Harlequin Enterprises Limited,
225 Duncan Mill Road, Don Mills, Ontario, Canada M3B 3K9.

This is a work of fiction. Names, characters, places and incidents are
either the product of the author's imagination or are used fictitiously,
and any resemblance to actual persons, living or dead, business
establishments, events or locales is entirely coincidental.

This edition published by arrangement with Harlequin Books S.A.

® and TM are trademarks of the publisher. Trademarks indicated with
® are registered in the United States Patent and Trademark Office, the
Canadian Trade Marks Office and in other countries.

TheNextNovel.com

 HARLEQUIN®

PRINTED IN U.S.A.

If you purchased this book without a cover you should be aware that
this book is stolen property. It was reported as "unsold and destroyed" to
the publisher, and neither the author nor the publisher has received any
payment for this "stripped book."

From the Author

Dear Reader,

After seven Teddi Bayer books and three online reads, what can I tell you that you don't already know?

How much fun it is to write this series? I bet you know that just from reading it.

How about just how much of the stories are based on my real life? For example, Jesse's friend Danny was my real son Asa's best friend throughout school. The two of them built guitars and forts and hid in our attic watching old home movies. Purple isn't only Dana's favorite color—it's also my daughter Arika's. The story about where babies come from came straight out of my own children's mouths.

Most of the nice things Drew does?

My wonderful husband did them first.

Teddi's best friend Bobbie? Loosely based on my friend Sherry.

Only June and Marty don't spring from my world. My parents were too wonderful to make for an interesting story!

Teddi's house mirrors our Syosset house—all hunter-green and salmon, with lots of sun streaming in. Bobbie's house mirrors my present house.

I don't know if I'm part Teddi or she's part me, but I know that my heart is in every book I write about her.

Welcome to my world!

Love,

Stevi

This book is dedicated to my wonderful husband, Alan, who is the inspiration for every hero I've ever written. He has read each word of this and every book I've written, dotted my i's and crossed my t's. He's made dinner when the writing is going well and sympathetic noises when it isn't. He told me it was wonderful when I needed encouragement and told me what was wrong with it when I wanted the truth. I know I couldn't write about love without him.

CHAPTER 1

Setting the mood in your house is more than just a matter of furniture. Lighting and music can change your room from calm to wild, from funereal to party-ready. Baking bread says "come on in."

TipsFromTeddi.com

The parking lot outside L. I. Lanes, the bowling alley I just finished redecorating, is dark and cold. It's almost midnight and a couple of the streetlights are blinking furiously, trying to illuminate the parking area, but they aren't up to the job. As far as I can tell, there's no moon and no stars. Inside, there's a party going on to celebrate the "Grand Reopening" and the music is loud. It's cold, I'm tired, and I should just take my bow and, basking in the kudos, go home and crawl into my bed.

Only, there was this phone call…

Which is why I've raced out here to the icy parking lot after my on again/off again boyfriend, Homicide Detective Drew Scoones, wearing ridiculously high heels that only an idiot or a hooker would wear in this weather. I must have been crazy letting my thirteen-year-old daughter, Dana, doll me up for this party so that Drew would realize how hot I am, so that he'd say, "Teddi, I want you and I'll accept you on your terms." These include not pressuring me into a second marriage mistake, accepting that my children have to come first, and forgiving me the mother from hell.

That's what I'd like him to say. Only what he actually says is, "Damn it, Teddi! Let go of the car." He's using his I-am-the-police-and-you-must-obey-the-law voice. He should know better, but it looks like he expects me to just let go of the door handle and back away. This, even though the phone call I heard was from Hal Nelson, Drew's partner, calling about someone named Peaches Lipschitz possibly being murdered.

Sounds juicy, no? The phone call, I mean. Not Peaches.

Except for the couple of times when he thought he was rescuing me from the very jaws of death, I've never seen Drew so rattled. Rattled enough, I think, to actually pull out of the parking lot with me hanging on to the door handle of his little blue Mazda RX7 as he goes.

Discretion being the better part of valor, I let go. Heck, I've got the keys to my own car in my pocket and how hard can it be to just follow Drew to this Peaches' place? As dark as it is, I'm pretty confident I can tail him without being noticed.

After all, I've learned from a master.

Him.

Maybe if it hadn't sounded like Peaches was dead. Or maybe if it wasn't that Hal—who I dislike intensely—appears to be involved. Then I could just let him go, do his job and hear the details later. I mean, having redecorated the whole bowling alley cum billiards parlor, I wouldn't mind hanging around for a few compliments.

Only, the thing is, I've gotten pretty good at this detective stuff and if I've learned anything from my close association with Detective Drew Scoones—besides where my own G-spot is hidden—it's that the first twenty-four hours after a murder are crucial to solving the case. It's that 24/24 rule that Drew is always talking about—the last twenty-four hours the victim was alive and the first twenty-four after she's been killed.

And I'm not missing out.

Maybe Drew is right. Maybe I *am* becoming a homicide junkie. But examining my psyche while trying to tail Drew like a pro is probably not the best idea I've ever had. And, trust me on this, I've had some other *not best* ideas in my time. And my time starts way before my first client died and I met Drew. All the way back to Husband Number One. Now there was a really, really *not best* idea.

Anyway, thirty minutes and a trip down motive lane later, Drew pulls into the driveway of a well-kept, two-story split-level in a nice neighborhood in New Hyde Park. I'm a half block behind him. I figure that's a safe enough distance for me to stop. I pull over to the curb and cut my engine. Drew gets out of his car and sends a glare in my direction which says that I didn't fool him for a second but that he doesn't have time to argue with me.

Despite the dark and the fact that he's the length of an entire Costco aisle away from me, I can still see his frown. I could be on the other side of Long Island and still see that frown, I know it so well.

I start to open my door, but he shakes his head. Nodding, I put my hands up in mock surrender, gesturing *no argument here*. Hey, if the man is gullible enough to believe I'm staying in the car, is that my problem? I mean, our relationship goes back three years now, and if he hasn't learned more than how to start my engines, he doesn't deserve to be driving my car, if you get my drift.

I lose sight of him as he heads up the front walk, my vision blocked by evergreens, the contours of the house and the darkness of night. I let myself out of my car, closing the door behind me. I do this as soundlessly as a six-year-old car will allow, which means that there is a bit of creaking. Actually, that may be my knees, since I've lowered myself behind my car just in case he steps back for a second look.

"Tire trouble?" a man's voice asks, and I jump, gasping like whoever murdered Peaches is out to get me.

Which, since I'm outside her house, is not beyond the realm of possibility.

"Didn't mean to startle you," he says, crouching next to me and studying my tire before assuring me that it looks all right to him.

By now, I'm standing up and stomping to keep warm, trying to look like I'm more than capable of taking care of myself and anyone else who comes along. I make up something about how the tire was kind of thumping, but that he is absolutely right—it does look fine. I run my hands down my clothes to neaten them and realize I'm still in the Hooker Barbie getup for the "Grand Reopening" celebration party back at the bowling alley—the same clothes my mother said made me look like a hooker housewife.

She'd said it in front of Drew just before he got the call from his partner, and he'd laughed. Then, after the call, he'd said something to the effect of *I don't know how you Bayers do it. A housewife hooker. Isn't that what your mother just said?*

If I was the type who put two and two together, which I am, I might put that comment and Peaches Lipschitz in the same sentence, and you know what I'd get?

Could Peaches Lipschitz be a hooker housewife? Or, make that *could she have been?*

The man beside me comes slowly to his feet, taking in every inch of me as he rises.

"You must be cold," he says, staring at me like I'm wearing even less than I am. "You, uh…?" He gestures toward the house in front of which I'm parked.

With as much dignity as I can muster, I tell him that I was actually going down the block, and I point my chin toward Peaches' house. The man smiles broadly. Too broadly, showing too many teeth of the better-to-eat-you-with-my-dear variety. "Let me walk you there," he says. "I happen to be—"

Instinct takes over. Some desire to protect Drew, if not Hal. To protect the integrity of the investigation… Oh, I *love* how that sounds. I decide that's exactly what I'm doing when I say, "Look, you seem like a nice man. Take my advice and go home to your wife." I'm protecting the integrity of the investigation.

The man stiffens, but his grip on my elbow doesn't loosen. He tells me he isn't married.

"Yeah," I say sarcastically. "And I'm not vice." I swear it just rolls off my tongue.

"No kidding," the man says, his hold on my elbow now painful. "I knew that right off. Wanna know how I knew?"

Sadly, I have an inkling. It's confirmed when he pulls out his badge and identifies himself. That happens just before he starts talking about arresting me.

"First off, *Officer*," I say, and I give that word all the contempt I can muster, "I in no way solicited you. In fact, I did quite the opposite, if you recall."

"Your outfit did the talking for you," he says.

Once more I think about killing Dana for dressing me up to make Drew jealous. But to do that I'll have to get out of this mess and get home. "Secondly, I'm here with Detective Scoones on police business and—"

"Scoones is here?" he asks, clearly taken aback. "What the hell is Scoones doing here? Besides screwing up my bust."

"So then Peaches really was one of those housewife hookers?" I ask as I ease my arm out of his grasp.

"*Was?*" he says, and I see his face go pale in the streetlight. "Whaddya mean *was?*"

IT SEEMS TO BE my lot in life to stand in kitchens with dead women at my feet and Drew Scoones staring at me like it's somehow my fault. The vice cop who escorted me into the house has the same look on his face, only he's directing it at Hal Nelson, who is nervously jiggling the change in his pocket and shooting eye darts at Drew.

In an effort not to make eye contact with, well, *anyone*, I study the kitchen. After all, kitchen redos are my bread and butter. Decorating is what I do for a living. I have to say that if Peaches Lipschitz really was a hooker, she had a great cover going in this house. There are no whips, no chains, no red velvet curtains or leather club chairs. In fact, rather than a bordello, I feel like I've fallen down the rabbit hole and wound up in Ozzie and Harriet's kitchen. I expect Ward Cleaver to come up the den stairs at any moment, asking where the *Beav* is.

"You know how long this operation has been going on?" *Vice Cop* asks Hal, who doesn't answer him. "Eight months. Eight months down the drain. What the hell was Homicide doing here, anyway? I didn't hear any call."

Hal looks at Drew. Drew looks at the floor. And it dawns on me and *Vice Cop* at the same time that Hal wasn't here in his official capacity. No one says a word. In the distance I swear I can hear Shelley Fabares singing "Johnny Angel." We're all so silent I can hear what sound like skips on an old LP.

Everyone's eyes dart around, each of us taking in the details while they bandy about things like TOD, which I take to mean time of death (approximately 10:00 p.m.); COD—cause of death (GSW, or gunshot wound); trajectory of bullet (straight and up close), etc. Drew is, not surprisingly, studying the blood spatters, though they will call in an expert. *Vice Cop* is staring at the curvaceous body on the floor—hopefully to determine the cause of death. Hal is blinking hard and keeping one eye on the front door.

And me? I'm carefully avoiding looking at Peaches Lipschitz, the hole in the back of her shirtwaist dress and the blood puddle oozing out from beneath her. Instead, I'm marveling at her Formica counters with the boomerang pattern, wondering where on earth she found the stuff, if it's genuine or repro. I'm noticing that her refrigerator is an old-fashioned separate-freezer-door-on-top one, with notes stuck on it that say things like "Remember to bake a banana cream pie for the weekend" and "I love my man, I love my life."

Shouldn't that be plural?

There's a newspaper folded in thirds on the counter the way a man might read it while riding the subway. I can see part of an article about the D.A.'s hopeless bid for reelection. One of the kitchen chairs has a banner that says King of the Castle. Next to it is a pair of men's slippers.

In the dining room the table is set for breakfast. There's a Betty Crocker mix on the counter, and I can smell the coffee in the coffeemaker.

And I'm thinking how wrong it is to be taking in decorating details when a woman is dead not ten feet from me.

And that's about when it hits me. The woman in the eyelet-trimmed cobbler's apron is somebody's wife. Maybe even somebody's mother. I think I sway a little. That or the room tilts. Someone swings a chair around and plants me in it. I expect a nasty crack from Hal about how at this point I usually throw up, but none is forthcoming.

"I told you not to come in," Drew says while *Vice Cop* pulls out his cell phone. "I'll call it in," Drew barks at him.

But *Vice Cop* shakes his head. "You had plenty of time," he says. And then we all listen as he reports the homicide and the fact that Detectives Nelson and Scoones found the body.

"Just Nelson," Hal corrects and I start to corroborate his story. I was, I tell him, with Drew when he got the call from Hal. *Vice Cop* isn't impressed, and Drew instructs me to go on home, take a hot bath and get into bed.

"I don't think so," *Vice Cop* says, and I agree, reiterating the fact that, after all, I'm Drew's alibi. Only Drew says *Vice Cop* isn't thinking about what to charge *him* with, and I remember how I'm dressed.

"I was at a party," I say. "At L. I. Lanes." And I start going over all the sordid details until the guy tells me to save it for the homicide squad.

I remind him that I am standing with two members of the homicide squad, to which he mumbles something on the order of *not for long.*

Drew says I wasn't involved and that I am leaving and that if *Vice Cop* doesn't like it he can lump it. Okay, he doesn't say that he *can lump it,* but I'm too embarrassed to say what he actually told *Vice Cop* to do. Suffice it to say that *Vice Cop* would have had to arrest himself if he did.

In the end, I wind up leaving, shouting over my shoulder that Drew was with me all evening just as two other homicide detectives show up along with some uniforms. I realize I should probably stop saying that, dressed as I am and walking out a hooker housewife's door.

Drew calls my name and I stop and turn. He tosses his coat to me gallantly. I don't know if he's worried I'll catch a cold or catch something else.

I slip into the jacket as I hurry to the car, a cat whistle or two following me as I go. I push my hands into Drew's pockets and feel a slip of paper in one.

Once I'm in the car, I take out the paper and turn on the dome light. "Keep your mouth shut, Teddi. *Please.*"

He's underlined please three times.

At least he's asked me nicely.

NOT AS NICELY, however, as Captain Schultz has asked me to open my mouth and spill my guts the following morning. And then there is the whole authority thing of being in the police station, in the Captain's office, his shield staring up at me while a clerk takes down my statement.

"Again, the reason you were at the crime scene?" he asks me.

I have to admit I followed Drew.

"And again, the reason you were dressed as…in…?" he asks, fumbling for a way to describe my hooker outfit, which is apparently detailed in the report on his desk.

I tell him about the party, about Dana trying to help me capture Drew's attention, about how surprising that is, in light of her desire for me to get back with her father. Basically, I tell him anything that pops into my head which has nothing to do with the case against Hal Nelson.

He asks me to describe in detail everything I saw at the scene.

I remind him I'm a decorator, and ask if he's sure he wants all that detail. And then I proceed to tell him name brands, color choices, guessing at paint brands and suggesting better choices Peaches could have made, discussing the quality of her furniture, estimating the age and the cost until the man's eyes nearly cross with boredom.

Drew is pacing outside the office, and I know that the longer I'm in here, the more sure he is that I've given away state secrets.

The Captain asks me if I noticed anything that might not have belonged there. "With your keen eye for detail, you may have seen something the murderer left behind that the officers might not have noticed."

I notice that he refers to "the murderer" and the possibility that it wasn't Hal, and I remark on it.

He tells me he is just being thorough, but that there's no evidence that anyone other than Hal had been in the house last night.

"Except, of course, that Peaches was murdered and that Hal didn't do it," I reply.

"Perhaps not," he says as he comes to a stand and reaches out to shake my hand, "but I wouldn't be too hopeful if I were you."

I smile, resist saying that there's always hope, and reach for my jacket.

"You be sure to call me if you think of anything at all that might help Detective Nelson," he tells me, adding that he's overseeing the case himself. "Nelson has a few enemies on the force and I want to be sure he gets a fair shake."

CHAPTER 2

*The role of the kitchen hasn't changed much over the years.
Not merely a place to prepare food or eat in, it's the heart of
the house. Important conversations happen in the kitchen.*

TipsFromTeddi.com

A week later, my mother, my neighbor and business partner,
Bobbie Lyons and I are all gathered in my kitchen, as per usual.
Well, the addition of my mother isn't usual, but then, neither
is my mother. We are drinking coffee and picking at a chocolate *babka* without actually cutting slices and putting them on
our plates. That way we don't get any of the calories.

And we are staring at the headline in *Newsday*, which reads
Hal Gets Hooked for Hacking Hooker Housewife. Below it is
a picture of Detective Harold Nelson, big enough to count the
hairs in his nostrils. I haven't gone soft on Hal, but it does seem
to me that there's been quite a rush to judgment here and the
fact that Hal is a cop is the only explanation I can come up
with. Unless you count the fact that the D.A. is running for
reelection on a less-than-stellar record and could use a high-
profile case to push him over the top.

The night of the murder I got a call from Drew telling me

to be completely honest about being with him when he got Hal's phone call, should someone from the precinct call for a statement. It seemed to me he was being extremely specific regarding what I should be honest about. A kind of *depends what the meaning of "is" is* sort of thing. At any rate, I gave my statement down at the precinct about being with Drew when Hal's call came in. Since then Drew's called once to see if I was okay after seeing yet another dead body, and then once more to say he'd call when he could. And that was it until this morning when he left a cryptic message about calling me later to talk to me off the record. He is supposed to call at two, before my three kids get home from school. This has, naturally, raised my curiosity level up to the *barely bearable*.

At least I can take solace in the fact that it appears he's in the clear, since there was no mention of him in the paper.

My mother, who has said ten times this morning how you can judge a man by the company he keeps, is poking Hal's picture with her freshly French-manicured nail.

"Did I tell you?" she asks. "Or did I not tell you?"

This is a rhetorical question which none of us answers, because, a) she never told us any such thing, and b) if she did, it was lost in the mountain of criticism she hurls in my general direction anyway.

"Teddi, you are well rid of the lot of them," my mother says while I pour us each another cup of coffee and refuse to rise to the bait. "They are so right about judging a man by the company he keeps." This makes at least a dozen times, and it's getting harder and harder to keep my mouth shut and not remind her that my last client was a good friend of hers and *he* turned out to be a murderer.

Instead I just sigh, shake my head and say, "Peaches Lipschitz. A hooker housewife. Can you believe it?" as if I knew her, as if our relationship went deeper than seeing her dead body.

The idea fascinates both Bobbie and me. We've talked about little else since *Newsday* did their two-page spread on Peaches' husband and kids and "Mom's" exploits while the kids were out at T-ball or visiting with their grandparents in Florida. It seems that the house Peaches was found in, which looked like it was blown in from Stepford by a tornado, was strictly used for a brothel. She actually lived with her husband and kids a few towns away. She'd gone to great pains to make it look as though your average American family—albeit circa 1950— lived there, down to the daily newspaper delivery and occasional bike in the driveway. Peaches spent several days a week there, smiling at the neighbors and waving to them. The story was that she was a divorcée and her husband had custody of the kids.

Well, now he does.

"You read about them," Bobbie says. "You hear about them. I once saw a TV movie on Lifetime about one…"

"But you just never believe they exist—" I start to say, only to have my mother interrupt me.

"Oh, grow up," she says and pulls out a cigarette from a leather pouch she's placed on my Emerald-Isle granite kitchen counter, custom-made for someone else's kitchen where, happily, it didn't fit. Just one of the benefits of being a designer whose sources stand behind their products. Mom puts the cigarette at the edge of her mouth—unlit—because she is not allowed to smoke in my house. "It happens all the time. There was a woman in our neighborhood when you were growing up—"

"Who?" I ask, all ears now to find out whose mother was turning tricks while we were hopscotching at the park. Okay, so we were necking, not hopscotching. At least we weren't charging for it. But Mom is busy poking out Hal's eye with her nail and hoping that Drew gets indicted next.

"I don't get what he was doing with a hooker. Didn't you tell me that he and his wife, what's-her-name, were like the couple of the year or something?" Bobbie asks, gesturing toward the paper, where Hal is nestled up against Peaches Lipschitz.

Uh, that is, against a *picture* of Peaches Lipschitz.

I explain that Hal and Hallie, if you can believe that, were united only in their utter disdain for me.

When I think about it, Hal Nelson and I didn't like each other from the day we met. Of course, that meeting wasn't under the best of circumstances. I'd just found my client dead on her newly installed terra-cotta tile kitchen floor, splayed there in only a Valentine's Day-type teddy from Victoria's Secret, and Hal and Drew were the detectives who showed up to investigate. Drew was intent on investigating me, while Hal was more interested in investigating the other *teddy* in the room. I couldn't keep my eyes off Drew. Hal couldn't keep his eyes off Elise Meyer's scantily clad body.

After seeing that, it's hard to imagine that Hal was interested in Peaches Lipschitz. You just never know, I guess. What

I do know is that it seems like whenever I see Hal there's a gun or a dead body lying around.

It's nearly two. I'm sure that Drew thought calling now would insure my being able to talk without the kids around. Good thought, but it didn't take into account the fact that my mother would be stitched to the bar stool in my kitchen, intent on telling Bobbie and me every last detail of Sydelle Silverberg's waterfront house and how we should pitch our interior design services to her now that she's called for an appointment.

"This could be your ticket," my mother is saying, removing the cigarette from her lips, tapping it on the counter and then using it as a pointer as she warns me. "That is, if you play your cards right. Not that you will."

I'd object, but then I'd have to hear about every opportunity I've ever blown, how my marriage was the biggest mistake of my life, how I had so much potential, and how many mistakes I've made just since breakfast—and I'd be dead ten years before she was even close to done.

"Anyone who is anyone goes to Sydelle's parties. Well-to-do clients you should be soliciting."

"Soliciting? You mean like Peaches Lipschitz?" I can't resist asking. "Soliciting didn't work out all that well for her, did it?"

My mother ignores my comment. "These are people who could get you where you want to go, Teddi," she says, slapping my hand when I reach for another piece of *babka*.

"Where is it you want to go?" Bobbie teases me as she takes a chunk of cake from the plate, breaks it in two and hands one half to me. "Jersey?"

Mom rolls her eyes. "Don't take my advice," she says sarcastically. "Screw up your life some more. Next you'll be telling me you're going to marry Spoonbreath."

"Not," Bobbie says, tapping her foot impatiently. She's annoyed that I'm not standing up to my mother. Let me tell you, if I could win this battle, I would fight it. But, like the best warriors in my son Jesse's movies, I've learned to choose my battles and only fight those I have a chance of winning.

"And speaking of screwing," she says, jabbing with her fingernail at the newspaper until Hal loses his other eye and is left blinded on my kitchen counter, "you'd be smart to stop that business right now, young lady. Before your name gets dragged through the mud along with his."

Now it's my turn to ignore her, which drives Bobbie crazy. Actually, everyone in my kitchen, with the possible exception of Maggie May, the dog I stole after her owner was murdered, is crazy. The telephone rings and Maggie jumps up onto her hind legs and does her *It's for me! It's for me!* dance. Okay, so the four of us are all crazy.

My mother manages to get the phone before I can and tells Drew that I don't want to talk to him. As I take it away from her I hear him say that'll be fine with him. He just wants me to listen.

"I haven't heard from you in days," I say. My mother exchanges a glance with Bobbie, a look that asks, *And this is a problem because…?*

Bobbie shrugs and I turn my back on both of them.

"I know, I know. I'm sorry. I've been busy," he says. I can tell he's in the squad room. There's chatter around him and someone keeps shushing someone else. "I can't really talk now, either."

I tell him I can well imagine how busy he's been. I tell him I bet the whole department's been busy trying to clear Hal.

"Yeah, well, not exactly," he says cryptically.

I ask what it's going to take to clear Hal of these charges, and my mother harumphs. At the same time, both he and she say, "A miracle."

"Well, we've worked miracles before," I say, though I'm not sure which of them I'm telling. My mother rolls her eyes. On Drew's end of the line there's silence. "Drew?"

"The sentiment around here is that if it looks like a dunker and smells like a dunker there's no chance it's something else." I'd ask what he means, but his bitter tone tells me he's not in the mood for small talk. So I take it he means it's a slam dunk— easy to prove, tough to beat.

I tell him, "I was thinking—"

Behind me both Bobbie and my mother sigh exaggeratedly. Suddenly they're best buddies, allies in the war to stop Teddi from making another mistake.

"Do me a favor," he says. He sounds tired, weary. "Don't. I've been ordered by the top to just stay out of it. The Captain's taking charge of the investigation and I'm off it."

I try to argue and he tells me—no, he *announces*—that he really doesn't want to talk about it. That he's accepted the edict and he's got other things on his plate. I get the distinct impression that he's not actually talking to me so much as putting on a show for the rest of the guys.

"So how's your day going?" he asks me, clearly trying to change the subject. I remind him that my mother is parked in my kitchen, so he can guess at what kind of day I've had.

"I'm not deaf," my mother says, hands on her hips.

"No, but I can dream, can't I?" I ask her and Bobbie tries very hard not to laugh out loud.

"Listen, I've been thinking…" he says, and there's that note in his voice that warns me that what he's been thinking about is *us*.

Do me a favor, I want to say, *don't*.

Seems we're both safer when we keep our thoughts to ourselves.

I remind him that my mother and Bobbie are both present. I don't have to remind him that neither are fans.

"What do you say we go away this weekend?" he asks. There's a false note of brightness in his voice. "What about your friend Carmine's house in the Hamptons? No one around and we can watch the ocean from inside that cozy room you decorated so great."

Okay, I realize this sounds like my dream invitation, especially when he says that he'll pay for a sitter if Bobbie or my parents won't look after the kids. But there's something fishy about it, don't you think? Hal's arrested for murder and he wants to go watch the ocean? I don't think so.

"Or if you don't want to leave them, we could take the kids with us. Snowmen on the beach. Wieners roasting in the fireplace. You, me, a king-size bed."

Since I'm wide awake this clearly isn't a dream. Which means that something is definitely wrong here.

"Am I in danger?" I ask him. "Do you need to get me out of town? The kids?"

He laughs that Drew laugh, that low one that sounds like I

amuse him immensely. "You're too much," he says, and I can picture him smiling a sad little smile against his will.

"Okay, are *you* in danger, then?"

He lowers his voice and says, "Yeah. Maybe." Then, apparently for the crowd, he follows that with, "Am I in danger? Yeah. Of falling head-over-heels in love, Teddi Bayer. And I may just sweep you away with me." I hear whistles and hoots and a muffled plea to shut the you-know-what up.

My mother is demanding to know what he wants. Bobbie is eyeing me with suspicion.

"So? Will you come away with me?" he asks. "Or are you going to make me go alone?"

"You'd go away without me?" I ask.

My mother has no idea where, but she assures me that of course he would. Bobbie, on the other hand, wants to know if it's someplace warm, and if she can go in my place.

"Sun? Surf?" she says. "I'm there."

Drew reminds me that a partner is like a spouse and losing one is like breaking up a marriage. "It's like I'm getting divorced," he says. "Who better to see me through this than you?"

I agree to go with him, and assure him that either Bobbie or my parents will watch the kids.

And now all I have to do is get one of them to agree.

THE SKY IS GRAY. So is my mood. The surf is pounding. So is my head. The street outside the cottage, where I learned last summer that Carmine and my mother conducted a torrid affair forty years ago, is deserted.

So am I.

Well, not completely deserted. I think there's some rodent in the bedroom. There's a sign hanging on the door telling me not to open it under any circumstances upon danger of being bitten. "Remember last summer," it says, and it's signed Drew. Just *Drew*, not *love, Drew*, not *I'll be right back*. Just *Drew*.

There's coffee brewing on the counter and an enormous bowl of M&M's next to it. Drew knows I have a weakness for them, but no one could eat that many in a weekend. Is he planning to hold me hostage here?

Until when?

And really, am I unwilling?

I've been here for hours, or so it feels. The thing about winter is that night starts at four o'clock, so by seven it feels like time to go to sleep. I try Drew on his cell phone and get his voice mail again, as I've gotten for the last two hours. I call the kids at home and get my father. I can't tell you how much better that is than getting my mother.

Unfortunately, he makes the mistake of using my name, as in, "Teddi! You get there okay? Everything—"

At which point my mother pulls the phone away from him. "It's a good thing I'm here," she tells me. "Your children were going to call in pizza for dinner. Dana doesn't have bad enough skin? She has to invite zits with an engraved invitation?"

I remind my mother that all thirteen-year-old girls have pimples. It goes with the territory. And they are all overly sensitive about them, so if she could just be a little more careful around Dana she might live until the end of the weekend.

"Speak for yourself, Teddi. I didn't have pizza and I didn't have pimples. I'm taking her to Dr. Silverstein on Monday. She's going to miss a social studies test, but I'm sure she can make it up. It was the only time he had open."

I tell her that Dana doesn't need the Island's top dermatologist, and certainly not if it means missing a test. I can't imagine how she managed to get Dana an appointment so quickly. "Are you giving her your appointment?" I ask her.

She tells me that's what a grandmother does. She foregoes her Botox injections in favor of her granddaughter's appalling skin condition. But, she reassures me, she's sure she'll convince him to take care of them both while she's there.

"As to Jesse," she starts, but I really don't want to hear it. In my head I'm humming Christmas carols, which has a doubly good effect. One, I drown her out. And, two, I enjoy the secret pleasure of knowing how aggravated she would be if she knew I wasn't exactly humming "Dreidel, Dreidel, Dreidel."

"You mark my words," she says. "Not that you will. You'll ignore me, the way you always do. And where did that get you, Teddi? Divorced. And without alimony at that."

The fact that I can and do support myself and my kids counts for nothing in her book.

"I don't know why the two of them can't be more like Alyssa," she tells me. "That child understands how life works."

That child is my mother's clone. So far I haven't been able to tease it, coax it or threaten it out of her. But I'll never stop trying.

My mother is railing about what a terrible example I am setting for my children, shacking up with some man I "hardly know" for the weekend. "Don't come crying to me when your daughter follows suit," she says. "Apples don't fall far from trees."

She may be right. She's spent a good portion of her life in South Winds Psychiatric Center and if I don't get off the phone with her in less than ten seconds, it's likely to be where I'll wind up.

Out the window I see Drew's sexy little Mazda RX7 pull up. "Your slutty daughter's sex partner just pulled up," I say. "I have to go find my whips and chains."

She's saying something about how I should never refer to myself as a slut—others might, but I shouldn't—when I hang up and rush to the front door, throwing it open and hurling myself into Drew's arms.

"This is a nice greeting," he says, trying to balance several bags and packages while being embraced by a drowning slut…uh, woman. "Just getting off the phone with your mother, I presume?"

I take two grocery bags from him and lead the way to the kitchen while he kicks the door shut behind him and follows me, remarking on how nice this is. *Nice* isn't a word that I'm used to hearing from Drew, and I turn to make sure this is the hard-boiled homicide detective I know.

Sure looks like him, but when I reach in to unload the groceries he's brought, he shoos me out of the kitchen, telling me he's got surprises in the bags and he wants me out of the way. "Go light some candles or something," he says. "Don't you know how to get romantic?"

I pull my sweater up and flash him a quick glimpse at my

lacy black bra. "A preview," I say. "But first I want to ask you about Hal's case."

He shakes his head and waves a bottle of champagne at me. "Find some glasses."

"I was thinking about that night, and did you notice—you must have noticed—that he had blood on his knee? I mean, there was no blood on his clothing except for his right knee, like he'd found her and kneeled beside her, not like he shot her."

Drew pulls two wineglasses triumphantly from the cabinet above the stove. "Glasses," he announces, like a)I can't see that's what they are, and b)I haven't said a word about his partner.

"And did you notice the way he kept looking at the door? Like he expected someone to show up? If he had a date with her for sex, he wouldn't expect someone else to come in, would he?" I think for a moment. "Or would he?"

Drew's look is wilting. Okay, so Hal wouldn't be expecting a ménage à trois. I didn't think so. Not really.

He's rummaging in drawers and muttering about a corkscrew. I remind him that champagne doesn't work that way. "Right," he says. "Right."

He seems nervous, which makes me nervous. He hands me the bowl of M&M's and tells me to put it on the coffee table in front of the fireplace. He follows me with the champagne and glasses.

He's got the fire ready to go, and he's anxious to prove he's a one-match man. It takes four matches and two grocery bags to get it going.

And all the while I'm pointing out little things about that night at Peaches' place. "You knew about the Vice investigation, right?" I ask. "I mean, it was your precinct, and I saw the look that passed between you and Hal."

"Damn it!" he says, pissed that the fire doesn't want to catch and stay caught. "The logs must be damp. I bought them at the market in town. Maybe I should bring them back while they're still open."

While I'm a big movie buff, I've never seen *Invasion of the Body Snatchers*. That is, until now. "Drew? I know that this thing with Hal—"

"You're not going to let this go, are you?" he asks me. I shake my head. "Okay, here's the deal. There's no way Hal Nelson offed Peaches Lipschitz. Not in my book. You can't be a man's partner for six years and not know what makes him tick, what he's capable of. Only the Department has been ordered to—" he puts his fingers up to put quotation marks around the next phrase— "'play it by the book.' The Captain wants a conviction and he's perfectly happy to railroad Nelson right into the Pen."

"But you won't let him, right?" I ask. As I said, there's no love lost between me and Hal, but I think Drew's right, if only because I think he's a great judge of character. Hey, he likes me, right?

He admits it's going to be tricky. He's been specifically ordered to have nothing to do with the case. "*Too close to it* is the official word. I'm off the case under penalty of suspension."

"Well, won't the rest of the squad—" I start to say.

Drew says they won't. "You ever hear of the sacrificial

lamb?" Drew asks, as if I didn't spend the best days of my youth in Hebrew school.

"Why Hal?" I ask. I mean, it's not likely that he annoys everyone as much as he annoys me.

Drew says that Hal reported a popular officer to IAB a couple of years ago and a few cops were still actively holding a grudge. "It's been subtle, nothing you could prove, or even put your finger on, but it's been there all the same. Hal's paperwork gets lost, his evidence misfiled…"

"And the cop he fingered? Did he get convicted? Or charged, or whatever they do with bad cops?"

Drew doesn't look directly at me. The way he explains it, the cop was actually part of a cleanup sweep and only looked dirty. A lot of fellow officers felt that Hal should have known the guy was clean, even while he was playing it dirty.

I pretend I see what he's getting at.

"And, right now a sex scandal would be a gift from the gods. The brass could use it to show the Department is willing to investigate and convict its own. Which they seem all too happy to do."

I'm well aware how much mud the press and the politicos have been slinging at the police and the D.A. You can't turn on the TV without some ad about corruption and crime. And on the off chance I missed any of it, there's my mother to re-iterate it in as bad a light as possible.

"And here's an open-and-shut case not involving corruption, fraud, bribery, cover-up. A chance to make the Department look clean as a whistle," Drew says.

I'm about to ask if the presumption isn't always that cops

are clean when I remember that Suffolk County cop who made women walk home naked or have sex with him. And I have to admit I've heard several rumors and accusations of bribes offered and accepted.

But they've just been rumors.

"So the idea is that they'll do it all by the book, convict, sentence, and get great press. And they don't want me fucking it up." Drew rarely uses foul language around me and it shocks me into realizing just how serious this is. He paces, looking like the proverbial caged animal. "And I've been warned what will happen if I step over the line."

I suggest that maybe the Department is just protecting him, preventing him from being tarred with the same brush. I'm about to add some other cliché when he reaches over and takes my hand in his. "Listen, I could lose my job over this, Teddi, but I have no choice."

"Maybe, maybe not," I say, a plan dancing in my head that I know he won't like. A plan that I'm going to have to broach very carefully.

"But that's not what this weekend's about," he says, waving the conversation away like so many cobwebs. "I'm trying to set a mood here, if you haven't noticed."

I pull off my sweater silently. If he wants to forget—for now—I know how to help him. I toss the sweater in his direction. "I've noticed."

The fire catches, he turns around, and there's a moment, just a moment, with the fire flickering wildly behind him, the wind howling outside, the depth of feeling shining in his eyes, that I want to freeze everything, stay in this place in time a bit longer, long enough to keep it with me always, to have it ready to pull out when I need it. Like when I'm old and alone, in the home and my children have ceased to visit me, as my mother assures me they will.

But Drew has other things in mind, and his name is all I can get out before he's crossed the room and I'm smothered with kisses. He guides me onto my back on the couch and traces the lace edge of my *take me! take me now!* bra. His hands caress my midriff and unsnap my jeans, part my zipper, attempt to wiggle my pants past my hips. He's like a man possessed, like he's drowning and I'm the only life preserver on the Titanic. As if we have only seconds and not a whole weekend to enjoy each other.

"Drew?" I'm not sure he hears me. He is kissing my midriff, yanking my pants, his knee making it harder as he tries to insinuate it between my legs.

I remind him we have all night as I still his hands and slip out of my jeans. He stares at me in the firelight as he strips himself to the bone and asks if I know how beautiful I am. And for the first time, I believe the words. I do feel beautiful, and the feeling surprises me—until I realize that I'm seeing myself through his eyes, eyes which don't care about a stretch mark here or some cellulite there.

For the moment, I'm fooled into believing that neither do I.

He reaches for the bottle of champagne and then stops himself. "Premature," he says.

"As long as that's the only thing that is," I say, reaching out and stroking him rather boldly. His shoulders sag, his head is thrown back, his mouth is slightly open. It's like I've answered his prayers, like his partner hasn't been arrested, like his buddies are behind him. Like he's totally content. I lean forward and with my tongue I tease his nipple. He breathes in sharply, but makes no move.

Do me, do me, his body is saying, and I'm answering with all I have, giving it all to him.

His breathing quickens, his moans sound almost painful until he pulls himself away from my grasp and turns the tables. My turn, and I luxuriate in the attention, the gentleness that threatens a loss of control—his, mine, ours.

When it's over, when I'm lying half under and half on top of this man, he tousles my hair and asks if I'm hungry. I admit to being positively starved, and he tells me he has lobster tails in the kitchen, cooked and waiting.

I reach for some M&M's and he playfully slaps my hand. "Later," he says and gets up, padding naked toward the kitchen while I reach for my clothing. "Don't," he says. "Stay just like that, in front of the fire."

I hear him in the kitchen, the rattle of silverware, the clinking of dishes, and I lie on the couch with my eyes closed until he returns with our dinner.

"Did you hear a car?" I ask, looking around for my sweater and imagining Carmine De'Guisseppe showing up as per my mother's request at the house I redecorated for him, hoping to interrupt our little idle.

Drew slips on his jeans and pads over to the window in bare feet. He pulls back the curtain and I can plainly see headlights as they are turned off in front of the house. "Oh shit," he says. "It's for me. Go into the bedroom, okay?"

I remind him about the note on the door.

"Just close your eyes," he says.

"And let something attack me?" I ask.

He assures me that the only attacking that will be done in that bedroom will involve two-legged creatures. We hear an authoritative knock on the door. "Go, but keep your eyes closed."

And like an idiot, I do. Of course, curiosity gets the best of me and I lean against the door to hear what's being said in the living room while I squint at the bedroom.

"Did you ask her?" I hear a male voice ask.

"What did she say?" another asks. "Where is she, anyway? Stand you up, Swoons?" *Did he say Scoones? Or Swoons?*

"Shut up," I hear Drew say. "She's in the bedroom." This, of course, gets a bawdy response, and I hear Drew tell them once again to shut up, only a little more colorfully.

Ask me? Ask me what? To help with the investigation? He'd hardly have to romance me for that. As my eyes adjust to the darkness, the room around me begins to look more and more familiar. But not as the room I decorated this past summer. It's another room, a room I feel as though I should recognize. There's a poster over the window of the South Seas. There are two pairs of slippers on the floor at the edge of the bed––his and hers. There's a nightgown laid out on the bed and a record player… It's *It's a Wonderful Life!* Drew Swoons has brought my favorite movie to life. It's that moment, after their wedding…

Did you ask her?

"They're gone. You can come out now," Drew says, tapping gently on the door.

Only I can't. I can't even breathe.

CHAPTER 3

A great place to get ideas is from television shows and movies.
Like what you see on Friends? Frasier? It's a great way to
define your own tastes and to express them to a decorator or
clerk in a store. Just stay away from E.R. or Seattle Grace!

Drew opens the bedroom door. "How'd I do?" he asks, sweeping the room with his hand. "You think you're the only one with a DVD player and a subscription to Netflix?"

"They aren't going to start singing 'I Love You Truly' under the window, are they?" I ask, trying to make light of the whole thing, though I can't figure out why. What's wrong with me? Why can't I accept this gesture for what it is? Why am I scared out of my wits?

Drew looks crestfallen. "I told you, they're gone," he says.

I take a deep breath, find a smile I hope doesn't look as phony as it feels, and tell him this is just incredible, touching. I tell him it's my favorite movie and he says he knows. He says he knows my favorite color, my favorite song, my favorite position.

"My *what?*" I ask.

He winks and tells me he knows all the moves I like, even offers to show me.

I remind him he already has.

He pulls me out into the living room, where our lobsters sit waiting for us. Well, they could hardly go anywhere, now could they? He offers to warm them up, mumbling something about wanting it to be perfect. I tell him it already is, and we sit down on the couch.

"Have they found the gun?" I ask him as he puts my napkin on my lap for me.

Drew reminds me he doesn't want to talk about Hal Nelson and hands me my plate.

"I'm no expert," I say, "but it seemed like she was shot in the back. I mean, there was a hole in her dress that—"

Drew says, "You're right. You're no expert." He is not a happy camper.

"It just seems to me that a man, especially a police officer, wouldn't shoot someone in the back."

One of Drew's eyebrows goes up. I've got his attention now.

"Unless, of course, he wanted it to look like someone else did it…" I muse.

Drew orders me to eat my dinner. I take a bite and the lobster is out of this world. He tells me Detective Winters has a brother in Maine who flew it down to a restaurant in Hampton Bays, where they cooked it for Drew and packed it up to be served immediately. He's disappointed about the delay and I get the feeling the whole Department was in on making this night special, all of which makes me feel uncomfortable, boxed in, like those women who get proposed to at Yankee

Stadium in front of fifty-five thousand people, or on some daytime talk show in front of millions.

Proposed to?

Good as the lobster is, I really can't enjoy it. What if he isn't planning on asking me? What if I'm reading the signs all wrong?

Don't be an idiot, Teddi. Of course that's what you're here for. And you're not scared he *won't* ask you. You're scared he *will*.

Drew asks if everything is okay.

I tell him that I hate surprises, I admit that I'm nervous. I say I'm worried about the snow that's begun to fall, about my kids, and global warming, not to mention the Middle East. I can't seem to stop myself. I babble on and on about not knowing how old Maggie May is and how soon she'll die, whether my parents will ever move to Florida, if the bagels I bought on Tuesday are moldy and if the kids will look before they eat.

He lets me go on and on, an arm around me, occasionally stoking the flames—mine and the fires—until I'm spent.

"I'm a basket case," I say, like I'm trying to dissuade him.

"I can take it," he says and hands me the bowl of M&M's.

I plunge my hand in to get it over with, I think, and come up with a handful of M&M's. Half an hour later, the colors separated into piles on the coffee table, the bowl is empty. So is the third finger on my left hand.

I don't feel relieved, which tells me a lot.

"Lie down," he says, and as I do, I warily let him pull my sweater over my head. He picks up the pile of red M&M's and lays them down my chest in a single line from my collarbone to my navel. Then he leans over me and eats the top one. "Yum," he says, and trails his tongue to the next one, which slips slightly. He chases it with his mouth and I try not to laugh and dislodge all the candies because this is too sensual for me to screw up.

He refuses to use his hands as he tries to slide an errant candy from where it's slid under the edge of my bra. As if I didn't already know, he proves how very talented his tongue is.

It's nearly impossible for me to lay still, but I try to confine my shifting to below the last of the M&M's.

When they're gone, he reaches for the blue ones while I wiggle out of my jeans. The line begins just below my neck once again, but this time it ends at the edge of my bikini panties.

Excruciatingly slowly, he circles M&M after M&M until he's at the last one. "More relaxed?" he asks me.

"Are you kidding?" At my answer he shrugs and reaches for a few yellow ones, but I take them from his hand and tell him that I'm the one with a weakness for chocolate.

"Be my guest," he says, shoving over the coffee table a few feet and pulling his shirt over his head without unbuttoning it as he lays down on the floor.

Now, sex with Drew is always good—*better* than good—but tonight there's an urgency, a hunger that's contagious. It's as if we can't get enough of each other, can't get it fast enough, can't go deep enough, can't be close enough. I have never felt this desirable, this worshipped. He's kissing and caressing places that I never knew were erogenous zones before. The inside of my elbow, the back of my knees, the hollow between my breasts.

He devotes what feels like hours to the back of my neck, behind my ears, kissing, licking, while his hands run down my back, reach around me, drive me crazy.

When it's over and we're lying there in the a haze of satisfaction, drifting somewhere between nirvana and oblivion, me wondering if he's ever going to pop the question, him wondering the same thing, I hear a cell phone ring.

"Mine," he says, and I reach for his jeans, which are tossed somewhere above my head. "I'll get it," he says with authority, like he's worried I'm going to answer his police phone.

Not.

He grabs his jeans away from me and something goes flying out of the pocket. Something small and dark, like a velvet box, thuds and scoots across the floor.

"Great," he says sarcastically as he seizes my arm and motions for me not to go after it while he opens his phone and says, "Scoones here."

"And here," I say, patting his privates. "And—"

He swats my hand away and puts a finger up, signaling for me to wait, but I know police business when I see it, and I get up and start to slip my jeans on, my eyes on the little velvet box.

I am just sliding up my zipper when I see the color drain from his face and he asks, "What hospital?"

"Who?" I ask, coming over to where he stands while reminding myself that if it were one of my kids, it would have been *my* cell phone that rang. I'm panicking nonetheless. My foot hits the velvet box and I pick it up and hold it out to him. He ignores me, making notes on a napkin from the coffee table.

"Okay," he says and he, too, is on his feet, slipping into his jeans and loafers, reaching for his jacket. "Can you get them to hold off telling Nelson till I'm there? Shouldn't take me more than forty-five minutes."

He's hustling me into my jacket as he's finishing up his conversation. When he flips the phone closed, he turns me to face him.

"Hallie's in Plainview General. OD'd on Valium. Looks intentional." Drew always drops words when he's in cop mode.

"Is she—" No matter how much exposure I've had to homicide since meeting Drew Scoones, I still have trouble getting the word *dead* past my lips.

Drew shakes his head. "Pumping her stomach as we speak," he says.

I can't figure out why Hallie would try to kill herself now. The shame? The publicity? Hallie always struck me as someone who'd want to be around to see Hal raked over the coals if he did her wrong.

"I've got to be there when they tell Nelson," he says. "I've got to be the one to tell him."

"Of course," I agree. Only there's the box, and we really shouldn't just leave it here in the house, right? I gesture toward it silently.

"Shit," he says. "I guess I should have put the damn thing in the M&M's, after all."

He snatches up the ring box.

"You want me to go down on one knee?" he asks. He's fidgeting and digging in his pocket for his car keys, reaching for his gloves, blowing out the candles and getting ready to leave our love nest.

"No," I say, buttoning my coat and putting on my earmuffs while I stuff my feet into my Uggs. "I want to remember this moment just the way it is. You saying *shit* and calling my ring a damn thing. That's just perfect."

Drew stops the world. No, really. The only muscle he moves is the one in his left arm, which stops me in my tracks with just a touch. "I'm sorry."

"Circumstances beyond your control," I say with a shrug. "Some other time."

"No," he says, and he's blocking my way to the door. Whichever way I try to go around him, he moves and stops me. "Teddi Bayer-Gallo-Bayer-Again, I love you. I love the way you make me feel, the way you make me laugh, the way you look at the world and make me see it. I love your children and I'm getting used to your mother and father. I want your family to be my family, your bed to be my bed and your heart to be mine."

I don't think I say anything.

"That's it. I think that was the whole speech," he says.

I tell him it was lovely and that we'd better get going.

"Well?" he asks.

"Well what?" I say. He hasn't noticed that he still hasn't asked me, hasn't offered me the ring.

He looks at me like he knows there's something missing.

"You need to ask," I whisper.

"Didn't I?"

I shake my head.

"Yes I did," he insists.

I shake my head again.

"Fine. I'll ask again, because I know I did. Teddi Bayer-Gallo-Bayer-Again, will you marry me?"

Before I can answer, his cell phone rings again. He shoves the box in my hand.

"Just take the damn thing and let's go."

CHAPTER 4

Stripes are best used subtly, paying special attention to their spacing and the contrast between colors, or you risk the optical illusion effect. Enter "optical illusion stripes" into Google and see what I mean. It can make your head spin.

TipsFromTeddi.com

The judge denied Hal Nelson bail, so we are in the visiting room of the Nassau County Jail. Hal is beside himself. I've never seen a man break down before, and I never want to see anything like it again. He keeps telling Drew that he has to get him out of there and Drew keeps promising that he will.

"Too far," he keeps telling me. "I pushed her too far." And he makes me promise to visit her, which of course I agree to.

Drew and I are in the car on the way to the hospital before either of us refer to his proposal again.

"This is not how I wanted this weekend to play out," he says, gripping the steering wheel tightly.

"You promised you'd get Hal cleared," I say. I ask how he's going to do that without risking his career.

"You worried I won't be able to support you and the kids?" he asks.

I give him a pass on that because he's obviously distraught.

"There are plenty of other things I could do," he says. "I don't have to be a cop."

"Uh-huh," I agree. We're both lying.

Drew pulls over to the side of the road. He leans back against the seat and breathes out heavily. "I don't know. I just don't know."

Very quietly, so as not to make him explode, I say I have a plan.

"Teddi," he says, a note of warning in his voice. "This is—"

I ask him to hear me out. In some ways this is a test, I think. Does this man think I'm worth listening to? Seriously? Are we going to be partners in this life? Because if not, I'm not really interested in seeing what's in that velvet box.

He twists in his seat so that he can watch my face. "Go ahead," he says.

"I haven't worked out all the details, but I have a plan. Okay, it's the bare bones of a plan. Maybe not even bones…"

The man has the patience of a saint. He waits while I circle the issue and beat the preamble to death.

"Okay, you can't do the investigation without risking your job, right? Well, I can. I can do all the stuff you tell me to and feed all the information back to you. They can't kick me off the force, right? And it wouldn't look too good if they went after me because *Newsday* loves me for showing up the police in the lottery affair, so the paper would make them look like they aren't interested in a good citizen's help."

It seems like a good idea to me, anyway.

"Wouldn't work," he says. "Everyone on the force would expect you to turn over all your information to me. They'd be on to your plan in a heartbeat."

"Not," I say, "if we've broken up." I just leave it hanging out there, waiting for him to shoot it down.

"It's a nice try, honey, and a damn sweet offer. The thing is, as you may have noticed, the whole Department knows what this weekend was about. I told Markowitz I got you a ring, knowing she'd tell the whole squad. I figured if they thought I was too busy with you, I wouldn't be working Nelson's case."

It takes him a minute to hear what he's actually said, that this proposal is some sort of distraction to divert suspicion.

"Not that I don't really want to marry you, Teddi. I do. I really do. I love you. I love the kids. But it also—"

"Even better," I tell him. "Everyone knows you were asking me, right?"

"That's my point," he says and throws up his hands like there's nothing we can do about it now.

"I haven't said *yes*, Drew," I say.

It's not shock that is all over his face. It's incomprehension.

"You could go back into the precinct and tell them all I said no."

He asks me if I'm serious. I don't say that I am, or that I half-am, or that there's a war going on inside me, my head saying I'm being used while my heart is dancing up and down at the mere thought of the velvet box and the lifetime it holds.

"Hey, if even you believed it, *they* certainly will, right?"

I can almost see the wheels turning in Drew's head. Still he asks me to spell it all out.

"Simple. You asked, I said no. You're done with me. You're licking your wounds, kicking up your heels, drinking, doing whatever scorned men do. I'm through with policemen, police work, blood and all that. Oh, I might try to get a few clients from some of the boys in blue, but I never liked Hal to begin with, so his arrest isn't of any interest to me."

He's thoughtful. Finally he says, "Okay, supposing anyone would believe that you would turn me down—"

"I just did." Man, it's so quiet in the car you can hear the keys swaying beneath the ignition. I let a full minute go by without saying a word.

He doesn't say anything either.

"See? It will work. You fell for it and you know I think you're the best thing that's happened to me, to Jesse, to the girls…"

Drew lets out a breath I didn't realize he was holding. "Put the ring on," he says. "Now. Put it on."

I take the box out of my pocket and hand it to him. "Maybe we should wait on it."

He shakes his head. "Put out your hand, Teddi." I slip off my glove and hold out my hand to him.

He opens the box and I can't see the ring until he slips it on my finger and says nothing has ever looked so right.

A small square-cut diamond glistens up at me. He's right. It's perfect. When the lump in my throat dissolves and I can finally speak, I tell him I love it.

And then I slip it off my finger, back into the box and tell him we'd better get to the hospital.

"A promise is a promise," I remind him as he puts on his blinker and gets back on the road.

"By the way," Drew says lightly, which sets off warning bells in my chest, "I've got a new partner. You know, until we spring Hal."

"And?" I ask. "What's he like?" I mean really, I can't like him less than Hal, right?

"He's a woman."

Oh. Wrong.

"I was thinking, I could, you know, appear interested in her, I suppose."

I suggest that maybe I need to appear interested in someone else, as well.

Drew solemnly shakes his head. "Life with you is going to be a pisser," he says.

LAST NIGHT WE TRIED to see Hallie, but she was still being evaluated and wasn't allowed visitors. We were told to come back this morning. I followed Drew's little Mazda RX7 back from the Hamptons this morning, imagining how it will feel to watch it pull into my driveway every night.

Which raises the question of whether Drew will move in with us, or if I will have to sell the house so that he doesn't feel he's a guest in the house that my ex and I lived in. Worse, the house that my father bought Rio and I soon after we were married. So many things we didn't work out last night after we got back to the cottage. All those things felt like they could wait, but in the cold light of day, in the hospital parking lot without Drew's arms around me, I'm realizing how important they all are. How critical. Could I move my kids? After all they've been through? Would they choose their house over a new dad?

Jeesh. I shouldn't have put it that way. Dana would probably choose new jeans over a new dad.

Drew pulls up next to me and lowers his window. "I'll call," he says, and then he's gone. It takes me a few minutes to set my story straight in my head and get out of the car.

Hospitals are never what you expect them to be. At least not what I expect. All the drama of television is missing and they are quiet, businesslike, and really, really ugly. Halls and rooms tend to be washed out no-color, if they actually were any color to begin with. As a decorator, I notice these things. It drives me crazy because for the same price of paint (okay, maybe more for the deeper hues, but a hospital could surely get a break on the price for the amount they'd need) they could make a hospital look joyous, they could make it hopeful. They could make it alive.

Hallie's hospital is none of these things. It could be a frozen-dinner warehouse and management wouldn't have to change a thing. It's even chilly enough to keep the food frozen. Anyway, I am walking down the corridor, listening to the loud-speaker paging a doctor whose name is unintelligible. Nurses' shoes are squeaking down the hall. My Uggs are slushy and I sound like a patient shuffling down the hall in slippers as I approach Hallie Nelson's room.

Hallie is one of those petite women you love to hate—you know she will never look old, fat, slovenly. The thing is, lying there in the hospital bed she looks tiny, shrunken, and it's impossible to hate her. The rails are up around her bed and her wrists are tied with gauze to the rails. The contents of my stomach threaten to come up my throat. Apparently I have a thing about bondage—with the notable exception of Drew's handcuffs—that elicits a visceral reaction.

At any rate, there is a young woman sitting beside Hallie, stroking her arm, murmuring soft, soothing words. I lift my knee and balance the flowers I've picked up downstairs at the florist on my thigh so that I can knock gently on the open door. Hallie's guest looks up and smiles as if she's been plucked from a river just moments before going over the falls.

"Hi!" she says, a little too brightly. "Come on in! Hallie, look, you've got company."

Hallie turns her head in my direction and then back toward the windows while the woman beside her jumps up and introduces herself as Hallie's sister, Sally.

Sally takes the flowers from me, oohs and aahs over them, and tells me that Hallie's going to be just fine. It's more a cheer than a diagnosis.

I come closer to the bed and quietly say, "Hallie? Is there anything I can do?"

Her words are slurred, but I believe her answer is, "Drop dead. Or is that too much to ask?" And she turns back toward the window while her sister chides her and says she doesn't mean it.

"Maybe she does," I admit. "I've never been a very good friend to her, and I guess this looks like I've come to pick her bones."

Hey, it's what I feel like.

Hallie turns slowly back from the wall and glares at me. "Haven't you?" she asks, her words slightly slushy.

"I've come because Hal asked me to. Drew and I saw him last night and he's worried sick about you."

"Yeah," she says sarcastically. "Sure."

"It has to be hard for him, Hallie, not being able to come here and look after you himself. Imagine if the situation was reversed."

Hallie tells me I don't know how close I've come to the truth.

"What do you mean?" I ask, but she dismisses the thought with a shake of her head and some mumblings about the goose and the gander.

"You wanna know what you can do for me, Teddi Bayer?" she asks. "You can tell me why a happily married man with a wife available every night had to go find some whore to screw up our lives with."

"Hallie, we don't know if he was even—" I start to say. "I mean, just because he was at Peaches' house that night…"

Jeesh. Even I don't believe what I'm saying.

Hallie looks at me like I'm the one whose wrists ought to be tied to the bed rails. "Oh, yes we do know. At least I know. And he knew I knew, 'cause he told me all about her, how she had no 'hard edges.' Get this… For months he swore he wasn't even screwing her. And I believed him."

"Well, then," I start. Only I've got nothing.

"That was before I had proof otherwise. What difference does it make now, anyway? Like I told him that night, our marriage is over."

I can't figure out what to say. Finally, I ask how he responded.

"Said he'd never see her again," she says, and I can't tell if she believes he actually meant it. My eyes meet Sally's. We're both thinking that it didn't take him long to break that promise. "But I told him it was too late."

I take in a deep breath.

"But, to be honest, I don't think he believed me. Hey, he had history on his side. And then there was the chance that just maybe it wasn't him, but me, and Peaches was maybe…"

I can see she's getting agitated, and that can't be good for her. Her breathing is coming in little gasps. I know I shouldn't ask for an explanation, but I can't help it. "Peaches was maybe what?"

"He wanted a baby as much as I did," she says earnestly. "Maybe more."

"Peaches could have been pregnant?" I ask. It comes out a squeak. "She must have used condoms, what with AIDS and all."

She murmurs agreement, but I have the sense that she was hoping against hope that there'd be a baby in it for them.

"He was going over there to end it," Sally says as she straightens Hallie's covers. "It was as simple as that."

"Really? You have to 'break up' with a hooker?" Hallie asks her sister after she takes a gulp of water from a straw which Sally holds for her. I must say, she's taking this whole restraint thing better than I would. "You don't just never show up again? You can't just say 'thanks, but no thanks, I'm getting it at home for free'?"

She has a good point.

"Maybe it was more than just—" I stop myself before I say what I'm thinking aloud. The room is very quiet. I think I hear Sally swallowing.

"You think he was in love with her?" Hallie asks me. She rattles the bed rails as she tries to yank her arms free. "Then why would he kill her? Either he loved me, in which case it was over with her and he wouldn't have killed her, or he loved her, in which case he wouldn't have killed her. Why can't the police see that?"

I think of the woman on the floor in the make-believe kitchen. "I don't think he was in love with her. Just with some fantasy of himself you probably didn't even know about."

Hallie smiles a forlorn smile, a smile that tells me she just might have known all about Hal's fantasies. And couldn't feed them.

"So if you already knew about the affaire, and he was breaking it off, he'd have had no motive for killing her. And you're right, if he wasn't breaking it off, he certainly wouldn't have killed her. What if she didn't take it well, this breakup? What if they fought about it and…" I wonder aloud.

Hallie and Sally stare at me.

"No signs of a struggle," I say. "One clean wound in the back."

"He didn't do it," Hallie says with conviction. "Trust me. He wouldn't have done it." I look at her tethers and I don't dare ask why, if she feels Hal is innocent, she tried to kill herself. But I guess the question is all over my face, like every other thought I have, because she tells me.

She tells me she doesn't want to stand by him, be the good little woman who swears her husband didn't do it while the world wonders why he was out getting it elsewhere instead of from her. She says she feels diminished enough as a woman. "I don't need to go through this. I can't go through this, too."

Too?

"Look at 'em," she says, gesturing with her chin toward the door. "All of 'em peeking in, wondering why. What's the matter with her that her husband didn't just stay home and—?"

I turn toward the door and see two nurses hovering. When they see me, they hurry off.

I decide she'd be better off with the door closed and cross the room, ready to do just that when who do I see sauntering down the hall but Drew. Next to him a tall woman is keeping stride with him. A tall, good-looking blonde with long hair and legs. She's got enormous blue eyes and a skirt that's too short.

And a detective's badge pinned to her waistband.

Now I'm the one muttering curse words under my breath. Did I really suggest we pretend to have broken up? I look at her and think I must have been temporarily insane. Or I soon will be.

You didn't know about her at the time, I tell myself.

He could have told you, I answer back.

He did.

Okay, true. But he didn't say she was joining the force after she was done shooting the *Sports Illustrated* swimsuit issue.

"Well, well, well. If it isn't Teddi Bayer-Gallo-Bayer-Again. I should have expected you'd be here," he says, by way of greeting. He sounds totally exhausted and fed up. "My weekend wasn't bad enough already." He introduces the woman beside him as O'Hanlon, his new partner. He puts the emphasis on *partner*.

The man should have become an actor. Just hours ago the name he called me sounded tender and intimate. Now it stings as if he's finding fault with me. There's no wink. There's no secret gesture, which I now think we should have arranged. A code word that means *this is all an act*. A movement that says *I have to do this, but I don't mean it*. A look that says *I can't wait until this is over...*

"I was visiting a friend," I say, but my voice trembles.

"A friend," he says. "Since when are you and Hallie Nelson *friends?* More like you just couldn't resist sticking your nose in, could you?"

The woman beside him clears her throat, as if she feels he needs to be reminded that she is there. With her looks, I don't think it's likely he's forgotten her. He mumbles introductions, referring to me as the *infamous Teddi Bayer*, and we nod politely at each other.

"Teddi and I used to—" The words hang in the air and embarrass me. Finally he tells his partner he needs to go in to see Hallie. To me he says, "Wait here."

"Is that an order?" I ask in response.

"Take it however you want, but I'd like to hear what she told you. Hal Nelson is my partner, you know." He casts a quick glance in O'Hanlon's direction, but doesn't correct himself, doesn't make it past tense.

"Detective Scoones," O'Hanlon says, and there is a note of warning in her voice, like she's his keeper and he is supposed to stay away from Hal's case or else. He flips her the bird with a look.

I tell him flatly, "You'll be happy to know that despite the fact that he was fooling around, she still says he didn't do it."

"What's the matter? You don't believe her? Think every husband who fools around is like your ex?"

That was a low blow I didn't see coming. I let the hurt show while telling him I couldn't care less. "I'd promised Hal I'd see her and I saw her."

"Nice," he says sarcastically. "The way you keep your promises."

"I always keep my promises," I tell him. "I don't make promises I can't keep."

Our eyes meet and hold for half a heartbeat, and then he looks away.

He's heard all about that last night, he says, implying that was the reason I told him I wouldn't marry him. He's good, he's really good.

This game isn't even an hour old and I already regret it. I'd like to forget the whole thing, except that too many pieces already don't fit in the *Hal Did It* edition of the puzzle. I know that the official police version is that Hal went over there and told Peaches that Hallie knew about them and he was ending it. Maybe he even threatened to bust her. And she said she'd blow the whistle on him. Cop using hooker, maybe pin a few other misdeeds on him, like extortion, drug abuse, money laundering. She pushed him to the breaking point, and he broke. But shooting her in the back? It just doesn't fit.

"So then, your Nancy Drew days are over? The Department can rest easy now?"

I tell him that as long as they aren't trying to pin a murder rap on one of my friends, the way they have in the past, I've no interest in crossing paths with them again.

O'Hanlon purrs that she's heard from the Department that I've done some great work.

"Oh, yeah," Drew says. "Just ask her. She's the Department's own little Miss Marple, aren't you, Teddi? Only our girl finds showing up a cop turns her on. Gets her juices flowing. Showing up the whole Department, well…"

There's nothing gentle in the eyes he rolls skyward. He's either turning in an Academy Award performance or he's uncorked the bottle on his feelings and the venom is spilling out.

"Showing you up hasn't been that hard to do," I say flippantly, because it's what I'm supposed to do. "Even in heels, backward, as they say."

Drew says he seems to remember me falling off a dock that way. "But you saved me from myself, Teddi Bayer-Gallo-Bayer-Again," he says one more time, as if it amuses him. "I owe you one for that. I suppose I got off easy. And I'll say this for you. At least you stopped us before we screwed up those kids of yours any worse, right? One divorce is probably about all they can handle."

Any worse? He really didn't have to do that. Or he could have at least warned me. I can't find my words. I don't know the script. I can barely breathe.

I remind myself that this isn't real. This is for his partners' benefit. Both his partners. This act is to convince O'Hanlon, the whole play is for Hal Nelson. Drew will call me later and tell me he loves me more than ever for what I'm going through for him.

But for this moment I realize what losing Drew would be like, and I have to lean against the wall for support. His hand comes out to steady me, but he stops himself.

"Look, I'm sorry, but—" I start.

"Yeah, you said that last night," he finishes for me. "Several times, if I recall."

"I was going to say that I'm sorry I can't stay and chat with you, but I've got an appointment with a client."

Drew looks embarrassed. He tells me I can go. At least he doesn't tell me where.

"Well, I'm going home," I say, turning away from him because, show or not, I can't really take it anymore. "Don't call me."

"I think your powers of observation are slipping," he says to my back. "I haven't been calling."

Yes, he has. Yes, he has. Relief washes over me. I fondle the box in my pocket and tell myself, *It's an act. It's an act.*

I shrug at him like what he says means nothing to me, but I hear his next words to O'Hanlon. "Well, that was cathartic," and they sting.

And again I have to wonder just how much of what we said was acting, and how much was venting.

And that hurts. It really, really hurts.

I SIT IN MY CAR for about twenty minutes before I check messages, hoping against hope that there is one from Drew in which he apologizes tearfully for saying things he doesn't feel, didn't mean. Instead, there's one from my mother informing me that my father is getting too much gas from the healthy diet the nutritionist put him on and asking me to pick up some good old Bromo Seltzer on my way over tonight. Her tone suggests that because I recommended the nutritionist I am responsible for my father's gas and the unpleasant night she spent in the same room with him.

My mother! How will I ever tell my mother that I've accepted a ring from Drew? Thank heavens it's a secret for now.

There's also a call from Susan Michaels with instructions about picking up the key to her house, which she wants me to work on while she is away. And another from Bobbie saying that she can't work on Sydelle Silverberg's proposal because they are having a sale in Loehmann's Back Room. Do I want her to look for anything for me?

Yeah.

A new partner.

Bobbie! How will I ever *not* tell Bobbie? Worse, I'm going to have to tell her that Drew and I have split up. And the kids. Jesse will be devastated.

It's with a heavy heart on Monday that I head over to Old Brookville to pick up the Michaelses' keys. Up a very steep driveway, I park next to a landscaper's truck and see Susan standing by her front door pointing this way and that and shaking her head. Susan is what you might call a formidable woman. She's stocky, has short thick hair, short thick arms and legs, and she's wearing a barn jacket and those pants riders wear that have an extra layer of fabric where the rubber meets the road.

As I approach, I hear her arguing that she's seen magnolias that bloom all through the winter and she doesn't see why this man cannot find them for her.

"I pay you enough to find palm trees in Alaska," she says, then looks at me. "You've seen winter magnolias, haven't you?"

The gardener looks pleadingly at me. *Tell this woman she's mistaken,* his face begs.

"I'm an interior designer," I say diplomatically. "What I know about plants and trees couldn't overflow a thimble."

Of course, neither Susan Michaels nor the gardener is satisfied with my answer.

I suggest an Internet search, which Susan seems to think is a wonderful idea, despite the gardener explaining that they'll sell anything to anyone on the Internet. He's right. I get offers every day to increase the length of my penis, and so far…

Susan invites me in, and I tell her again how I adore the feel of her house, wish I had done it myself, and can't wait to make the screening room fit in seamlessly. She reminds me that is precisely what she is paying me for as she leads the way to the new room.

"I would have naturally used Miss Lehman to do this room as well, had she not gone to that big D&D building in the sky," she says, looking reverently upward. "It's a loss I take personally," she adds.

"I suppose you were very close to her," I say. Miss Lehman was a legend and I wish I'd met her, even once.

"You'd suppose wrong," Susan says. "The woman died before we even bought this place. She worked for the previous owners, but her work is what sold us on the house. And I feel close to her every time I notice a detail that escaped me at first. Like just yesterday I realized that the flush handle on the commode in the guest bath off the mudroom resembles a Herm Sprenger *bradoon*."

"Really?" I say, pretending I have any idea what that is. "I wonder if she had it custom-made."

Susan assures me that of course she did. After all, those bits aren't exactly run-of-the-mill.

I promise her that the new room will have no run-of-the-mill-ness to it.

"It had better not," she warns me.

We are standing in her new space, meant to become a media room, which is the hottest craze on Long Island. Everyone wants a huge-screen TV, leather theater chairs (with cup holders, of course) and surround sound. They want a minibar, at the very least, room-darkening shades, remotes for everything (including the shades), and a popcorn maker that makes the room smell like the movie should start shortly, and not like it was shown yesterday.

Which is all well and good, except that from the Michaelses' media room windows there is an incredible view of their pasture where I can see three horses who are so perfectly groomed and so stately that I have to wonder where the blankets of roses are stored. I tell Susan it's a shame to ever draw the shades on that scene. "People put views like that on their TV sets as screen savers," I tell her.

She loves the idea and will hire a photographer to take the picture and install it on her system.

I remind her she has the real thing.

"Sometimes it rains," she says. I imagine the horses standing in the mist. Or better still, with snow falling… "Have you any quarter horses?" she asks.

Go fish, I think.

It's as if she's doing that bit in *The Philadelphia Story* where Katherine Hepburn and her little sister are trying to put one over on Jimmy Stewart and Ruth Hussey by acting higher and mightier than they already are. Susan phrases and paces herself just like Kate.

Only Susan has a Long Island accent.

I admit that, alas and alack, I have no quarter horses, no eighth horses, not even any horsehair sofas.

"While I'm gone, you must think of these studs as your own!" She claps her hands as if she has just solved a very vexing problem. She should only know how I'd like three studs to call my own. "I was reluctant to leave them alone with Eddy, since he's new and, well, just a groom, but this is a wonderful solution. You may ride them, if you ride English, naturally. Regardless, I expect that as long as you will be here supervising the work on the house anyway, you will come by and treat them to carrots and apples and sugar cubes."

She signals for me to follow her and we trudge out to the corral. Okay, I trudge. She glides. I want this job, *need* this job so badly that I don't dare tell her that horses terrify me. The only time I rode one, I searched in vain for a seat belt and finally pretended to have been hit in the head with a branch so they'd take me back to the corral and help me down off old *Tennessee Ernie.*

Do you have any idea how tall horses are?

"Take a handful," Susan tells me as we pass the stable and she reaches into a bin filled with carrots that look better than the ones I've been serving my kids lately. Since they don't eat them anyway, I don't see why I should pay extra for the good stuff.

I follow Susan's lead and stick out my handful of carrots, thinking about how I could possibly staple sheets to walls, trim lampshades with beads, paint flowers on accessories, all with a finger or two missing.

"Zorro," she calls, snickering at one of the horses, and he comes running. He has velvety soft lips that tickle as he takes the carrots from my hand. Just when I think this isn't so bad, he snorts and the force of his breath and the suddenness with which it comes has me jumping backward and stepping on the end of a rake which just misses hitting both Susan and me in the head.

Susan shakes her head. "Eddy. I swear that groom is out to get me. He's always leaving things where they are bound to injure someone. If the horses didn't like him so much—" she pauses to nuzzle Zorro's head, which is like the size of a small club chair "—I'd replace him. Not that you can find grooms all that easily around here."

They refer to the people of Old Brookville as "the horsey set," so I don't know where she'd be likelier to find grooms, except, perhaps Kentucky.

She walks me through the stables, if you can call an out-building lined in Southern yellow pine with a custom-made chandelier, built-in cabinets and a lounge area a stable. She's showing me the barn to impress me, and it works.

After I promise to visit the horses faithfully, noticing that there are security cameras installed in the stable and on strategically placed poles around the corral so she will know if I don't keep my word, we return to the house, where I agree to keep the tone in her new room once again. We talk of bits and bridles and girths (not mine, thank goodness), and I fake it the best I can. Then I take the key and a small note card embellished with what looks like a bee on it and on which is written her security code, and I head for home where my children should, hopefully, be waiting for me.

"ANY CALLS?" I ask the kids as I unburden myself, easing my portfolio to the floor, my samples bag next to it. My handy dandy imitation Bottega Veneta bag—which Bobbie insists I carry because that's what cool people use even though it's impossibly heavy—hits the floor with a thud. Naturally I'm hoping that you-know-who has called.

He hasn't.

"Since you're home now, can I go over to Kimmie's?" Dana, my thirteen-thinks-she's-eighteen-year-old daughter asks. She comes bounding down the steps, seven-year-old Alyssa in her wake, in leggings and a T-bag shirt that reminds me of my old maternity tops. This is the "in" look of the moment, and while it drives me crazy, it beats looking like you're trying to *get* pregnant, which those crop-top-look-at-my-belly shirts seemed to say. "It's an emergency."

She's already halfway out the door. In an effort to be an engaged parent, I ask what the emergency is. Seems Kimmie, one of Bobbie's twin daughters and Dana's best friend, has lost her iPod.

"Oh my God," I say sarcastically. "How will she live without her music?"

I get the *Mother, you are such a complete and total dork* look. "We already loaded all my music onto her old MP3 player," Dana tells me. "It's the other stuff."

Of course, I have no idea what "the other stuff" means.

In that voice kids get somewhere around nine or ten that automatically implies anyone older than twenty-five has crossed over into the realm of senility, she adds, "Like when she gets her period, and her locker combination, and…"

"You mean her iPAQ," I say. "You can't put that stuff on an iPod."

She rolls her eyes. "Right, Mom," she says. "You're the iPod expert who can't even turn off Shuffle, but you know the difference and I don't. Can I go?"

She doesn't wait for an answer as she swings her backpack over her shoulder.

"And Jesse's in his room with the door shut. *Again,*" she says. "My guess is you won't have to worry about ever getting him a car. He'll be blind before he gets his learner's permit." And with that, she is out the door, leaving me to explain to Alyssa why Jesse is in danger of losing his eyesight.

Thank goodness I am saved by the bell. I reach into my purse, but it isn't that phone ringing. Lys and I play look-for-the-phone and finally find it on the kitchen table. It's not my phone, and I wonder if Dana has been entertaining some boy here while I've been out. We've been there, done that, and the idea doesn't sit well as pick up the phone and grouchily answer it.

"Who is this?" I ask.

"No 'hello'?" The sound of the familiar voice washes over me.

"Oh. It's you," I say. "How did you…?"

"Don't worry about it," he says.

I wasn't until he said that.

"Untraceable, but still don't expect me to call too much. And don't call me, Teddi. Don't."

"You know this is ridiculous," I say. "There's no reason we—" Jesse walks into the kitchen. His cheeks are flushed as he reaches for the refrigerator door. I wish there was a man in the house for him to talk to. Or for me to talk to about him. Or for me just to talk to…

"The kids around? I don't want to upset them any more than they have to be. I still think you're wrong about not letting them in on this."

I remind him that Alyssa is seven. And loves Grandma June with all her heart. I make it sound like I'm ordering a personalized T-shirt or something.

"You're telling me she couldn't keep it a secret," he says.

I make it clear that telling Alyssa is the same as telling my mother, and that I think a "surprise" would be a better way to go. I motion to Jesse to take a glass rather than drink straight from the container.

"Actually," Drew says, "I'd like to be there when we spring our 'surprise' on Grandma June. I wouldn't miss seeing you break the news to her that the breakup was all a ruse and we're going to get married for anything."

"You want to see her face?" I ask.

"No, I just think I ought to be between you and the bullet," he says gallantly.

"So what do I do now?" I ask him.

He suggests that I get into Hal and Hallie's place and poke around. See what I can find that might help us. "In the meantime, couldn't we just tell Jesse?" he asks me.

I admit that I wish we could. I tell him that I just hope this gets taken care of quickly. I say something about making it a rush order.

"And we'll make it up to them," I say.

Jesse looks at me strangely and asks who is on the phone.

I make some face like it's a telemarketer for the GOP and they've got a chocolate bar's chance in a gynecologist's office of getting a dime out of me. His brow furrows. "Cancer Care," I say. "I'm getting a 'Grandmas Don't Smoke' T-shirt for Lys. You want one?"

The offer effectively ends his curiosity.

"And there's string cheese, Jess," I say as he reaches for the Fritos. "That's better for you than those chips."

Jesse asks why I buy them, then. It's a valid question and while I try to think of an answer, Drew tells me, "I'll call when I can. O'Hanlon's hanging pretty tight."

Just what I wanted to hear—how it's hanging.

And then I hear a click.

"New phone?" Jesse asks while I stare at it. "Isn't that one of those disposable ones? How come you got one of those?"

"It was a gift," I say. "From someone who seems to think I'm a disposable kind of gal."

"Oh," Jesse says. "Dad?"

CHAPTER 5

*You can learn a lot about decorating from restaurants. A meal
tastes better with a cloth napkin on your lap. A child behaves
better at a fancy restaurant than he does at Friendly's. Surroundings can subtly influence behavior with their expecta-
tions. Look around your house. What does it say you expect?*
                                                    TipsFromTeddi.com

A few days later I figure it's time to tell the kids and Bobbie
that Drew and I have broken up. Not an easy task for someone
whose nose turns red and blinks when she even hedges about
how many cookies she ate, never mind when she tells a real
whopper.

We are at Empire Sechuan for dinner, which seems a good
place to come out with it. There's less chance of histrionics,
and hopefully Bobbie will have the good sense not to ask in-
delicate questions in front of the kids. Or in front of Charlie,
our waiter.

Of course, with kids, there are no guarantees.

We order the same meal we always do. A pupu platter with
no shrimp toast, extra dim sum. A plate of spareribs for Alyssa.
Steamed veggies for Kristin, Bobbie's vegetarian daughter who

flirts periodically with anorexia. Sweet and sour chicken for Dana and me. Orange beef for Jess. Enough food for leftovers so I won't have to cook tomorrow.

While we munch on crisp noodles dunked in duck sauce and wait for our order to arrive, I clear my throat. "You may have noticed…" I start.

They haven't noticed anything, not even me talking. Alyssa is putting sugar into her water glass. Jesse is squirming uncomfortably. Dana and Kimmie are text messaging—no doubt with each other, despite sitting across the table from one another. Remember when we used to spell things out in front of *them* so they wouldn't understand? Now they are doing it in front of us.

Bobbie is trying to convince Kristin that the noodles haven't been fried in animal fat and that duck sauce doesn't come from ducks.

"As you may have noticed," I try again, with much the same result, "I need to tell you all something."

You'd think that would get a reaction. It doesn't. Well, I do get a just-a-minute finger up from Dana.

"While this only affects any of you peripherally—" what am I doing, conducting a board meeting? "—I think that you should know…"

"Spit it out, Ted," Bobbie says, looking impatient. "The business is going under, right?"

"Mom!" Dana's mouth opens wide. "Will we have to move? I can't move. It's the middle of the school year. I'll live with the Lyons. Right, Bobbie? I can stay with you, can't I?"

"No, it's not—" I try to wedge in, but they are all off on a tear.

"I can live with Grandma," Alyssa says. "And go to her beauty parlor every week like she does. And we can shop at the store that gives out lollies and…"

"I'll go with you, Mom. Maybe we could move in with Drew. I mean, until you guys get married and—"

"There's nothing wrong with the business. In fact, I have two new clients who I actually expect will pay us."

"So then?" Bobbie asks, somewhat less interested. I think she was kind of hopeful the business was the problem.

"Well, actually Jesse brings up a point." Boy, when I flounder, I just flop around on the deck on my way to certain death. "I don't know where you got the idea that Drew and I are ever getting married, actually. The fact is, we aren't seeing each other anymore."

"Can I still move to Grandma's?" Alyssa asks, while Dana says something mildly sympathetic like *that's too bad*, and goes back to her cell phone.

"When did this happen?" Bobbie asks. What she really wants to know is why I didn't tell her sooner, and privately so that she could ask for all the gory details.

Before I can answer her, Jesse throws down his napkin and stands up. He looks at me like I've given away his secret stash of *Playboy* magazines—something I'm contemplating. "I knew you'd wreck this, just like you wreck everything. I knew it."

Charlie comes sailing out of the kitchen, our dinners stacked on his tray. Jesse almost runs him over.

I excuse myself and go after Jesse. I find him in the vestibule, where the winter cold seeps in through the door. "I'm sorry, Jess," I say. It's the best I can do, with his knife sticking out of my heart.

"I hate you," he tells me.

I can't blame him. Right at this moment, I hate me, too.

I DON'T LIKE ME much better when Captain Schultz calls me first thing in the morning to say he was sad to hear about my breakup with Drew and wanting to assure me that I'll always have a willing ear at the police Department.

"You doing okay?" he asks me.

I assure him that I am.

"Hope this won't mean you're off our team," he says. "I was telling Mrs. Schultz the other night how helpful fresh eyes can be. Especially pretty young ones."

I tell him he's just the medicine I needed tonight and thank him for his concern.

"You haven't had any breakthroughs on the Nelson case, have you?" he asks me. "Haven't remembered anything else and had no one to tell, what with you and Scoones…"

I tell him that, as of yet, nothing's come to mind, but that I'll be sure to give him a call if I come up with anything.

"You do that," he tells me. "You call me anytime."

Which is tempting, since I spent most of last night wishing I could talk to a different policeman on the force. I examined the phone and there was no way to return a call, no way to call up a number for the received call. I can't tell him what we're doing to Jesse, can't have him convince me that it's the right thing and it's only temporary.

No, I am on my own.

Which is hard enough when it comes to my children, but impossible when it comes to helping him with Hal's case. I don't know what I'm supposed to be doing. I've read all the file material he could slip me, and all the newspaper accounts. Now what?

I'm full of questions beyond *what was I thinking?*

Like: Did Mr. Peaches really know what the misses was doing with her spare time?

Like: What's Hal's explanation for what he was doing there?

Like: What exactly am I looking for at the Nelsons' place?

Not that I can do anything about any of that today, because today I have my big presentation to Sydelle Silverberg, my mother's friend. If she turns out anything like the last client who was a friend of my mother's, I'll be lucky to come out alive.

Pulling up to the Silverberg place, I can see what my mother means about Sydelle getting me where I want to go. Can we say *The Riviera?*

The house I grew up in (affectionately dubbed the House of Horrors by my brother and me) was nothing to sneeze at, with its marble staircase over which hung a Fortunoff chandelier intended to intimidate anyone who might have the audacity to stand under it. It had four bedrooms, five bathrooms and a den with a bar where my father and I used to watch baseball, me pretending I cared who was batting and what each swing would do to their average, while enjoying his attention.

But Sydelle's house makes my mother's look quaint. It is a house built for entertaining, for impressing, for astounding.

Sydelle, on the other hand, is short, frumpy and has flour on her cheek when she greets me, coming to the front of the house after the housekeeper has shown me into the hall. At least I think it's flour and that she hasn't been snorting coke and missed her nose by a few inches.

"Come into the kitchen," she says, waving me to follow her. "I'm making Chinese dumplings to die for. You like Chinese? Of course you do. You're Jewish, right? So of course you like Chinese. You cook? Or you're a businesswoman? Not that they're mutually exclusive, but it's not easy to be both. Believe me, I know."

You may have noticed I haven't gotten a word in yet. We are now in the largest noncommercial kitchen I've ever been in. There must be several hundred little dumplings on trays around the counters.

Sydelle continues her monologue. "So your mother tells me you're a decorator and a detective. That's quite a combination. I'm guessing you don't cook. You have children? What do they eat? Do they like Chinese? You'll take home some dumplings. They'll love them. What's not to love? A little pork, God should forgive me, a little *schmaltz*. You know *schmaltz*? Of course you do. Here, taste."

She hands me a little plate with two dumplings on it. One looks like a half-moon ravioli. The other, a beggar's purse.

"You're not kosher, are you? Oh, right. You married that Italian boy. How could you be kosher? Eat, darling! So tell me, your mother says you know that terrible Harold Nelson. She's right?"

Her timing is impeccable. She pauses for my answer when my mouth is full of steaming dumpling.

"Good? It's the ginger. May that man be accosted by every man he ever arrested and may they do to him…" She rolls her eyes at the ceiling. "Not that anyone did that to Dennis, but it would have been on that man's head. Here. Try another."

I have fallen down the rabbit hole. Alice drank that bottle, I ate the dumpling.

"Your mother says you're going to nail him good. Tell me, darling. How can I help?"

I swallow quickly. These are, without doubt, the best Chinese dumplings I've ever had, but I want to get a word in before she starts again.

"An abuse of power," she says, just as I'm opening my mouth a moment too late. Worse, she opens a smoking stainless steel steamer and pulls out several more dumplings, adding them to my plate. "That's what it was, an abuse of power. Eat, darling. Everyone knows pot shouldn't be considered a drug. Only a few ounces, our Dennis had. A slap on the wrist he should have gotten, but no, your friend Harold Nelson throws the book at him. Thousands, tens of thousands, it cost us to get him out of it."

Why can't my mother have any normal friends? Ones that ask me in, sit down on the couch with me, look at my sketches and say, "I'd like my house to look like that."

"Any enemy of Harold Nelson is a friend of mine. What I want is for you to warm up this kitchen. Wood, tile, something not industrial, for God's sake. What am I, a professional cook? No, I'm just a housewife."

If she's "just a housewife," what does that make me? A pissant?

"But I'll tell you this, Miss Teddi Bayer… I still can't believe your mother really named you that. If we'd been friends back then, I'd never have permitted it. You must have hated your ex-husband a great deal not to keep your married name. I'll tell you this, Teddi Bayer. You get Harold Nelson sent up the river, and my Lester and I will give you such a bonus your head will spin. College for your oldest. How does that sound?"

I swallow the pot sticker whole and start to choke.

Sydelle gives me a glass of water. "So?" she says when I've caught my breath. "How do you like them dumplings?"

BOBBIE SITS IN MY KITCHEN, wanting to talk about Drew. I don't. She wants details. I don't have any. Not that I can give her. And not showing her my ring is killing me.

I busy myself with Maggie May, trying to teach her to speak, since half the time my kids don't want to talk to me.

Maggie gives up and leaves the kitchen, but Bobbie doesn't.

"So what happened?" she wants to know.

I tell her Drew asked me to marry him and I said it was not a good idea. Not now. He didn't take it well. In fact, things got very ugly. Especially in front of his new partner, which showed me just what kind of man he really is.

"So then the whole Drew thing has just been to irritate your mother?" she asks me, which I deny. "Are you in love with the guy or not?"

"It will be a long time before I'm over what Rio tried to do to me," I say. "Drew isn't willing to wait. He wants me to trust him as though I've never been betrayed. That's too much to ask. Too much, too soon."

Where did that come from? I wonder. It sounded almost as if I meant it.

I steer the conversation away from Drew, telling Bobbie she missed the show of a lifetime at Sydelle's. No matter what she saved on shoes at The Rack, and no matter how much she'll be able to get for them on eBay, I say it wasn't worth it.

"And she wants us to redo a kitchen that's bigger than the parking lot at the mall. Right now it's stainless steel and industrial shelving and she wants it all to look Country French. Painted wood and hand-painted tiles and a fireplace with a hearth in the kitchen where she can make pizza and bread and… The woman is just amazing."

Bobbie doubts it's merely a coincidence that Sydelle wants to hire a woman she believes is bent on proving the detective who arrested her son to be a murderer.

"Oh, please! That was back when Hal was a beat cop. Over ten years ago," I say. "That's a long time to wait for a decorating connection, don't you think?"

"Yeah, if your prime objective is to redecorate," Bobbie says. She's using my laptop to post shoes on eBay and only half listening to me.

Still, she has a point. There really is nothing wrong with Sydelle Silverberg's kitchen as it stands now. She doesn't even seem all that interested in redecorating it, leaving all the details to me, despite the fact that the woman seems to spend her life in that room.

Could she want revenge so much that she'd pay me to redo a perfectly fine kitchen to get it?

"Do you know how to turn off these stupid CNN breaking news e-mails?" Bobbie asks. "They're always interrupting me."

"That's because they're important," I say. "They're supposed to interrupt less important things, like selling shoes."

"The only thing more important than selling shoes is buying shoes," Bobbie tells me with a huff as she gets down from the bar stool and opens my refrigerator, staring into it. "Don't you have any good food in here?" she asks.

I tell her to throw some of the dumplings in the microwave (not the way Sydelle recommended I reheat them, but really… I do have a life!) and I click on the CNN update:

A gun has been found in the murder case involving Nassau County Police Detective Harold Nelson and Peaches Lipschitz, known as the Housewife Hooker.

I click on the link and learn that the gun was found in the storm drain outside Peaches' house.

"Now, really, what kind of cop would throw away the murder weapon where it was bound to be found?" I ask the air.

The site doesn't say how long ago the gun was found, and Drew hasn't mentioned it to me, though he must know. Which tells me that whatever evidence they've gotten off the gun isn't good for Hal, or he'd want me to know, right?

I feel a strange vibration in the pit of my stomach and I wonder if it's connected to all these questions I have, or merely to hunger. It's nearly electrifying. I know it's not hunger, after all those dumplings. It's…it's…

Oh, shoot! It's the *Dick Tracy* Secret Phone from Drew that I tucked into my pants pocket, now vibrating. I make some excuse to Bobbie about the bathroom and go running upstairs, pulling out the phone as I go and opening it so I don't lose the connection.

"Be back down in a minute," I yell so that Drew can know what's going on.

In the bathroom, door closed, water running, I say hello.

"It's Hallie's gun," Drew says. I can hear cars zooming by.

"Where are you?"

"Pretending to take a whiz off the parkway," he says. "The one place O'Hanlon won't come with me."

"The gun is Hallie's?" I ask, not wanting to go near the *well-O'Hanlon-isn't-sleeping-with-you-is-she?* question.

"Time to visit your best buddy again," Drew says. And then I hear him yell that he's coming. He damn well better not be.

"Drew—" I start. But the line is dead.

Okay, now if I'm Hal and I am screwing around with Peaches and I wind up killing her with Hallie's gun… I back up to the night of their argument. Hallie finds out about Hal's affair. She's furious. She threatens to expose the pair of them. Hal's caught between the two.

Kill one and frame the other for the murder?

Uh-oh. I can see that. Hal would have had access to his wife's gun. He probably bought it for her to begin with. When? Did he have framing her in mind when he bought it? What would stop him from saying that Hallie knew about the affair before she bought the gun?

Call me back, Drew, I tell the phone.

Unfortunately, you need a connection for that to be of any use.

"You okay in there?" Bobbie asks from outside the bathroom door.

"Must have been the dumplings," I say, thereby keeping the call a secret and saving the rest of those little delicacies for myself. I am one tricky woman.

I should be able to keep this farce up for oh, at least another few minutes.

HALLIE IS STILL in the hospital. They'd actually released her to go home, but her sister said she was afraid Hallie might try to kill herself again and that she couldn't move in with her. She has a family of her own. So apparently they gave Hallie the option of staying in the psyche ward—I don't think they actually told her she was committing herself, but, been there, done that at South Winds and I recognize the lay of the land.

I tell the nurse I'm Hallie's sister. She looks at me skeptically so I figure she's already met Sally. "Tali," I say, extending my hand. "I'd have gotten here sooner, but you don't get to meet the Dalai Lama every day, and I just couldn't get a flight out until yesterday. I've come straight from the airport."

The nurse looks me over. Apparently, despite fixing myself before I left my house, I look convincingly like I've been flying for days. Great.

I recall a line from *Annie Hall* and tell her that the only word for it was *transplendent*… "It was *transplendent!*"

She buys it and leads me down the hall and presses the buttons beside Hallie's door. "You know the rules," she says to Hallie, leaving the door open with a stern look. Hey, I know them, too. I spent an eternity one weekend at South Winds

Psychiatric Center due to my ex-husband's imitation of the movie *Gaslight*.

"Teddi?" Hallie looks up from her dinner and suspiciously eyes the door. "How did you get past Nurse Rachett?"

"Tali," I correct her. "I'm your long-lost sister. I hope that's okay with you."

"I'm so starved for company, even *you* look good," Hallie says. I see that her meds haven't softened her loving disposition. "So it's true then, what I heard?" she says.

"What is?" I ask, feeling self-conscious as she stares at me.

"You look like shit, so I guess you and Swoons really did break up." She smiles as if this is, in any way, her doing.

"Swoons? Is that like Dr. McDreamy?" I ask.

Hallie tells me he was "quite the player" before I came on the scene. "They all rot," she adds. "And Swoons is the worst of them, not even trying to find out the truth about that poor woman's murder."

Poor woman? I don't think that if my husband was fooling around with another woman I'd refer to her as a *poor woman*. I'd call her a slut. Oh, wait. I did. But I don't bring that up. Instead I ask Hallie if she knows something the police don't.

"You bet I do. I know Hal couldn't have done it. He wasn't mad at her. He wasn't afraid of her. He had no reason to kill her, and every reason not to. Every reason. And he wasn't the kind of man who could shoot some defenseless woman in the back."

"Every reason not to?" I ask, noticing how she emphasized that. I get the sense she's lobbing me secret messages and I'm missing the ball entirely. I wonder how many strikes she'll give me before I'm out. "It's not looking good for him, Hallie, so if you don't have more than that—"

"Why? What would you do with it? Unless you and Swoons aren't really kaput, and he's sent you here to pretend to be my friend—"

"*Sister*," I correct. She's on meds and in a hospital, yet she's the one who's managing to hide the truth while I give away every secret in my arsenal. "What makes you think that Drew and I haven't really broken up?"

"Because I heard your fight outside my door and what he said was off. I mean it sounded like *he* was breaking up with *you*, and not the other way around."

"He asked me to marry him and I said no. He was hurt and angry."

Hallie says the word around is that I said I wasn't ready for any commitment and Drew wasn't about to hang around until I was.

"Look," she says. "I've known Drew Scoones since he was a rookie. I've seen him sleep around, I've seen him go after a dozen women and catch every one of them. And I've seen him throw them back."

This is not exactly what I want to hear.

It gets worse.

"Maybe he wants to get back to fishing," I say weakly. Hallie ignores me.

"I've seen him with women who turn heads, women who belong on magazine covers, one who actually did pose for *Playboy*. Big-breasted ones, wasp-waisted ones, blondes and redheads and…"

"I get the point," I say. "I'm not in their league."

She says that isn't her point. "I've seen him infatuated, I've seen him taken, I've seen him smitten. I've never seen him in love…*before*."

"He's not—" I start, but she puts up her hand to stop me.

"He is. And he'd wait. I know it just like I know that Hal didn't kill that woman."

I wonder what makes her so sure about Hal. I can't believe it's just faith in her husband. It's got to be more than that. It was, after all, her gun. And it was, after all, thrown away in a panic not worthy of an officer.

Could it be that it's the old jealous wife crime? She did it, he's appearing to take the fall and they'll pull the old witness-for-the-prosecution thing at the trial?

"I know it looks bad for him. I know he went over there. But he had no reason to kill her. I mean, he almost worshipped her. I think he really believed that she'd help solve our problems. And why kill her when I already knew? And Andy knew—" She closes her eyes tightly. I get the feeling she wishes it had been her mouth.

"Andy? Andy who? Do you mean Andy Lipschitz? He knew his wife was a hooker?" I ask.

"Well, don't you think he must have?" she asks evasively. I admit that no, I don't. "Well, maybe you're right, then. Maybe he didn't."

"Do you know Andy?" I ask, my mind racing. Now I've got the two of them in cahoots. They get rid of his wife and then they get rid of her husband by pinning the murder on him. Hallie gives Andy her gun. He kills Peaches and dumps the weapon where he knows it will be found, implicating Hal. Then Hallie and Andy ride off into the sunset together.

Shoot. Why is it that every scenario seems to work?

"So, do you know Andy Lipschitz, Hallie?"

"Andy Lipschitz? How would I know him?" Hallie says, a little too quickly. "I can't really think with all these drugs."

I figure I better move on. Who knows how long I'll be able to get away with this, anyway?

"So tell me, Hallie," I say. "Because maybe there's some way I could help Hal. No one else seems to want to. Who else would have had access to your gun?"

She looks at me blankly. For a second I think it must be the medication they have her on, but then the nerve endings appear to connect. "My gun? Oh my God. My gun?"

I nod.

She swears she hasn't checked on the gun's whereabouts in months. Hal bought it for her after the Captain's house was burgled. "He took me to the range and taught me how to fire it. Then we put it on top of the closet. Like I told all the girls, I'd probably be overpowered and wind up getting shot with my own gun. I never looked at it again."

"Well, now that the police have it, they'll be running prints," I say, lying through my teeth, since I have no idea if its been wiped clean or not. "I guess they'll know soon enough."

"Prints? I wouldn't think they'd need them to clear Hal. They must have checked him for residue, right? They must know he didn't fire the gun." Ah, new question. Did they check Hallie? Just how soon after the arrest did she wind up in the hospital?

"Who else knew about the gun?" I ask, just as the nurse comes in.

"So this is your sister," she says amiably. A little too amiably. "Funny that your *other* sister, Sally, says she has only one sister. And here you have two."

"I should go," I say. "You're tired, sis."

The nurse tells me I can drop the "sister" routine.

"She's involved with a cop," Hallie tells her. "Believe me, she's part of the sisterhood."

I hug her goodbye, for the first time feeling that Hallie and I could be friends.

That is, if only I didn't suspect her of murder.

CHAPTER 6

Even the most formal house needs to have a sense of humor, something to make you smile. Accessories are a good place to exercise your individual quirkiness, whether it's in the bathroom or the kitchen. Rubber duckies by the tub, one of those Felix clocks where the eyes and tail go back and forth on the kitchen wall, something that says "don't take life too seriously."

TipsFromTeddi.com

"I realize that this is totally off point," I tell Drew when he finally calls on the Bat Phone. For some reason that term cracks him up, but he won't tell me why. Must be a guy thing, I guess, and I let it go.

At any rate, it's been a long day, punctuated by an even longer evening, during which getting Alyssa to bed proved a challenge I wasn't up to. She's sleeping now in the hallway outside my bedroom door because the monsters of her babyhood have apparently been booked for a return engagement in her closet—and *we don't have my daddy, or even a policeman to protect us anymore*. "But I need your advice as a man."

"Shoot," he says. It always unnerves me when a man carrying a gun says that.

"It's about Jesse."

Jesse, until now the kid we never had to worry about, has a special place in Drew's heart. He's fond of my girls—fonder of them than I am at this moment, but Jesse's stolen his heart. It's a mutual thing, so the response is rapid-fire. "What about Jess? What's wrong?"

This is a pretty delicate matter. Too delicate to talk comfortably about it with my dad, who, according to my mother is having his own difficulties in that department. And there is no way I'd talk to Jesse's dad about anything that even remotely involves sex, because I know where that conversation would no doubt go. By the time he was Jesse's age, Rio was probably seducing his teachers. And his solution for Jess would no doubt be to hook him up with someone who could "relieve his tension." *You don't want him to get blue balls, do you, Teddi?* I can imagine him saying.

"Teddi? Is something wrong with Jesse? Should I come over?"

I explain in my usual round-the-bush sort of way that Jesse is spending a lot of time alone in his room. At first Drew doesn't get it.

"He's probably just upset about us. It's time we leveled with him. You realize what this must be doing to the kid? Even worse than not being able to just pick up the phone and call you, worse than not being able to just drop over, worse even than the no sex…is knowing Jesse believes I'd just walked out of his life because of you."

As Jesse's mother, I find that incredibly touching. As Drew's main squeeze, not so much. So I don't tell him how maudlin Jesse is. I tell him that Jesse hates me, not him, blames it all on me, and that once we clear Hal we'll make it right.

"Besides, he's not in there sulking, Drew. He's...*entertaining* himself. And I know that's supposed to be normal, but I've lost count of the number of mismatched socks..."

Drew chuckles. I wish I could see his face, the way the crinkles beside his eyes suddenly appear, the way he smiles off to the right just a little. Or is it to the left? I feel as though it's been forever since I've seen him.

Even longer since I've seen him smile.

He assures me that it's perfectly normal and I should be relieved that Jesse's *energies* are *inwardly directed*. "A boy his age can get in a lot of trouble—"

I ask if he can't sort of "use it up."

"Later, when he's older," Drew says. "But not at his age. Look, I'll have a talk with him when this is all over, which can't be soon enough for me."

I say nothing, and so he asks what I found at Hal's place.

I admit I haven't been there yet. "I'm not really a breaking-and-entering specialist."

"I don't recall you having any trouble getting back into the Meyers' house. No trouble getting into your friend Howie's place, or Jerry Kroll's. You realize that once they release Hallie from the hospital..."

I tell him I don't even know what I'm looking for.

"You'll know when you find it. You always do."

I think that's actually a compliment. I tell him that I'll try to stop there tomorrow.

"I get the sense that you're not in much of a hurry," he says. There's an edge to his voice, an accusation.

I remind him that I do have mouths to feed and a roof to keep over my children's heads and I'm supposed to meet with a client who thankfully may provide a way for me to do that. I don't mention that this client has it in for Hal Nelson and wouldn't mind my being late if it meant that I was gathering evidence to prove his guilt rather than his innocence.

The truth is that I may be dragging my feet just a little. I mean, what do I really know about this man that I'm going to bring into my children's life?

Excuses, Teddi. I can't believe you're using the kids as excuses. Shame on you, a voice in my head chides. *This is a good man and you know it.*

I remind the voice that I thought Rio was a good man, but there is no answer.

"Teddi?" Apparently I've missed something Drew's said while listening to the gullible Teddi, the one that's ready to leap into another marriage…

"I said I'd get some money wired into your account," Drew says. "That'll tide you over until—"

Oh, God. Is *my* money going to be *his* money? Is his going to be mine? Marriage was so much less complicated the first time around.

He's not real happy with me when I politely decline. In fact, he's what you might call pissed.

"Maybe you don't care what those kids eat," he says, to

which I reply that we went out for Chinese more than once already this week. "Or what they're wearing on their feet." A sorer subject, to be sure, since the kids want Nike Dunks and not whatever's on the rack at Payless.

"They're not barefoot just yet," I tell him. "But I promise if it comes to that, I'll holler."

"Like hell you will," he says. "When this is over, I'm taking Jesse out for those sneakers he wants. Regardless."

I wonder what *regardless* means here. Whether I want him to or not, or whether we're together or not?

"I can take care of my children, thank you very much," I say and it's clear I don't mean it nicely.

There's dead silence for a moment and then quietly, rationally, without rancor or bitterness, Drew says that he doesn't think of them as *my* children anymore. "Maybe I'm jumping the gun a little here, but they've gotten under my skin and into my heart, Teddi, and being away from them is hard. I want to take care of them."

I expect his next sentence to be that he wants to take care of me, which has me riled. Only that isn't what he says at all.

"I want *us* to take care of them."

I bite my lip to stop myself from crying. Finally I find my voice and tell him that I won't be buying the kids those sneakers.

I'll wait for him to do it.

"Good," he says. "Good. Have you told Bobbie yet?"

I tell him I've been good and kept the secret.

"Oh," he says, and he sounds disappointed. I assure him that I wanted to tell her, but was afraid that once I told her I wouldn't be able to stop myself from telling everyone. It sounds like an excuse, but he accepts it.

"One more thing, Ted," he says before we hang up. "And I hate to say this, but watch your back. It's not impossible you're being tailed."

"You're just saying that to justify this ridiculous faux break-up," I say, praying that when this is over it'll turn out to really be faux.

"Now why would I do that?" He sounds like he's teasing me, daring me to mention his new and very sexy partner.

I won't go there, and I don't bite.

He tells me that he'll call me tomorrow so I can tell him what I've found out. And he adds that he's counting on me.

"I'm having dinner at my folks'," I tell him. "Call late."

"Perfect."

Now Drew knows how any time spent with my mother turns me into a raving lunatic, so I'm surprised by his reaction. "Why *perfect?*" I ask.

He hems. He haws. He mumbles something about going out with the guys to celebrate someone's divorce.

"Does *the guys* include your new partner?" I ask.

I can sense his shrug through the phone. "Sure. A lot of people will be there," he says.

I don't really want to talk about Detective O'Hanlon. I don't want to think about Drew spending days and nights and stakeouts in a car alone with her. But I don't want to hang up, either. This is the longest conversation we've had since Hal was arrested and, nestled under my comforter, I'm relishing every moment of it. So I ask whose divorce they're celebrating.

There is a very long silence. Finally he says, "Just, you know, one of the guys."

"This guy have long blond hair, a killer figure and wear skirts that don't reach her knees?"

"She claims it's not that the skirts are so short, but that her legs are so long," Drew says. "She does have long legs."

THE MORNING FINDS Alyssa in my bed. This is supposed to be a big no-no when there are two parents involved because it interferes with parental intimacy. Not a problem here. I think it's still a no-no for single parents, but whoever is writing these books is made of sterner stuff—both physically and emotionally—than I am. Carrying a sleeping seven-year-old back to bed? Can we say deadweight? Can we say female equivalent of hernia?

Do we even know what that is?

At any rate, I do manage to get them off to school before my mother calls to ask, oh so innocently, why I wasn't home last night when she called.

"I was not seeing Drew Scoones, if that is what you are asking," I tell her.

"Did I ask?" she says, feigning great offense.

I tell her I was just saving her the trouble. "We've broken up, Mother. I'm sure you're very happy to hear that."

She admits she is, but only, she says, because she wants me to be happy and she knows that I couldn't be happy with Drew.

"Not in the long run. Now that you're free, Teddi, I know a very nice man, a widower, who knows about fidelity."

"Mom—"

"I'm telling you, the man's wife was sick for months. Wasting away. In agony. And he had round the clock nurses for her. For her! Not that she didn't deserve them, but… You remember Paulette, may she rest in peace…"

"Paulette Jenson? Didn't you just go to her funeral a few weeks ago?" I ask. I could swear I had to take my mother to buy black shoes she could wear to a cemetery. *Now here's a man who knows about fidelity.* Fidelity Bank? Fidelity Trust?

"It's six weeks. Perfectly respectable when you add in how long she was dying. And a man his age can't wait forever, Teddi. He isn't getting any younger. And he'll be snapped up in a heartbeat if we don't get right on it." She goes on until she senses that I'm not listening.

"Fine," she says. "Let another one slip through your fingers. But remember, Teddi, you're not getting any younger, either."

I wish I could argue with her there, but this morning in the mirror it looked like a flock of crows spent the night performing *Riverdance* by my eyes.

"I spoke to Sydelle," she tells me. I doubt this is the case. She must mean she *heard* from Sydelle. Even my mother couldn't get a word in a conversation with Sydelle Silverberg. "She says you are going to use that detective's balls for—"

"Mother!"

"I'm only quoting Sydelle. I don't know what you did, Teddi, but for some reason, she actually likes you."

How is a daughter supposed to respond to that? I ask you.

"So it's very important now that you don't blow it. Keep your mouth shut and tell her exactly what she wants to hear."

I don't bother pointing out the impossibility of that.

"I changed your appointment with her. She's going to be home all day anyway, so we're seeing her this morning. I can meet you at her house at ten. I think that my input could be invaluable."

"I can't be there at ten," I say. It's easier than telling her *she* can't be there at ten. "I'm planning on seeing her later this afternoon."

"But I have my massage this afternoon. And nails and toes. You know that. Every other Friday, Teddi, for as long as you've been alive." I hear her take a drag of her cigarette and exhale exasperatedly.

"And you've got Dr. Cohen Monday at nine," I say, referring to the shrink she's been seeing for almost forty years. "And you get your hair done Tuesday in the afternoon. Then there's waxing on Wednesdays before Canasta, and Thursdays there's mah-jongg…"

"Congratulations. You know my schedule, Miss Smarty Pants. Then you know this morning is the only time I can give you," she tells me.

Sadly then, I will have to do without her. I'll have to go it alone. Not have her there to tell the client about the time I had a hallway painted the wrong color. Not there to have her say I have garish taste, but I can tone it down. Not there to say that all houses should be done in beige or taupe or ecru, and that there is a vast difference between them and their effect on the psyche.

It seems fate has stepped in and decided to send me off to Hallie's place this morning.

Now all I need is a plan.

"OKAY, WHAT IS SO important that it couldn't wait until after I posted my new stuff on eBay?" Bobbie asks me as she shrugs out of a little mink-lined denim jacket. She has on black leggings, an oversized cashmere tunic which is belted with a gorgeous gold belt with a stone buckle and boots with heels at least four inches high. Her hair is perfect and her lipstick has been freshly applied.

"You dressed like that to work at your computer?" I ask her, waving at her attire as she reaches for my coffeepot and a clean cup.

"You thought I'd wear what? Sweats?" she asks before she grabs my left hand and points at the ring on my finger. "What is that?" she demands.

I make her swear that she will keep this a secret, and because we've been friends forever and seen each other through the trenches, I believe her when she crosses her heart, which happens just before she jumps up and down.

"I thought you didn't like Drew," I say, confused at her excitement.

"Because he wouldn't pee and he wouldn't get off the pot," she says.

"Men don't have to be *on* the pot to pee," I remind her.

"Isn't that the truth," she says. "I didn't think he'd come through. I really didn't." She wants to know who else knows, and why it's a secret.

"No one," I say, and explain how we're pretending to have broken up so that I can investigate for him and help clear Hal.

Bobbie is beside herself. I'm working for the underdog again, I'm getting married again, and I'm about to irritate the hell out of my mother again.

She has only one question, she says. "How can I help?"

TWENTY MINUTES LATER my ring is back in the safe in my bedroom, and Bobbie and I, in each other's cars, are headed in different directions on the Long Island Expressway. She's headed west toward the city in my car while I drive her car out to the Nelsons' house.

"Hello?" I say into the air, amazed that with Bluetooth I can keep both hands on the wheel and still place phone calls. "Bobbie? Is anyone following you, do you think?"

"Something's wrong with my phone," she says. "It says *unlisted number* and your picture doesn't come up." I hear her hit the phone against the steering wheel.

I explain I'm using a different phone and ask again if she is being followed.

"How would I know, Mrs. Detective Scoones?" she asks me.

"They call him Detective *Swoons*," I say. I can't help giggling about that. It's so Drew. "What do you see in the rearview mirror?"

"Um… My hair looks really good this color," she says. "I like the blond highlights with the red. I'm going to wear it this way to your wedding. And, oh my God, do I need to get my eyebrows waxed! How long do I have to keep driving? I really need to pee and get my brows done and I still need to check my listings on eBay."

I tell her that I probably need an hour. We have to meet at Sydelle's at noon to try her new recipe for stuffed cabbage and show her our ideas. And I remind her that she was supposed to be wearing a hat so that if someone was actually following her they wouldn't realize it wasn't me.

She swears she was going to, but that her hair came out too good to ruin it with a hat.

"If I get arrested for breaking and entering, you'll look really good at my arraignment," I tell her.

She tells me she doesn't know why I am bothering anyway. "We all know he did it. I mean, the man cheated on his wife—"

She stops herself. Not only did my husband cheat on me, but Bobbie's husband, Mike, actually left her a couple of years ago for another woman. He came back, tail between his legs, repentant, and she took him back.

"—which, I'll admit, doesn't make him necessarily a murderer," she concedes. "But the cops wouldn't have arrested him unless—"

Again, she stops herself. She herself was arrested when all the evidence in the Meyers murder seemed to point to her. Yes, it was a bogus arrest and they were trying to entrap the head of the smuggling ring, but still. And then there was the near arrest of our good friend, Howard Rosen.

"Okay. I'm in. I'll drive down to Cedarhurst and pee at your mother's. That ought to give her a real thrill. And I'll put on the damn hat."

I thank her and remind her that my mother absolutely can't know about Drew and me.

"No problem. Teddi, aren't you excited?"

Now that Bobbie knows, it feels a lot more real.

"Of course I am," I say, which comes out flat. "Okay, well, nervous, too, I guess." Of course, that could have to do with breaking into someone's house....

I PARK AROUND the corner from the Nelsons' place. I figure if it's being watched, I don't want to pull into the driveway, do I? I know that Drew has a key to this house. Most cops have keys to each others' houses. It's a sign of trust. Heck, they're cops. They know how to get into a house without a key.

At any rate, Drew hasn't given it to me because that would blow his stupid I-told-her-to-stay-out-of-it plan, so I'm dashing through the backyards and standing at Hallie's back door.

I've never been here before, but, as a decorator, I'm pretty good at sizing up layouts. This is a traditional high ranch with an upper and lower entrance at the back of the house. The lower one connects to the family room and happily is all but hidden under the large deck that was added a few years ago. I figure they don't use the family room much since a)they don't have a family, and b)they've effectively cut off all the natural light by adding the deck.

At any rate, I feel around the top of the door frame for a spare key. I figure that in the same way that lawyers never read the fine print because they know they can weasel out of any contract, and doctors smoke because they think they'll know the warning signs and will be able to quit in time, cops think that no one will break into their houses, and if they do, well, hell, they'll just shoot 'em.

Actually, that particular thought doesn't sit real well as I look under the flowerpot beside the door where I'm pretty sure a key must be hidden, since the plant that was in it started dying the day after they installed that deck.

Voilà! Sometimes I'm so smart I impress even myself. I slip the key into the lock and slide the door open. No security bar, no two-by-four in the track. Amazing.

The room is dark, gloomy and has no charm at all. Personally, I think it perfectly reflects its owners. The first thing I notice is that it looks like someone has been sleeping down here. There are sheets on the couch and a pillow and blanket piled up on the chair. So, Hallie wasn't lying about them having had a fight. She's lying about something; I just don't know what. Had Hallie made up the bed for Hal? Or was *she* sleeping down here?

I climb the stairs to the kitchen and look around there. All the appliances are stainless steel. The sink is stainless steel. The walls are white, the floor is white. The window blinds are slats of, you guessed it, stainless steel. It has all the warmth of an operating room. Not exactly Peaches' homey kitchen.

It looks to me like the cops have already been over this place with a fine-tooth comb, though nothing is out of place. They always leave telltale signs, I think for other cops to find.

What am I looking for? I wonder as I tiptoe around. On the wall next to the refrigerator is a framed calendar with lots of careful writing on it. Doctor's appointments, bold red X's every four weeks, bold red O's spaced evenly between them. Not hard to figure out what was on Hallie's agenda.

An angry red X that all but obliterates February 21 explains a lot more than Hallie told me at the hospital.

I slip out my camera phone and take a picture of the month on high resolution so that I can enlarge it on my computer. But I know that anything Hallie might have been hiding from Hal, or vice versa, isn't likely to be posted on the fridge. What I need is a personal date book, a BlackBerry, a Palm Pilot, something like that.

I put the calendar back on the fridge, noting a picture of Sally with her husband and her three kids, others showing one officer or another along with their wives and kids, a kid's drawing held on with a fertility clinic magnet. I think of my three darlings, one of which kept me up half the night, and remember how lucky I am to have them. Their father may have been a mistake, but a mistake worth making since it got me them.

Up another flight of stairs I find a wood-paneled office with a computer and file cabinets, clearly the domain of Hal, with his citations framed on the walls, his trophies on a high shelf, looking rather meager and lonely. Two appear to be for softball or Little League—they look just like Jesse's. There's an old baseball glove up there, probably being saved for his son, or for himself to have a catch with that elusive child.

God, I hate it when my heart goes out to someone I've decided to hate.

Makes sense now. Hal's always chiding me for being reckless when I have children to think about. Of course, I don't for a minute think he'd give up being a cop if he and Hallie had gotten lucky.

Which reminds me of when my kids were very little and Dana, being older, had somehow learned that sex makes babies. "But I don't understand," she'd said. "You and Daddy have sex all the time, but you don't always make a baby."

"You have to be lucky," I told her.

And little Jesse, who couldn't have been more than four at the time, piped up with, "And you don't want to be lucky, do you?" The "do you?" came out like a threat.

I fire up the computer, put in my two-gig flash drive and direct the download of Hal's Documents and Settings files. That will have to do for now, I figure, as I head for the bedroom, clearly decorated by the same Spartan who did the kitchen.

The walls are papered in a soft grey suede. I'm thinking that if I could find that in buckskin it would be super in Susan Michaels' media room. The furniture is grey Formica with mirrored knobs on the drawers. A modern curved glass frame holds Hal and Hallie's wedding picture on the dresser. On one nightstand is a bottle of antacid, one of those squishy balls you squeeze to relieve tension, and the remote to the DVD player. On the other nightstand is a box of tissues, some jars and tubes of hand cream, foot cream, night cream and the cable remote.

In the wastebasket I find a copy of *Hustler* magazine, no doubt for Hal's "command performance" issues, a small bottle of K-Y Jelly and a thermometer.

I pretend that this is any of my business because otherwise I'd be way too uncomfortable to look any further, and I open a bureau drawer. I hit on Hallie's underwear first and feel around beneath it. If I was hiding something from my husband, that's where I'd put it. Somehow husbands only like undies when they're on women. That and, of course, taking them off said women.

Her underwear is varied and I feel like a voyeur as I sift through brand-new white cotton panties with the tags still on them, well-used black silk ones, a jeweled G-string, half a dozen thongs. Clearly she was willing to suit whatever mood might do the trick for Hal, while he was interested in a whole different kind of trick across town.

Just as my hands encounter something definitely not underwear, I get the nasty feeling I'm being watched. It starts at the back of my neck and shimmies down my spine. Without moving, I shift my eyes toward the doorway where a uniformed cop, his hands crossed over his chest, leans on the door frame.

"Find what you're looking for yet?" he asks me. His calm is downright eerie, and scares me more than if he were pointing his service revolver at me.

After gasping, I try to recover and seem just as calm as he is. "I didn't realize anyone was still here," I say, like seeing him wasn't a major shock to my system that probably took five years off my life. "Hallie just needs a few things at the hospital. Fresh undies, that sort of thing." I hold up a pair of her panties—unfortunately, crotchless ones—and stuff them into my purse, along with the little notebook from the bottom of the drawer.

"I see," he says. I'm sure he does. And having shown him those undies I can't help wonder exactly what he's seeing. I stuff in a couple more pairs, including those new white cotton ones.

"A nightgown," I say, trying the drawer beneath her panties. "And what else?"

"A robe?" he suggests.

I nod.

"Slippers?" He's a regular Mr. Helpful.

Again, I nod. I'm doing good. I reach down for the slippers she's left by her bed.

"A copy of what's on her husband's computer?"

Shit. Okay, not so good.

"A photo of her calendar? She sentimental about February?"

"Uh… Uh… Actually, I think she's just a little confused. You know, the drugs she took, the ones they're giving her. I guess she just wanted to get certain things straight in her mind."

He sticks out his lower lip and nods. He's still filling the doorway. "Nice try," he says. He puts out his hand, palm up. "Your phone, please."

I hand it to him without argument. I watch *February* disappear.

Handing me back the phone he tells me that it was real nice finally meeting the famous Teddi Bayer. "Or should I say infamous?" he asks.

"Depends who you ask, I suppose," I say.

He isn't saying who told him I'd be there, and I don't know if it's friend or foe.

"Drew Scoones would say—" I stop myself. Drew is supposed to hate me now. "Well, I guess for him I'm kind of an historical figure." I watch for a reaction. The man could be a guard at Buckingham Palace, or the Tomb of the Unknown Soldier. Nothing shows on his face.

"I'll see you out," he says, and moves so that I can pass him in the doorway. I head for the computer, but behind me I hear, "Uh-uh-uh," which I take to mean *no*. Well, another two-gig flash key beats the dust.

He leads me back down through the family room and slides the door open for me. Once I'm on the outside of the door, he lowers the safety bar into place.

Okay, so I'm not so smart. I fell right into their trap.

So why didn't they spring it?

Why let me leave?

CHAPTER 7

Decorating a house doesn't start inside the front door. It doesn't even start at the porch, where a few wicker chairs or an Adirondack bench can do wonders for setting a mood. It starts at curbside, with the mailbox, the driveway, the walk up to the house. The mood outside your house—crafty, formal, country—can be set before the key goes into your door.

TipsFromTeddi.com

At eleven fifty-five I am in Sydelle Silverberg's driveway. Bobbie is not. Nor is she answering her phone, even when I use my traceable one to call her. My first inclination is to call Drew and tell him about what happened at Hallie's house and ask him if he knows whether anything has happened to Bobbie. My second inclination is to just kill Bobbie for standing me— and the client—up again.

I try my mother's house, since Bobbie was supposed to make a pit stop there. My mother says she left "hours ago," and wants to know why I can't dress like my friend. "She always looks so well put together," my mother tells me. I look down at the pants I'm wearing, which have dog hairs from the knees on down. The pants are brown. My parka is green.

Why *can't* I dress more like Bobbie?

My mother starts in again about Paulette's husband. She's hardly been dead long enough to call him a widower. "He has good teeth. All still his own," she says. I don't ask how she comes to know this. Someone in her spy network must use the same dentist he does. "He's on Halcyon, because he's having trouble sleeping since Paulette died. I told you—he knows fidelity."

I promise to at least think about it, a promise I have no intention of keeping, and hang up.

Eleven fifty-nine, according to my cell phone which everyone knows is atomic time. Or whatever. I figure I'll give Bobbie sixty seconds more, and slip Hallie's little booklet out of my purse, where it's nestled up against her panties. Turns out it's a date book. A date book she has taken pains to hide from her husband.

Eureka! I have hit the mother lode.

Or possibly it's been planted by the police for me to find.

I look at the day of the murder with skepticism. In the little square for February 20 is a notation which reads 6 p.m. until?— Inn Between with L.C-W., S.B., T.L. and R.S. Below that, in tiny, almost invisible letters are the initials A.L. followed by a question mark.

I think that these are the initials of several detectives' wives on the squad. Ron Williams' wife is Lynette Chappell-Williams, Dan Brody's wife is Susan. I can't remember the others, but I think this is what Hallie would refer to as the sisterhood.

A knock on the car window startles me, and the panties that are still in my right hand go flying up as I jump in my seat.

Sydelle's mouth makes a little O.

I lower the window and gather up the panties at the same time, shoving them beneath my seat as inconspicuously as I can, which isn't very.

"I don't care what they say," Sydelle tells me before I can say hello. "That's not the way to a man's heart. You come in and try my *holishkes*. That's what a man will love. Can a man eat those panties?" She turns three shades of red, all of them clashing, as she realizes what she's said. "So, maybe I'm wrong."

"I—"

"But could both hurt? I mean, I'll pack you up some cabbage and you can do a test, yes? Have them cooking on the stove so he—your policeman friend, maybe?—smells them, then…" She points toward the seat of my car. "You're coming in? That partner of yours isn't here yet, but we can start without her. I have stuff on the stove."

"And I have wonderful preliminary sketches to show you. Just some clippings and things to be sure we're on the same page." There. I've gotten out two whole sentences. I feel like the conquering hero.

"What's so difficult? Country French. You could do it in your sleep, I betcha. Come. I don't want them to burn."

I trot after her into the house, looking over my shoulder for Bobbie, who is nowhere in sight.

We spend what feels like hours talking about stuffed cabbage and Country French. Okay, she talks about stuffed cabbage and I try to steer the conversation back to Country French.

"So tell me," she says after a while. "How are things going with our *butcher in blue?* I read the paper every day and there's no news. Why isn't the arraignment scheduled? What's the holdup?"

Okay, I've been down this road before. I had a client who kept pumping me for police information and he turned out to be the murderer. Now it's a stretch and a half to think this little woman wielding pots and, okay, yes, butcher's knives, killed Peaches Lipschitz. But then, I'd have said the same thing about seventy-year-old Jerry Kroll being a serial killer, and look how that ended up—with me in the Long Island Sound treading water for my life.

"Your mother says things aren't so good between you and that detective anymore. The one who used to be the butcher's partner—"

"Detective Nelson is not a butcher," I say. It just comes out of me, and if it costs me this job, then so be it. I mean, any man who saves his old baseball glove for his son deserves to be cut a little slack. I'm not saying he didn't fool around with Peaches, and I'm not even saying that he didn't kill her. I'm just saying he's not a butcher.

I'm just saying.

"But you're still investigating?" Sydelle asks me. "I only want you to find out the truth, which I know will be that he did it. They always get hoisted by their own petard. You know what I mean? The mightier they are, the harder they fall, I say. Well, *everyone* says, really. Anyway, as long as you're still looking into it, I know you'll find out he did it, and you'll help the police, like you did before. My Dennis showed me a couple of articles about you online. You're someone to be reckoned with, alright."

"You're sure you want light blue for the accent in here?" I ask, waving in the general direction of the stove, not wanting to talk about Hal while my feelings are so jumbled. "I was thinking of a sunny golden color. Kind of antique-harvest-gold, only with some more buttercup in it."

"Blue," she says. So many of my clients are drawn to blue. Sometimes I feel like I must be the only woman in the world who hates the color.

In the end she picks three clippings she likes, two tile companies she adores, and poo poos the idea of granite for the counters in the kitchen. I leave with enough cabbage rolls to feed the Mormon Tabernacle Choir, should they want a *bisel nosh* from the old country, and the distinct feeling that I am being hired to convict Hal Nelson. And if by chance I feel like decorating this kitchen, we can do that…on the side.

In the car yet again, which is where I seem to live these days, I call to check up on the kids.

"Roger's here," Dana says. "Just so you know and don't think I'm doing anything behind your back or anything." This is a reference to her last boyfriend, the twenty-something Rio had to beat up and who Drew threatened with the law. It's nice when my men can collaborate, don't you think?

"And what are you two doing?" I ask, trying to make it sound like idle conversation.

"Homework," she says. "DBQs for social studies." I have no

idea what a DBQ is, but I'm embarrassed to say so. We didn't have DBQs when I went to school. We were just getting into acronyms, like AIDS, STDs…

"And you know what Jesse's doing," she says, and I hear Roger snort in the background. "And Alyssa is watching SpongeBob. And I know you don't like SpongeBob but she doesn't listen to me, and you're not here and if you don't want her to watch it, then you should be here telling her."

"Do I deserve that?" I ask her and she is immediately contrite.

"Sorry. I guess you're feeling pretty crappy these days, boy-friend-less and all. Don't worry, I'll find a DVD she likes, Mom," she says. "Roger will get her to watch something else. She's crazy about him."

"The little flirt," I hear Roger say in the background. "Hey, Squirt Flirt…"

I tell her I'll be home soon, and punch in Bobbie's number. I don't want to hear her excuses. Don't want to hear about the Jimmy Choos she scored while I'm trying to earn enough to buy my own kids Cons and knockoff Nikes and Sketchers.

"I'm sorry," she says when she answers the phone.

"You're all right?" I ask.

"I stopped at your mother's and then just lost track of the time," she says. It hurts. It hurts down to my very soul that I can't rely on her anymore, can't trust her, can't count on her. And then I think, why should I? I'm a big girl and can rely on myself. Isn't that what this business was all about? Bobbie isn't interested in it. She's got nothing invested in it. No matter how great a job we do, no matter how satisfied our customers are, the truth is that the triumph is mine, mostly because it's so important to me.

I haven't gotten an urgent call from my mother threatening to disown me, so I know that Bobbie has kept my secret.

"She knows all these great places to get vintage stuff and designer stuff. Apparently she and her friends give the stuff to charity all the time, and she told me about this resale store in Manhasset that has designer shoes sometimes and—"

I'm going to have to let her go—in the boss-employee sense, and in the roots and wings sense. I'm going to have to let her fly.

"So? Did you get great shoes?" I ask.

"There was a pair of almost-new Manolos there. At the Cancer Thrift Shop in Manhasset," she tells me. "Five bucks! I should get at least two hundred for them!"

"Good for you," I say, and I mean it. "Listen. Can you order *Witness for the Prosecution* and *Anatomy of a Murder* from Netflix? The kids have a million stupid ones in our queue."

"Oh…are we having a Girls' Night In? Can I invite Diane? We haven't had one of those in ages."

I tell her I'm counting on Diane being there. I need to pick her cop sister's brains. "I have a theory," I say, but before I can give it voice, my pants start to vibrate. I enjoy the sensation for a minute, knowing who's causing it, even if it's not intentional. And then I dig the phone out of my pocket and answer it.

"Hold on," I tell Drew, and then I say goodbye to my partner, in more ways than one.

"Where are you?" Drew asks me when I come back to him.

I tell him I'm about ten minutes from home, heading up the Meadowbrook Parkway. "Sweet," he says and tells me to pull into the Coliseum parking lot, head in like I'm going to the Craft Fair there and then go out the back and meet him in the Marriott. Room 341.

I think about the two containers of stuffed cabbage in the back of my car. "Are you hungry?" I ask him.

"Only for you," he says.

I reach under the seat and pull up the crotchless panties. With a shrug I tuck them in my purse and turn on my signal to exit the parkway.

DREW ANSWERS MY KNOCK and lets me in. He's got on jeans and a very tight T-shirt. No socks, no shoes, no belt. I figure less than a minute to stark naked and spread eagle. Unfortunately, that doesn't seem to be his plan.

"Did you get into Hallie's?" he asks me, helping me out of my jacket and tossing it toward the bed, where I'd prefer he was tossing me.

"You know I did," I tell him, feeling like I'm being used. "Why didn't you just have the patrolman let me in? You like having me scared half out of my wits? Those are five years I'm not going to get back in this life, you know."

Drew looks at me blankly. Drew never looks blank. This is not a good sign.

"The cop who was there? The one who must have left the security bar up for me? The one who…"

He hasn't a clue. I start at the beginning. Somewhere in the middle he sits down on the bed.

I finish with the cop insisting I leave the flash key and seeing me out. "He was clearly expecting me, Drew. And yet he let me leave."

"Were you followed here?" Drew asks me, getting down on all fours and trying to look under the door. I assure him that I was not. "You're sure?"

"I spent twenty minutes in the Craft Fair talking paint with a furniture artist. I then went to the ladies' room, cut into the middle of the food line and then slipped out the exhibitor's entrance," I say, sitting down on the bed and taking off my boots. "Believe me, no one followed me."

"Okay, look. They are trying to trap *me*, not you. But they're using you to do it."

Now I'm the one with the blank stare.

"They plant information for you to find, expecting you to pass it on to me. When you do, they've got me by the short hairs."

"You mean like her date book? You think that was a plant? And got you for what?"

"If I go against the Department, I'll be seen as a rogue cop," he says, shrugging in answer to the date book's veracity. "You know what they do to rogue cops?"

I shake my head.

"I was at the scene of a homicide with the prime suspect and I didn't call it in. Can we say 'accessory'? And I don't mean your purse and shoes."

"But—"

"You wanna guess how long it would take a smart D.A. to make it look like if Vice hadn't shown up Hal and I would have been able to cover up the whole affair? Not hard to make it look that way. Not hard at all."

"Cover up the affair and the *affaire*," I say, catching on. "Remove any connections between Hal and Peaches."

"Maybe even remove Peaches," he agrees. So now I finally get why we're meeting in secret and why he can't work on the case openly.

"So then they're out to get you, too?" I ask. He shrugs agreement. It's a possibility. "Then we just need to figure out who wants to get you, right?"

"I'm just the bonus—the cherry on top. Not that they'd mind nailing me for sticking by him. Collateral damage, as they say. We need to figure who's behind this frame-up fast. Nelson's arraignment is coming up in less than a week."

"If it's a frame-up," I add.

He assures me that it is, and says it's been a bad year for local law enforcement, what with a sheriff's officer arrested for fraud and grand theft. "They're going all out to show the county they can clean up their own. All out," he repeats.

I ask him how we know what information we can trust and what's been planted, and he looks at me as though for the first time I understand what it's like to be a cop.

"So let me see the book," he says, holding out his hand. I reach into my bag and along with the date book, out comes Hallie's undies.

Drew ignores them and takes the book. I point out to him the notation on the day of Peaches' murder. He confirms that the initials are all cops' wives. "A.L., too?" I ask.

No one pops into his mind. "Could be just someone's girlfriend," he says. "Maybe they were thinking of inviting her and that's why there's a question mark."

"Maybe," I agree, balking at the reference to *just a girlfriend*, but letting it go. "Or maybe it's Andy Lipschitz. Maybe she was meeting him after the party."

Drew puts down the book and looks at me. "Interesting. Brains and beauty," he says, and suddenly he remembers the panties, picks them up off the bedspread and holds them up between us. "And look, as I said, there is a kinky side to you, after all."

I explain that they are Hallie's, that I probably couldn't get one leg into them, and any further explanation is interrupted by lips and hands and soft parts and hard parts and oh…

In the middle of which Drew bolts upright—not the part of him that's supposed to do that in this situation—and says that it could be a trap. Something to send him down a blind alley while they railroad Hal into the pen.

"Did I remember to tell you that Hallie told me Andy knew about Hal and Peaches' relationship?" I ask. "But then she denied knowing him?"

I'm back to *beautiful and brainy* and on my back. Then on top. Then on my back again.

Forty-five minutes later I'm lucky to be able to talk, and walking will be out of the question. And I'm starving. So, probably, are my kids. I tell Drew that I've really got to get going, but that I'm working on his case. I admit that I got into this just to help him, but that now I'm finally convinced that Hal wasn't the murderer.

"Too many things just don't fit," I say. "I have this feeling that we're all being had. By the Department, by Hallie and Hal. By the real murderer…"

Drew is over the moon that I've seen the light. I assure him that it's not that I think Hal is that nice, that honest, that law-abiding.

I simply don't think he's that stupid.

"That's fine, that's good," Drew says. "Especially in light of the fact that he's just confessed."

CHAPTER 8

Decorating can make or break a diet, so those of you who want to trim down, take note. An old-fashioned kitchen with cheery canisters, a covered cake plate, a cheerful kettle on the stove, all say EAT in capital letters. A gorgeous bowl filled with fresh fruit on a center island, a watercooler with fresh lemons atop it, a small herb garden in a greenhouse window say EAT, too, but eat HEALTHY!

TipsFromTeddi.com

"He confessed," my mother says. She has managed to work us into her Monday schedule and has turned up at Sydelle's for my next client meeting. We are all, of course, in Sydelle's kitchen. I can see why she wants it warmer and friendlier. If ever a kitchen was the heart of a home, this one is it. "The pressure got to him. It always does. If I know about anything in this life, it's pressure." She checks her watch for the third time. The pressure my mother knows is that she's got an appointment she doesn't want to miss with a golf instructor she's thinking of hiring. If they ever do move to Boca, she wants to be ready.

Me?

I've been ready for that move for twenty years.

"So? Details?" Sydelle asks me. Frankly, it's hard to think with the smell of *rugelach* surrounding me. Oh, how I intended to stick to my diet today. I tried on Hallie's panties over my lonely weekend, and they were only a smidge too small. I really think five pounds…seven, tops, and I could—I mean, if I wanted to—wiggle my way into those panties. "All *Newsday* says is that he confessed and that the arraignment has been moved up. Eat, darling, they're still hot. So, I want to know when the public flogging is. I want to be there, God should forgive me, to cast the first stone."

"Is this one chocolate?" I ask, examining the little pastries on my plate and not wanting to fool my mouth into thinking it's getting chocolate and then finding out it's just dark raisins.

"Have you any idea of the calories in these things?" my mother asks, taking the one I suspect is chocolate off my plate and popping it into her mouth to my astonishment. "What?" she asks me innocently. "I'm already married. When you're married again you can get as fat as you want and I won't say a word."

It's the most tempting inducement for marriage I've heard yet.

"So did you help get him to confess?" Sydelle wants to know. She puts two chocolate *rugelach* on my plate to replace the one my mother stole. "She's skin and bones, June. Eat, darling. So, did you find some incriminating evidence? Some incontrovertible proof? Did you make him see there was no way to wiggle out of this one?"

I know it may cost me this job, but I have to say it. "I don't think, actually, that he did it."

My mother gasps. She actually drops the pastry onto her china plate with a thud.

Sydelle isn't affected in the least. "Do I care?" she asks. "If he didn't do this, he did something else. He thinks he's above the law, or outside the law, or maybe beneath the law."

Paging Steven Seagal. I have two new titles for you.

"A man confesses, he did it. End of story," my mother says, checking her watch again and coming down from the bar stool at the counter. "You're replacing these, I hope?" she asks me, looking disdainfully at the modern chrome stools that are so uncomfortable.

I assure her that the stools will be the first things to go, while Sydelle asks why I doubt Hal's guilt. "Why would he confess if he's innocent?" she asks me.

Why, indeed. Well, the most obvious reason is to protect someone else, or stop a greater misdeed from being revealed. It's hard to imagine a greater misdeed than murder, so I'm thinking he's protecting someone. He's got a wife. He's got a mistress. The mistress is dead. Leaves just little old hospitalized Hallie. Hallie who tried to commit suicide after Hal was arrested.

Could it be as obvious as the nose that used to be on my face before my mother insisted I have a nose job?

I've got to go talk to L.C-W., S.B., T.L. or R.S.

I make my excuses, get my bag of goodies to go, promise I'll have more sketches next time, and hightail it out of the Silverbergs' house. On my way out I nearly run over a man so thin a breeze could blow him to China. He's dressed in white shorts that swim on him and one of those sleeveless undershirts that grandpas and "wife beaters" wear. A Tony Soprano undershirt. But he looks more like Uncle Junior after the cancer got him.

"Lester, are you back from your run? Come taste this," Sydelle yells from the kitchen.

"Coming, dear," the man says while I stare at him. "Eat and run," he says to me and winks. "Eat and run."

LYNETTE CHAPELL-WILLIAMS, Detective Ron Williams' wife, had no interest in meeting with me. Not, that is, until I told her that I managed to sneak in to see Hallie and that Hallie mentioned the evening at the Inn Between. Now she's sitting across the table from me at the Inn, playing with the rim of her coffee cup and waiting for me to dish some dirt. Lynette's one of those women who expects intimacy just because you're the same gender.

She's all woman, voluptuous, dark hair, dark skin, dark eyes. Sitting across from her I feel not merely unfeminine, but sexless, neutered by motherhood and responsibility.

She's waiting for me to dish.

"She looks awful," I say.

"Well, what did you expect?" Lynette says. She recites the litany of what's happened to Hallie in the last month, finding out Hal was cheating, his being arrested for murder, her suicide attempt…

"Her failed attempts to get pregnant," I add. Lynette seems surprised that I know about that. "We're close," I say almost apologetically.

"Those hormones they're pumping her full of…" Lynette shakes her head. Other parts of her shake along with it. "She's not the Hallie I knew, anyway."

"She kept talking about that night, when you were all here," I prompt, hoping Lynette will tell me what Hallie never did.

"Oh, she was really a mess that night, what with the fight with Hal and all. She was jumpy, like she knew something was going to happen."

I admit that Hallie knew Hal was going over to see Peaches, to end it.

"Only Grace told her that men never end affairs, they just cover their tracks better. She wasn't talking about Hal, of course, but we all figured that's how Hallie must have taken it."

"Grace?" I say. I know the names of lots of the wives and girlfriends from Drew, but Grace doesn't ring a bell.

"Schultz. Captain Schultz's wife. She's got a wicked tongue, that woman. Especially when she drinks. And she was drinking like a fish that night. Hallie wound up taking her into the john to heave halfway through dinner."

"So Hallie was here the whole time?" I ask, and Lynette clams up. "I mean, the way she was talking about it, I had the sense that more happened than just dinner and drinks."

"Plenty more happened," Lynette says. "Like her husband wacking his ho mistress."

"Well, yeah," I agree. "But—"

"So what I want to know is, is it true you dumped Drew Scoones? Detective Swoons? Ron says it's over between the two of you."

I nod sadly.

"Thought you guys were going to get married," Lynette says. "The whole Department thought so."

"Yeah," I say. "So did he. Funny thing. No one thought to check with me."

"You really said no?" She eyes me sharply and I get the feeling I'm not the only one at this meeting with someone else's agenda on my plate. "You're trying to tell me that you two are really kaput?"

"Dead in the water," I say.

"Come on. That man is hotter than a Harley's engine after a long, long ride." It's quite an image, that hot engine vibrating between my thighs. "You don't really think you're going to do better, do you?"

Oh, the look she gives me, like I'm something she'd scrape off the bottom of her shoes.

I tell her it's not impossible, that there's a widower I'm thinking about seeing. But that the real problem is that I'm not ready and Drew isn't willing to wait.

"Wait? What in God's name are you waiting for? You aren't getting any younger."

I agree that I am not. "Does that mean I'm supposed to settle? Or to rush into something I'm not sure of? What happened to forty being the new thirty?"

"Ha. Forty is the same old forty, crow's feet, sagging boobs and all. Unless…" Her eyes light up and she leans over the table and puts her hand over mine. "You can tell me the truth, Teddi. He's not that great in bed, is he?"

I lean forward, too, so that our noses are nearly touching. I am so tempted. So, so tempted. But I resist. "Oh," I say, "he's that good."

"Then I don't buy—"

"I'm not desperate. I think he thought I was, just like you do. Like my mother does. Like everyone assumes a forty-year-old divorcée to be. Well, I own my own home, my own business, I put food on the table for three children, and I don't need someone to take care of me or mine. When I marry again, *if* I marry again, it will be because I want to share my life with someone worthy, and not because I want someone to take care of me or warm my bed."

Lynette just stares at me, like I'm speaking a foreign language. Finally she sputters and asks me, "So what are you doing with a cop? You know, *to serve and protect?*"

I tell her I don't care much for the division of labor: me serving him and him protecting me.

She admits she had me pegged all wrong. "You are so not the woman I met when Drew first brought you around."

She's right. I'm not. I've grown up since then. "Drew is a great guy," I say, because I'm good at the truth. "But the timing isn't right and he doesn't want to wait."

"Damn," she says. "And I was so hoping he was a lousy lay."

The waitress slaps the check down between us. I reach for it. "No such luck."

I EXPECT GRACE SCHULTZ to be a tough nut to crack, but she seems to have all the time in the world for me. Odd, don't you think?

I do, anyway.

"My husband talks about you all the time," she tells me as we sit in her company-only, don't-put-your-feet-up living room chatting amiably over tea. Who serves tea outside of England? My guess is the woman has been watching too much PBS and BBC.

"I suppose I'm the bane of his existence," I say, without even a hint of the pride I feel at the thought.

"Well, I'll admit he doesn't like the way the newspapers characterize your exploits," she says. "As if you're cracking cases the Department can't. But, of course, he likes to see justice served. And he seems to think you do have a knack—he says a clumsy one—for helping the Department do just that on occasion." She dabs at the corner of her mouth with one of those fancy napkins you get at museum shops and wonder if anyone uses. She may be the only one in America who actually does.

Grace looks like she'd be comfortable in some tony golf club's clubhouse. She looks like she could walk around naked in the locker room there without feeling the least bit self-conscious. It's not that she looks good—just confident. She looks like she doesn't care what anyone makes of her.

I find it unnerving.

I compliment her on her lovely taste, gesturing toward the generic-but-overdone window treatment, the couch and love seat which match each other rather than coordinate and she tells me that they are thinking of moving to a bigger place.

"Maybe you'll help me decorate it," she says.

I tell her I'd be delighted, but ask why they'd need a bigger place since their children are grown.

"Entertaining," she tells me. Apparently she plans to do a lot of it.

She tells me that the Captain is worried about me since he's heard I've broken up with Drew and we do the breakup thing again. I'm getting better and better at it. And then I ask if she'd mind if I asked her a question or two about the night that Peaches was murdered.

I've clearly ruffled her tail feathers, but she just sniffs it up. "Of course," she says. "Anything I can do to help the investigation. It's the Captain's top priority, you know, so of course I want to help. But, dear, don't you think the police are up to the task?" She reminds me the case is so clearly high profile and as she goes on I hear loud and clear between the lines that any glory to be had in this case will land squarely on John Schultz's shoulders.

"You can rest assured, dear, that justice will be done in this particular case. After all, it's one of his own men who stands accused, and the Captain is overseeing it personally."

She says that as if she has no connection to him, in the same way that royalty refers to themselves in the third person. I expect her to say, "The Captain's wife has complete and utter faith in his ability and discretion."

"Oh, I'm sure that's the case," I say, all innocence and gullibility. "It's just that I feel somewhat torn—I'm both connected and disconnected, if you know what I mean." I hope she does, since I don't.

"Because you know Detective Nelson?" she asks.

"Because he was Drew's partner, and so was I, in a way, and now we're both…" I shrug. "Anyway, with our split, it looks like my source has dried up. And now I have to just wonder alone." I tilt my head pathetically and sigh.

"And what is it that you wonder?" she asks me, refilling our cups with tea that was only tepid to start with. Everyone knows that you have to warm the teapot first by pouring boiling water in it or the tea will not be hot. I know that and I'm not even a tea drinker.

"The night that you were all at the Inn Between—" I try to do this delicately "—and you were taken ill, Hallie helped you to the bathroom, right?"

She doesn't correct me, though she doesn't really answer.

"Did she go right back to the table with you? Or take you out to your car, or—"

"Actually, you have it wrong. Hallie was ill, not me. I took her back to her place and put her to bed." Her body language looks uncomfortable, but she has no trouble maintaining eye contact. I have to remember to ask Drew what that means. He's always telling me how to know when someone is lying.

"But you'd had a lot to drink yourself, right?" I ask, trying not to sound accusatory. "I mean, everyone was indulging, right?"

"Perhaps I had a few too many," she says, somewhat embarrassed. "I hope you won't tell John. He doesn't really like me going to these things. Unseemly, you know? 'Imagine if you were pulled over, Grace,' he's always saying. That's why I always take a cab to and from the dinners."

Well, I suppose that explains the rubbing together of hands.

"So you called a cab to take you and Hallie back to her place?" I ask.

She nods, and I think, *Alibi*. In a car at the time of the murder. I don't know why that pops into my head. I guess Drew is right and I've got a very suspicious nature.

"And you two waited together until it came?"

Grace seems to think about this. I guess she wants to be sure that Hallie's whereabouts are fully accounted for. "Yes," she says. "Now I remember. She was by my side constantly. She even sat with me by the door. I remember now because some man tried to pick her up. She was very unnerved by it."

"Did the man seem to know her?" I ask.

"Maybe," she says. "Why exactly are you asking me this?"

As I've told you before, I'm lousy at lying. I tell her the truth. "I don't know. I just think it might be important."

IF I WAS A COP, or still had easy access to one, I'd have a picture of Andy Lipschitz and I'd have a picture of Hallie Nelson and I'd show them to the bartender at the Inn Between and ask him if he was on duty the night of the murder and if he remembers them talking to each other.

But my motto is I will not be thwarted, and I do have a computer and Internet access. It's downright scary what you can find when you search for a person and hit "images." *Newsday*'s article on Peaches' murder has a family portrait, from which I crop Andy with Photoshop. Susan Winters, Detective Winters' wife, has a blog with pictures from the last picnic the Department had, complete with Hallie Nelson.

It's around eight o'clock, and Alyssa is winding down. She's given up on the monster business and has decided that now it's a burglar who lurks in her closet. A burglar, she says, or a

Mormon who wants her for another wife. In desperation I have taken the closet door off its hinges and convinced her that bad people need doors to hide behind, so she is safe. It's times like this that I wish Rio still lived here. Oh, wait. Rio burgled the house and he had two women.

It's times like this I wish we had a resident police detective.

Better.

Much better.

After I've got Alyssa tucked away with all the lights in her room blazing, her closet "undoored," and the door to her room wide open, I head for Jesse's room and knock on his door.

"Just a second."

Crap. This isn't going to go away. "It's me, Jess. We need to have a little talk."

"Finally!" I hear from Dana's room, while Jesse unlatches something and then opens the door. I enter the room and pretend I am just closing the door for privacy and not to see what he unlatched.

"This has to come off," I say, finding one of those hook-and-eye sort of closures on his door. "It's a fire hazard, for one, and it says you don't trust me not to allow you your privacy, for another."

Jesse's cheeks redden. I expect him to say that it's Dana he wants to keep out, or Alyssa. He says nothing.

"You'll remove this as soon as we're done," I say. When he still doesn't answer, I add, "Or I will."

"I have a right to privacy," Jesse begins. "It's guaranteed by the constitution."

"And it vests when you are an adult," I finish for him,

looking around his room at all the evidence of his age. There are still two Transformers on his shelf, a pewter wizard does battle with a pewter dragon. There's a poster of Natalie Portman as Queen Amidala across the room from his bed with a target drawn on her. "Would you let a baby play alone in a locked room? How about Alyssa? Would you let her lock herself in?"

He reminds me he's not a baby.

Nor, I tell him, is he an adult. "Look," I say. "This parenting stuff is hard. I've never been the mother of an eleven-year-old boy before. But I've read. I don't live in a cave, I know what you're doing in here. And I don't think you'll go blind, and I don't think that the occasional—" I stumble around for the right words "—relieving of your...urges...is a bad thing."

"So?" he says. He's biting the inside of his cheek.

"So enough is enough, Jess. I'd feel the same way if you were in here 24-7 playing video games. Sweetheart, I'd even feel the same way if you were in here 24-7 studying or reading *War and Peace*."

"Are you going to get back with Drew?" he asks.

Well, that came out of nowhere.

"I don't know," I say, adding "Maybe," to soften the blow. "What does that have to do with the price of tea in China?"

Jesse won't meet my eyes. I cross the room to him and take his chin in my hand, forcing him to look at me.

"What does my relationship with Drew have to do with your obsession?"

His Adam's apple bobs against the heel of my hand.

"Jess?"

He looks up at me, blinking away tears.

"Jesse, honey. What is it?"

He scrunches up, his knees against his chest.

"It's not working right," he says, and I follow his gaze...right into his lap.

CHAPTER 9

*One reason to hire a decorator is that she knows more tricks
than the average home owner. She can use a lightweight base,
gild it and then place it under a heavy glass top to make a
coffee table that appears to cost thousands. She can hide a
door in a wall, or make one appear to be where one isn't. A
decorator can be, quite simply, a magician.*

TipsFromTeddi.com

On Thursday night, the bartender at the Inn Between confirms my suspicions. I play with a stack of business cards for the Mid-Island Taxi Cab Company while he tells me that not only did Hallie and Andy meet that night, but they'd been there together before. No boyfriend-girlfriend stuff, he said, no footsies under the table, no accidental meeting of hands, brushing of boobs, meeting of eyes or lips or any other parts.

"Like business associates," he'd said.

I'd asked him to take a guess what kind of business.

He'd stroked his chin, thinking hard. Then he'd said, "Mortuary, maybe?" and offered me a Bloody Mary.

FRIDAY MORNING. I have three *Absolutes* for today. Since I'm suddenly all about taking care of me and mine, I absolutely must go to Susan's house, say hello to her horses and confirm the measurements I have for the window and door openings before I place my order for custom moldings and cabinets. The plan I have worked out depends on being perfect to the inch.

Miss Lehman, eat your heart out.

And I'm meeting my painter, Sal, there at noon for him to try some faux effects on the wall. I'm hoping for a leather look without skinning an animal to get it. Though, of course, Susan wants leather chairs. I think she really believes that they only use the hides of animals who have died peacefully in their sleep.

Second *Absolute,* and higher on the list: Ask Rio to come over and see if my phones are being tapped. Last night I was on with Bobbie and I kept hearing clicking. Rio has his own security company, thanks to my mother's old beau, who shall remain nameless but who makes offers people can't refuse, and he has the kind of equipment that can check for these things. There's nothing Rio would rather do than bring his "equipment" over here, so I'd like to be out when he shows up. Only that would mean either leaving him a key, which I don't trust him not to make a copy of (and I don't even want to think about what he'd do with free access to my house), or allowing him to come when the kids are home.

Now, that option is tempting, because he could talk to Jesse about his own "equipment," which is actually *Absolute* 3. Only I'm thinking that I would rather have Drew talk to Jess about it because for all I know, Rio will laugh at Jess and scar him for life.

Ah, for the life my mother believes I lead. I only wish.

There's actually a possible *Absolute 4*, which I think is an oxymoron. Can you have a *possible Absolute*? This involves breaking into the Lipschitz Love Nest, as Drew and I refer to it. Today is Hal Nelson's arraignment, which seems like the perfect time to slip in, seeing as how the Department will be in turmoil. It's been police-taped up since the murder, and who knows what went on in the other bedrooms.

Funny, no one is coming forward with that information.

I call Rio and tell him I want him at the house at four. I figure the kids will be there and so will I, so if he messes with Jesse's head I can do something about it. I wonder if there's room in Hal's cell. Makes me think of Sartre play, *No Exit*. Hal and I in a cell together...

Rio gives me the usual hard time. He's too busy, he's got paying customers, he's got no one to watch Elisa, the baby he conceived with Marion when he was still married to me. Now he's the father of four and the husband of none.

Anyway, I give him an "or else," which involves just the slightest mention of his boss (my mother's old boyfriend, the one with the mafia connections, who's staked him in his security business because he adores me). I don't have to say all that, just that I expect to be seeing Carmine soon, and Rio agrees to check my phones, though he can't imagine why anyone would want to tap them.

Why does it seem like I am always surrounded by people whose imaginations pale in comparison to mine?

At any rate, he'll be at my house at four.

Then, with my handy dandy Secret Cell Phone for Bat Calls, I head out to my car to go to Susan's, praying that Drew will call me. Don't take this as some sort of anti-faith thing, but not surprisingly, prayer doesn't work.

Neither, it seems, does my car.

Now, the car is getting on in years, but to be totally dead on a day when I have so much to do? And some of it involves Peaches' murder?

Coincidence? I think not.

Tapped phone? Dead car battery? Is someone sending me a message?

I traipse over to Bobbie's and ask if I can borrow her car. She's got to go to the post office to mail out eBay crapola, and she was hoping to hit the outlets this afternoon.

"Why can't all your eBayers hit the outlets themselves?" I ask.

"Look at the addresses on these boxes," she tells me, waving at the stack of cartons with her hand. "Japan! Arkansas! South Dakota!"

I take that to mean I can't borrow her car, though she does push me into agreeing to start looking at wedding dresses with her. I give the AAA a call, watching out Bobbie's window for any sign of a dark sedan that might be watching for a sign of me, while she pulls up wedding gowns on eBay for me to consider.

"You don't really expect me to wear something like that," I say, looking at what appears to be a wedding-cake topper with a woman standing in it.

"Actually," Bobbie says, and I think she's issuing a challenge here, "I expect you to acquiesce to your mother's demands and wear taupe. I expect us all to wear taupe."

"Bobbie," I say, getting up off the couch and heading for the door to meet the tow truck coming down the street. "If I acquiesce to my mother's demands, there won't be any wedding. At least not to Drew."

"There's always that widower," Bobbie shouts out the door after me. "Don't marry Drew and you could get stuck with him."

I turn around and stare at her, raise my hands like *what are you thinking?* and tell her to "shut up!"

She quickly covers her mouth with her hand. Then she apparently thinks she can fix it. "I mean, if you change your mind about Drew, and he agrees to take you back and…"

Her voice trails off while I flag down the tow guy and point toward my garage.

Mistake telling Bobbie, I think, but it did make Drew happy to know that I couldn't hold it in.

Anyway, after having to hear that I *must have left your lights on, ma'am,* the tow guy finally gets my car started and I am off to Susan Michaels, hoping against hope that Drew will call me so that I can ask him about Jesse's situation.

The horses are in the barn, in stalls marked with their names: Tonto, Silver and Zorro. They are beautiful animals, especially from afar. Up close they are very big and a bit slobbery—like St. Bernards. Their teeth, which they are happy to show me, look like piano keys. And someday, when I am a

rich and famous decorator like Miss Lehman, I will never have
to be this close to one—never mind three—again.

"Nice horsey," I say, picking up some apples that look mushy
and rotten compared to the ones that were in the bin when
Susan was on the premises. This is not going to make Mrs.
Michaels happy. If I was a nasty person, I'd let the camera see
them. I might even say something like, "Susan really will have
to talk to the groom about keeping these apples fresh when she
is away." Only I'm not the kind of person who would make
trouble for someone whose name I don't even remember. "I'll
bring you fresh apples next time," I say softly, my back to the
camera as I hold out an apple to Zorro and pray I have my
fingers when he's done.

I'm not going to say a word until I notice that Zorro's stall
could use a good cleaning out. "Where is…your person?" I ask
the horse. "I don't think you should be standing in that muck."
Hey, I'm willing to bring fresh apples, but I'll be damned if I'll
rake out my client's stalls.

My duty having been done (and having witnessed Tonto do
his, if you get my drift), I head for the house, realizing that I
should have done my measuring first, rather than track in
yucky stuff from the barn. I slide my shoes off just outside the
door and slip the key in the door.

Inside the house I hear the shrill sound of the alarm system
waiting to be turned off. Reaching for my bags I realize that
I've left my Bottega Veneta workbag in the car and only have
my handbag with me. I drop my purse and, knowing the cops
are sure to come, I am already rehearsing my story as I race
toward the driveway to get the code from the car.

Only the car isn't there. It's careening down the driveway backward, heading for the street. At which point the alarm system loses its patience with me and goes ballistic.

And my car hits the front end of a tan vehicle marked Old Brookville Security.

And I am standing in the middle of the driveway in wet socks and no purse or ID when three Nassau County Police cars pull up the driveway.

The only thing to go right is that one of the officers who emerges from the cars is Diane, Bobbie's sister. Unfortunately, she, too, has her gun unholstered and it is pointed at me.

CHAPTER 10

Virginia Wolf had it almost right. Writers need a room of their own. But then, so do all mothers. A place where they can shut the door on the children, the husband, the dirty dishes piled in the sink and the to-do list on the fridge. They need a place to regroup and face the world with renewed strength, to eat ice cream at eight o'clock in the morning if that's what it takes, rather than be on constant display, always setting a good example.

TipsFromTeddi.com

Drew snickers right along with the other cops as I am all but perp-walked through the precinct house. Several officers are in their dress blues. Everyone seems on tenterhooks.

Captain Schultz comes out of his office and the snickering stops. "Knock it off," he says after the fact, putting an arm around me protectively. "You all right?"

I tell him I'm fine, that I wasn't in the car, and that I shouldn't be here.

"Of course you shouldn't," he says. "We'll just have someone take your statement and see if we can't get this all cleared up."

I thank him, notice Grace is standing in his office door and nod hello to her. She nods back.

"Scoones," the Captain says. "Why don't you take Ms. Bayer's statement? You don't mind, Teddi, do you? The rest of the officers are getting ready to go over to the courthouse. In fact, I'm on my way over there now."

"Don't go taking anything else while you're in there," someone says as Drew shows me into an interview room. "I mean now that you're not—"

I miss the last word as he shuts the door.

"Drew, I—" I start to say, but his eyes dart to the glass wall.

"That's *Detective Scoones*," he corrects.

"Oh? I thought it was *Swoons*," I say contemptuously.

Does he feel the same way I do? Is it killing him to sit across the table from me and pretend I'm just some wacko?

It can't be too hard, this pretending I'm a wacko. I'm beginning to believe it.

"I was not breaking and entering," I say. "I had a key, I had the code to the alarm, I had the permission of the owner. I was there to take measurements. As you well know, I'm a decorator and—"

"Is that what you're calling it these days?" he asks, looking me over from head to toe, clearly enjoying himself. I choose to think that he's so happy because I've just missed being in an accident and here I am fine and in one piece. He sits down all businesslike and taps his pencil against the file. "Decorator. Is that some new word for *tease?*"

My jaw drops. Drew Scoones, *Bad Cop?*

"That isn't the necklace I gave you, is it?" he asks, pointing at my throat like he'd like to put his hands around it.

"Gonna accuse me of stealing it?" I ask.

He puts his hand out for me to give it to him. Which, under other circumstances, like if he'd actually given me the necklace, I suppose I would.

"It was a gift," I say. I leave off from my dad to my mom, who didn't think it was an important enough piece for her to wear.

He curls his hand in a gesture that says *gimme*.

"And then I can go?" I ask. *And you can meet me later and give me back my mother's necklace?*

He laughs. This is not the man whose ring I put on every night after the kids are asleep just to look at it and marvel at my luck.

I reach up to undo the necklace and before I've gotten it unfastened he asks if I can't do it myself.

"No," I say softly.

With a humph he gets up and comes around to stand behind my chair. "Get up," he tells me.

I stand and hold my hair up off my neck. He comes close enough so that I can feel his breath.

"Pretend you're annoyed," he whispers.

"It has a lousy clasp," I say loudly.

"I miss everything about you," he says into my hair. Then loudly he says that he didn't expect to be taking it off.

There's a hand caressing my rear, proving that I've been right all along. The man has three hands. And then I realize that he's got both hands on the necklace.

"Uh," he says, like he's trapped.

I grab up the file from the desk and push it at his waistline as I yank the necklace off and hand it to him. "Happy now?" I ask, and it's all I can do to keep a straight face.

"Immensely," he says, the word dripping with as much sarcasm as he can muster under the circumstances.

He sits back down, playing with the necklace in his hand as he peruses the file. "Says here you weren't in your vehicle when it made contact with the second vehicle? Is that right?"

I tell him what happened. Someone comes into the room and drops a file in front of Drew, makes a crack about lovebirds, and tells him that O'Hanlon's almost ready. Drew nods. The cop leaves the door open behind him, like his coming in was just a rouse to get that door open. *The better to hear you with, my dear.*

"So you forgot to put on the emergency brake," Drew says, like it's a fact.

I correct him, telling him that I most certainly did put on the brake. That once when my brother David and I were little we were in my father's car which was parked on a hill and we were fooling around and David took off the emergency brake and we—

Two officers are standing outside the room, nearly doubled over laughing.

"I put on the brake." I cross my arms over my chest, signaling that I am unwilling to negotiate the point.

He closes the file, then reopens it, flips a page and says, "According to the officer at the scene, the brake was not on."

"Then someone took it off," I say. Drew's eyes flash up to meet mine.

I need to talk to you, I try to telegraph.

Not here comes back loud and clear. Cat whistles and yelps come from outside the room.

"Cut it out," an official voice calls.

The yelling dims to murmurs of "Looking good, honey. Looking sweet."

Somehow, sadly, I don't think they mean me.

Detective O'Hanlon leans into the doorway so that only her face is visible. "Her story checks out. We reached Susan Michaels on her cell. Says she gave her the key and the code."

Drew shuts the folder. "Okay, then. Insurance will cover the car business. Guess you're free to go, Ms. Bayer."

"I don't have a car," I say quietly, hoping he'll offer to run me home. Ten minutes in the car with him is all I'm asking for.

"I'll run you home," he says, and I try not to look as thrilled as I feel. He tells me that most of the officers are going over to the courthouse for the arraignment, but he's on assignment. At this point Detective O'Hanlon steps full into the doorway. She is wearing fishnet hose, a leather skirt that barely covers her privates and a blouse that doesn't reach what my father would refer to as her *pipic*.

And her *pipic* is pierced.

"On loan to Vice," she explains. She flips her hair off her shoulders seductively. The woman breathes seductively. I'm betting she brushes her teeth seductively, and pray that Drew can't confirm that.

"Drew?" his partner asks. Not *Scoones*, the way everyone at the station refers to him, but *Drew*. She comes into the room and puts a hand on his shoulder possessively. "You ready?"

Drew bites at the side of his lip. If I were a suspicious woman I'd say what crosses his face is guilt, pure and simple. "This is my new partner," he says, as if we haven't met before.

"The upgrade," someone says from the squad room, to plenty of laughter.

"I know what she is," I say, looking him up and down conspicuously. "But what are you? Her pimp?"

You can hear all the low oohs echoing down the hall.

"You want a ride or not?" he asks me, looking at O'Hanlon and at me and appearing very uncomfortable as he pockets my mother's necklace.

I think of Drew's little Mazda RX7 which seats two, and wonder where he has in mind for me in this little drama we're putting on wherein I'm the clunker he traded in for the Ferrari. The trunk, maybe? Or could we tie O'Hanlon to the hood like a trophy?

"Well?" he asks as O'Hanlon puts the strap to her little purse over her shoulder, letting the bag swing down by her hips.

"I'd rather walk," I say, while the background noise swells and I storm out in a self-righteous huff to a smattering of applause from some women who are glued to computers.

Of course, that leaves me just off Jericho Turnpike with no way home. I stand there only long enough for Drew and his partner to speed past me fast enough to break my heart.

"YOU HAVE TO STOP at the post office for me," Bobbie says when we get back to the house. "I can't lend you my car unless you promise me on your life to get these packages out."

Can shoes really be a matter of life and death?

"It's all about your seller rating," she tells me. "Mine slipped to ninety-eight percent because I believed the size on the box of a pair of dynamite imported shoes." I look at her blankly. "Was it my fault they were way smaller than the size they were marked? Of course, Italian shoes…blah, blah, blah."

I'm sure she explains this better than I am, but that's only because I totally don't give a damn about shoe sizes.

After I promise and cross my heart, etc., she loans me her car. I figure that driving her car gives me an extra layer of cover, which I no longer think is ridiculous. I know I didn't leave that brake off when I parked my car at the Michaelses'.

I know it.

I know the way to Peaches' Love Nest, since I followed Drew there a few weeks ago. My plan was to park behind the house, like I did at Hallie's, but it turns out that behind the house there's a private golf course, so that's out. Several doors down someone opens a garage and pulls out of the driveway. I wait until the car is out of sight and then pull into the driveway as if I live there. I pop Bobbie's trunk and, no surprise, find a shopping bag, which I carry with me as I walk around to the back. I leave the shopping bag behind the house and walk through the yards until I get to the Love Nest.

I study the back of the house, wondering how I'm going to gain entrance. The first thing I do is ring the back doorbell. I don't want any surprises, like the police, or any other hookers once I get inside. No one answers, but I see that there is a keypad rather than a traditional lock on the door.

Ten numbers, including zero. How many combinations would that make? I could be trying here until I'm old and gray.

After seeing Detective O'Hanlon dressed for the streets, I admit that isn't a very long time away.

Okay, think! I tell myself. This keypad is meant for men to be able to come and go without being seen entering the front door. So they'd have to remember the numbers. What would be an easy series of numbers a man would remember? Maybe something that would make him feel cool. *One in a million* isn't likely. How would you key that in, anyway?

I stand there, staring at the keypad, pretending I know more about detecting than I do. If only I was a supersleuth, a James Bond, or Jamie Bond, anyway…

Oh my God!

It's worth a try.

I press the zero button once. Twice. And then the seven.

A little green light blinks.

What john out cheating on his wife doesn't fancy himself James Bond?

I'M DOING MY CAT burglar thing, donning gloves, socks, and knowing that if I screw this up, Drew isn't going to be able to get me out of it very easily. Not without losing his job. So I'm thinking of it like *Mission Impossible*. He'll have to disavow any knowledge of me.

I just know that what I'm looking for is under my nose—some computer disk, some date book, like I found at Hallie's.

You can tell the cops have been here. There's fingerprint residue everywhere. I try to disturb nothing.

In a small alcove off the kitchen, where I clearly remember seeing a computer, I see only an empty desk. Apparently the police took anything that could tell them who might have had a reason to kill poor Peaches Lipschitz.

Funny how she's become *poor Peaches* in my mind, even though she was sleeping with married men and charging for it. I suppose being murdered changes things.

Anyway, I'm creeping up to the bedroom, hugging the walls like that will make me invisible. And all the while I'm thinking about how Peaches had a normal life going at the same time she was doing this. She was the vice president of the freaking PTA.

I wonder if Andy was ever here. Did he help her pay for the place? The house's title—thank you, Internet search of public records—was only in her name. And I can't help wonder if she did it here with him, for kicks, or if she saw this place as strictly for business.

The master bedroom, as it usually does in split levels, faces the front of the house, maybe so Mom and Dad can watch whose car their kids are getting into. I stare at the double beds with the nightstand between them, disbelieving. Fuzzy pink scuffs are parked beneath the bed with a pillow which says The Little Woman on it. The other bed sports a pillow, which claims to be Reserved for The King of the Castle. What did Hallie tell me? That Hal swore he never slept with Peaches?

Could he have been telling the truth?

I run my hands along the footboard of Peaches' bed and encounter a pink ribbon tied to the corner. Another at the other corner. Is that a third I see dangling from the center of the headboard, looking as if a bow had just come undone?

You bet it is. And I'm figuring Peaches came undone under it.

That woman definitely knew her business.

I am going through the drawers in the nightstand that separates the beds—lubricant, a rubber band of some sort that I don't even want to guess what she did with, and a jewelry box tied with a ribbon. I open it and there's a gold remote with her name on it, just like the ones in *The Stepford Wives*. Was that her idea of a joke, or some john's? I'm reading the buttons, which say things like "fetch beer," "massage back," and several more intimate suggestions, when I hear voices. The closet is across the room and I'll never make it before I can be seen in the old-fashioned mirror above the dresser or one of the two cheval mirrors that flank the beds, so I fling myself under "The Little Woman's" bed, wiggling when I have some trouble getting all the way under.

Sydelle's cooking is going to be the death of me, or at least the arresting of me.

"I don't get it," a female voice says. "I mean, where are the whips and chains? Where are the fuck-me pumps?"

"I don't know," a man's voice says. "It's kinda kinky in a way. Like doing it in your parents' bed. I can't picture old Hal Nelson doing the dirty here." I can see the bottom of his uniform and his shiny black oxfords.

"Not and paying for it," the higher, feminine voice says. "Be like screwing your mother, don't you think? I can't believe we're stuck here while everyone else is at the arraignment."

"Sucks to be us," he says and they both laugh.

I can't see her shoes, but I feel the bed sag above me.

"So what do you think Peaches had that Hal's wife doesn't?"

"A dog collar?" From under the bed skirt I can see up to about the cops' waists in the mirror. I see one of the pink ribbons move. "I wonder who tied up who."

"Read the pillow. Looks like it was The Little Woman who was fit to be tied," she says with a laugh. "You know, I've seen the wife. She's cute. I don't get why he couldn't just—" She bounces a couple of times on the bed. Is she demonstrating what he couldn't just do?

"What's really kinky is that they found her fingerprints here," he says. "You think she's one of those types that likes to watch?"

My fist hits the carpeting. Drew *Freakin'* Scoones isn't telling me squat. Hallie's been here? I try to fit that into what I already know while above me the bed sags lower.

Hallie Nelson knows the victim's husband. She's met with him at the Inn Between. Her gun was found at the scene. Her fingerprints are here.

Yet Hal Nelson confessed.

"You look good like that," the guy above me says. "A picture of 'The Little Woman.'"

"Another few weeks and I'll outrank you," she says, clearly pissed. "You'll be 'The Little Man.'"

"Get your thong outta your crack," he says. "I'm just giving you a compliment. You look good."

She thanks him reluctantly.

"You know," he says, "there's something… Don't you feel it?"

"Feel what?"

"I don't know…naughty?"

"Naughty? You mean because we're supposed to be making sure the place is secure?"

He tells her it's the place. Makes him feel, "I don't know. Like I'm gonna deflower you or something."

This does not bode well for me, stuck under the bed.

"You gonna tie me up, big man? King of the Castle?" she teases.

He kicks off his shoes, nearly getting me in the face. I want to remind them they're supposed to be watching the place so that someone like me can't get in and tamper with evidence. She tells him about as much.

"I got my eyes and ears open," he says.

Which leads right into what she says she's got open. Suffice it to say, what went on in that bed when Peaches was alive, goes on in that bed now. Only this time I'm under it.

They find a button that makes the bed vibrate.

I think I'm going to vomit.

I hear the smack of flesh on flesh, the groans of exertion, the succulent sounds of… You get the picture. My eyes are shut tight rather than see anything in the mirrors. My ears, however, can't miss the release of a little gas.

"Jack!" she says and laughs. "That was gross."

"Sorry," he says. "You know what we need?"

"Tums?"

"Music. We could use some music," he says.

That would be nice, I think.

Loud music, I wish.

Feet land near my head, pants still around the ankles. He tries to take a step, stumbles.

"Shit!" he shouts, his hand halfway under the bed, a lock of my hair caught beneath his palm.

"What did you expect?" She laughs at him. "Take your damn pants off, King."

He says something about the possibility of needing to pull them up quickly, but he kicks his remaining shoe out of his way. It hits the wall. Bare legs in black socks pad across the room. "Hey, there's an iPod in here," he says. I think he's looking at the old radio. "Only it's dead," he says.

"Give it to me," she answers. "You probably just don't know how to work it, Your Majesty."

He argues that he knows what he's doing and that the iPod is dead, but I sense that he tosses it to her. "Too bad. She's got Bose speakers and everything."

"It's not just dead," she says. "It's busted. Otherwise it would play in that thing. Forget it. Just come back to bed," she says. "And bring your joy stick with you."

I'll have to remember that one, should I get out of this mess and have the opportunity to use it. The expression, not Jack's stick.

Three minutes later they're done and dressing. I've had the foresight to move his shoe out from under the bed so that he doesn't come looking for it.

When I think they are out of the room I start to wiggle out from under the bed, only to hear footsteps and her saying, "What are you doing there?"

I'm ready to explain that...

No, actually, I'm not ready to explain anything.

But I don't have to because he says, "Maybe it just needs charging."

"You can't take it," she says. I can see her feet by the doorway, his by the dresser. "Jeesh! You're an officer of the law, not some thief."

"I wasn't stealing it," he says. "I was gonna bring it to the station house. It's evidence, don't you think?"

"Yeah," she says sarcastically. "A broken iPod. If it was evidence the forensic boys would have taken it. Leave it, Jack."

"It's not like she can use it," he says, but I hear him slip the iPod back into the holder.

"And zip up, Jack, for God's sake."

I hear the sound of his crisp shirt being tucked into his pants, his fly being closed. "You hungry?" he asks.

A woman after my own heart, at least in this, she replies that she is *starving* and I hear them bound down the steps. I slip out from under the bed and hide behind the door. I think I hear the front door open and close. And then a couple of car doors slam.

I lift the old radio case and pick up the iPod, which is, as the cops so eloquently put it, busted. Well, why not? Hal's busted, isn't he? But maybe it's just dead—like Peaches. Only it wasn't broken the night Peaches died. How could it break just sitting in a cradle?

If anyone can get it to work, it's Dana. She's a whiz at these things. And then, like she's in the room with me, I can see that look she gave me the other day when Kimmie's iPod got lost. *When she gets her period…*

Jesse, when he'd finally emerged from his room, had told me that you can sync your calendar to your iPAQ. Who knew that?

So if, on the off chance we could get this to work again, and on the even more remote possibility that Peaches Lipschitz knew you could do that, and actually did it… Hey, it's worth a try.

I MAKE IT HOME just before five o'clock, to find Rio eating the last of my favorite chocolate *babka*, the piece I was saving for tonight, for when I'm in bed alone with my lies and feeling miserable. Having escaped with the iPod and my freedom after the mattress-dancing cops left, I'm in no mood for my ex-husband and his games.

"Did you check for bugs?" I ask him.

His response? "Do I look like an exterminator?"

I look him over carefully. I take my time, trying to figure out where the kids are while I consider his question. "Yes," I finally say. "Where are my children?"

"According to the message on your machine—"

"You checked my messages?" I am livid. I am beyond livid. Livider. Lividest.

He looks at me like he can't see what's wrong with that. "Your mom's as whacko as ever. She's more than pissed that you refused to go out with some guy named Jenson. Resorting to fix-ups from June? What happened to your little cop friend?"

"Where are my children?" I repeat.

"Jesse got detention and Dr. Meredith wants to see you about him."

That ought to be a great conversation.

"Dana says she's waiting around for Jesse, which sounds suspicious to me, and Lys is babysitting Elisa."

"She's what?"

He tells me that he hired her to watch the baby at a quarter an hour. No doubt he'll renege on even that. He set them both up in front of the TV and they both fell asleep.

I tell him I don't want him ever touching my answering machine again. "No problem," he tells me. "I changed your code to 666 so I can do it without even being here."

My jaw drops open.

"Just kidding." He tells me I should have seen the expression on my face.

I can't print what I told him.

I check my watch and figure I'd better get over to the school and get Jesse released and find out what Dana's up to. Rio offers to go, but the last thing I want is for him to discuss Jesse's problem with the school principal.

He agrees reluctantly to stay with the girls until I get back.

I throw my purse over my shoulder and am about to head for the door when I hear something clatter on the table. I turn around and see Rio playing with something that looks like a watch battery.

"So," he says. "You want to tell me who bugged your phone?"

CHAPTER 11

Let's face it. TV is a part of our lives, more the fabric of them than cotton. Whether you call it the media room, the den or the TV room, there are certain essentials involved—the ability to regulate light, a comfortable place to sit or recline and face the set, someplace you can put up your feet, put down a drink and a spot for that elusive remote that always slides between the cushions.

TipsFromTeddi.com

It's all over the six o'clock news.

Not Jesse's little problem, which was only marginally involved in his detention. It seems he took one of those *Playboy* magazines to school and got caught showing it around.

"Not the first young man to do that," Dr. Meredith said patronizingly to me. "But not something we can ignore."

I assured him that I would not ignore the situation and then had to listen to the middle school principal lecture me about the importance of a male role model in cases of divorce.

All that wasn't bad enough. I then found Dana with Roger's hands on her butt—made me want to go back to the principal's office to tell him that apparently I need a female role model, as well.

I almost didn't let her go off to Melissa Mandel's birthday party, but in the end I relented.

Jesse, apparently embarrassed to within an inch of his life, elected not to come down to his grandparents' house, either. I took him at his word that he would not spend the evening locked in is room "practicing his technique."

The poor boy looked so crushed I almost didn't leave him. I wouldn't have, except that my mother was threatening to send Paulette Jenson's widower, the man she wants me to marry, over to get me.

Happily, Mr. Jenson is nowhere in sight and my mother doesn't mention him when Lys and I arrive. The aroma of dinner is conspicuously absent when we enter the house, where we find her and my father glued to the TV set, watching the six o'clock news. Harold Nelson, decorated former Nassau County Police Detective, has just been formally charged with the murder of PTA vice president and part-time hooker, Peaches Lipschitz, and his guilty plea has been accepted by the court.

His sentencing is scheduled for March 24.

My mother is dancing in the aisles, or at least she's smirking in her TV room, nudging my father with her elbow saying, "Did I not tell you? Did I not?"

My father is agreeing and doing what he can to protect his ribs, while I watch the TV and tell myself there's still time. March 24 is almost two weeks away. We can find the real murderer and prove it in that time, right?

I look at my mother, delirious, and wonder how far and how fast she'll plunge into depression when I a) prove Hal didn't do it and then b) announce that I'm marrying Drew Scoones. I can hear the ambulance now, see the men coming with the little white coats, and all I can think of to say is, "Don't forget to get your nails done next week."

They don't let the manicurist come to South Winds.

My mother is in fact, so happy, that she doesn't even pitch a fit over the fact that my father has brought in chicken for Lys and hot pastrami sandwiches for the rest of us.

"Your daughter is probably hungry," she tells me, not taking her eyes from the screen. "Don't you think you ought to feed the child?"

"I'm not hungry," Lys says. She's coloring contentedly in a *My Little Pony* book my mother keeps here to entertain her.

"I'd go set the table and warm up dinner," my mother says vaguely when I don't take the hint, "but I don't want to miss this."

I get up and turn to my father, offering him a hand up off the couch, as well as an excuse to escape. "Wanna help me, Dad?" I ask, though what kind of help it takes to put three sandwiches and containers of potato salad, coleslaw and pickles on the table is beyond either of us.

Still, he all but leaps at the chance. I tell Lys to stay and keep Grandma company and I can see my father's antenna come to full attention.

"What's doing, Toots?" he asks me as I open my mother's casual dish cabinet.

"Where to start?" I wonder aloud.

"How about why Bobbie's car is parked in my driveway?" he suggests.

I agree that's a good place, and I tell him about the mishap at the Michaelses' house. I don't want to worry him, so I don't tell him that I think the accident was engineered.

He offers, as I hoped he would, to loan me my mother's car while mine is being repaired and assures me that he and she can get along with one car for a little while. I know I should tell him he'd better run it by her, but if he doesn't know that after all these years, my telling him won't do a whole lot of good.

"So what else, *Maydala?*" he ask me.

"I guess you've heard about Drew and me," I say, and he pats his shoulder and offers it to me, saying it's a shame, a damn shame. He's bonier every time I see him, and I can't forget that he's past seventy now and has heart trouble. "I just want you to know that I'm okay about it," I tell him. I hate like hell to give him more to worry about, especially when it isn't even true.

He raises an eyebrow, not believing me.

"Really, Drew isn't the problem," I say. "That will work itself out. It's Jesse, but asking you about his…activities…is really awkward."

My father smiles. "Perfectly normal," he says. "All boys do it. Sometimes it comes in handy," he adds with a wink and a gesture that I'm not going to get into here. Every man I've spoken to, from Drew to the principal to my dad all seem to think there's nothing more ordinary than a boy spending every waking hour in self-discovery.

Who am I to argue?

Not much later I drive off, my father following me and my mother following him so that she can take him back home.

By the time I've kissed them goodbye it's nearly nine o'clock, but it's not a school night and since Lys had a nap on the way home, she isn't tired. I'm pooped, but I've got too much on my mind to sleep. I check on Jesse, who is either exhausted from the day he's had or is pretending to be asleep, which is okay with me.

"Mind if I get some work done?" I ask Lys. Peaches' iPod is burning a hole in my handbag at this point, Hal's confession notwithstanding.

The iTunes software on my computer syncs with Dana's iPod and I have been warned not to so much as touch the cable for it. But Dana is still at the birthday party at *L.I. Lanes* with her new boyfriend, Roger. I assume Lys knows less about iPods than I do, and since she's got the TV tuned to the Noggin station, I figure I can at least see if I can get the iPod to work.

Because this should be quality one-on-one time with her, I put up a batch of guilt chip cookies to share with her. And then, with my heart in my throat because there is nothing worse than the wrath of a thirteen-year-old premenstrual daughter (and it seems they are always premenstrual at this age), I head for my office.

I sit the iPod on my desk, Dana's iPod cord dangling temptingly beside it. I remind myself that a man's life could be at stake and decide to plug the damn thing in. Nothing happens. I turn the computer off and reboot. The iPod remains dark.

I try changing the USB port. Nada.

I smell delicious cookies.

I try unplugging and re-plugging the iPod, pushing the menu button to no avail.

I smell delicious cookies getting well done.

I shake the iPod. No go.

I become obsessed with the idea that the answers I seek are hidden in a gizmo that, if it was made of chocolate, wouldn't fill a cavity.

Speaking of chocolate, I smell no longer delicious cookies getting too well done.

I run to the kitchen, iPod in hand and meet Alyssa there. She shakes her head at me sadly.

"Too little, too late," she says, parroting my mother, who, unfortunately, she resembles a little too closely.

I pull the fairly burnt cookies out of the oven and offer to scrape the burned part off the bottom.

I get the *thanks, but no thanks* grimace. "What were you doing that was more important than me?" she asks, showing that she has completed my mother's course in Jewish guilt with flying colors.

"I was trying to get this to work," I say, showing her Peaches Lipschitz's white nano.

Alyssa takes the iPod and slides the little button across the top back and forth, back and forth. "Hmm," she says. "Okay, sometimes this works." She holds the device in one hand and hits it hard with the other.

"Alyssa!" I'm ready to hold her in one hand and…

Only the screen comes to life.

"How did you…?"

Lys tells me that lots of the kids in her class get their older siblings' broken iPods and someone found a blog on the Internet about how to get them to work again. "It's like you always say, Mom. You can find everything on the Internet."

I decide that she's earned a fresh batch of cookies and I promise her I won't burn them. I put them up and break my promise twenty minutes later when I'm knee-deep in iPod-land in my office. These stupid little things are completely counter-*my*-intuitive.

But I do find the contacts list and the calendar under Extras. Who knew? Well, considering Lys helped me, apparently even a second-grader.

Now all I have to do is wait for Drew to call so that I can see how my list compares with the one the police must have taken off Peaches' computer.

The phone rings and I pounce on it as if Publishers Clearing House is checking to see if I'll be home to receive their check.

"Sorry," Bobbie says sarcastically when disappointment tinges my voice. "Just wanted to let you know your movie came and Diane is on for tomorrow night."

I MANAGED TO MAKE the most of the following day, despite hearing from the Captain once and my mother sixteen times, begging me to go out with what's-his-name and warning me that this is my last shot at a decent marriage.

When she reports that she has to stop calling because she and my father have dinner plans with friends, I think I actually say, "Thank God."

It feels delicious when Diane, Bobbie and I settle down in

the den I now adore for a very late Girls' Night In. Maggie joins us and goes directly to the doggie bed I decorated just for her, circles around twice and then nuzzles herself down in it like a bird on a nest.

Being a front-to-back split, the ceiling in my den is only seven feet. It used to make me feel closed in, so I had Sal, my painter, paint the ceiling to look like the sky. He did an incredible job, putting just enough peach into the clouds to make you feel like it's spring and if you're lucky you just might spot a robin. Then we painted everything white—the brick fireplace, the knotty pine planked walls, the bookcases, so that it all matched and looked clean and spacious. I went to a mill end warehouse for the carpeting and was able to snag some winter-white carpet that has green leaves trellised on it, and little peach flowers thrown here and there. It is gorgeous.

It is a room that says my ex-husband doesn't live here anymore. I've got a huge bowl of popcorn and we are getting set to watch the movie, which I'm hoping will help me figure out who may have killed Peaches, and why.

Hey, it worked when Rio was trying to drive me crazy and we watched *Gaslight* with Charles Boyer and Ingrid Bergman. Sigh.

Don't you just love Ingrid Bergman?

Anyway, Diane is drinking Sprite instead of Coke so that when she spills soda on my gorgeous carpet there'll be no harm done. Notice I don't say *if* because with Diane there is no question that at some point in the movie she will get mad at the way the police are portrayed and slam her glass down, or miss the coffee table altogether.

I'm surprised I don't get an argument about the no-Coke rule. I'm also surprised by the looks Bobbie keeps giving Diane, especially since she's sworn that she has kept my secret.

"Stop poking me," Diane says, and slaps at Bobbie like they are still both kids.

"Do I have to sit between the two of you?" I ask them, hands on hips like I'm the mom.

They ignore me—again, like I'm the mom. Bobbie asks if Diane is going to tell me or if she should.

"Tell me what?" I ask, slipping out of my shoes, plopping down next to Bobbie and putting my feet up on the coffee table.

"Nothing," Diane says. Then to Bobbie she adds, "Knock it off, *Barbara*."

So now they have my curiosity piqued. I pretend it's not, but I'm not great at that. I don't need to be, because Bobbie isn't going to let it rest.

"They're talking about you and Drew at the station," Bobbie says.

"Thanks, *Barbara*. I knew I could count on you to be discreet," Diane says sarcastically. Great. Now we're all counting on Bobbie to be discreet.

"Well, that's not surprising," I say. "But there's nothing to talk about. It's over." I jump up and get us coasters, not because I'm worried about the furniture, but because I'm uncomfortable lying.

"No one really bought it at first," Diane says. She leaves off what happened to change that.

"But they're buying it now," Bobbie says. Diane shoots her

a look. "What? Believe me, Diane, Teddi needs to know. Before it's too late. Don't you think?"

Diane says that she obviously didn't think so, or she'd have told me. "Too late for what?"

Bobbie looks at me.

"Too late for me to get him back, she means," I say. What else could I say at this point?

"You know he has a new partner?" Bobbie asks. "Which gives new meaning to the word, actually."

I try to act like I couldn't care less and haven't gotten her not-so-subtle meaning, while admitting that, yes, I know he's been assigned a new partner, and yes, I've seen her, and yes, she's a knockout.

"And you didn't tell me this because...?" she asks.

"Because he's a professional and he isn't going to do something as stupid as—"

"The pool is up to twelve hundred dollars," Diane says, not meeting my eyes. "Not *whether*, but *when*."

"—and because it doesn't matter to me, anyway."

Bobbie says that she can see that. And she points to the fringed pillow I'm hugging to my chest and unfringing.

"Things are tense around the Department," Diane says. "This is just a way to blow off steam."

"Oh," Bobbie says. "So it's just a blow job."

Diane says she never said that. "Though I do admit, Teddi, that your boy and O'Hanlon do seem to be taking advantage of the opportunity your rejection has given them."

"Who's this jerk O'Hanlon, and what's the matter with him?" Bobbie asks.

"That's his new partner," Diane says.

"And as for what's wrong with her," I say. "Apparently, nothing."

ANYWAY...

I remember there's a twist at the end of *Witness for the Prosecution*, but I can't remember what it is. Something about the wife manufacturing letters and pretending the husband did it and then losing credibility as a witness...

Three-quarters of the way through the movie I am nearly asleep when I feel the familiar flutter down under. Finally! I jump up and head for the stairs.

"Now? You're taking a bathroom break *now*?" Bobbie asks. "When they're gonna get the wife to testify against the husband?"

"Pause it," I hear Diane say. "No, back it up." I can hear them arguing most of the way up the stairs, where I peek at Alyssa, sleeping in her own bed for a change, on my way to my bedroom. I shut my door and sit down on my bed, flipping the phone open.

"I thought you'd never call," I say. "Nothing yesterday and now it's almost midnight."

The connection must be bad. I can hardly hear him.

"Drew? We have to meet. I have a list of—"

And then, oddly, the call-waiting clicks. I click over to the new call.

"Did you lose me?" I ask.

"Hello?"

"Couldn't you hear me before? I could hardly hear you," I say. "Drew, look, I have—"

"Sorry," I hear him say. "I must have the wrong number."

"No, it's—"

And I hear a click. It takes me a minute to figure out what just went down. And then I get it. The first call wasn't Drew. Someone is on to us.

Oh, shoot. Shoot, shoot, shoot. What did I say? Did I use his name?

I try to replay the conversation in my head, but I don't know how much I actually got out.

I wait a few minutes but Drew doesn't call back. Reluctantly, I drag myself back downstairs to the smell of fresh coffee.

"Want a cup?" Bobbie asks me, playing hostess in my kitchen.

Diane is sitting at my kitchen counter. Both women are staring at me.

I figure I have to take a chance, I have to trust someone. Not too far, mind you. Just enough.

"I miss him," I tell them. I look straight at Diane. "Can you tell him when you see him that I miss him?"

Bobbie tells me she doesn't want to sound like my mother, but...

Diane says nothing. She continues to study me, carefully. Finally, she tells Bobbie she left her pager in Bobbie's kitchen and asks her to go get it. Bobbie looks at her like she's left her mind there, as well. "It's the middle of the night, Diane. I don't go wandering around alone in the middle of the night."

"Go," Diane tells her, waving her away.

Bobbie looks down at her straight-leg J Brand jeans, her crisp white shirt with tiny pleats from Barneys in Manhasset and her new linen-and-leather Prada flat riding boots. She adjusts the wide alligator belt that sits on her hips and asks if she looks like Wilhemina's errand boy, Marc.

A fan of *Ugly Betty*, Diane knows just who she is talking about as she sizes her up. "Yup," she says. "Only he's got better boobs."

Which doesn't exactly get Bobbie moving. But Diane just waits her out, something I could never do.

Bobbie looks at me, waiting for me to say it's all right for her to stay, but I don't because I don't know what Diane has in mind. With a huge sigh and a nasty "Fine," Bobbie goes, looking over her shoulder to see what Diane could be up to when she leaves.

When she's out of sight, Diane suggests we pretend we are planning a surprise for her. "Her birthday's next month. Make it seem like we want to surprise her somehow."

"But really we're…?" I ask.

"Really we're passing a note under the teacher's nose," she says. "I'm willing to be your go-between. I might not have the rank yet, but I'm not a bad detective. And I'm not buying that you and Drew have really split. And I'm saying you can trust me, Teddi. If you want to."

I don't say anything, which is, of course, the same as speaking volumes in this case.

"Even Bobbie won't know. I promise."

Do I tell her that Bobbie does know? Do I admit that Drew and I are playing the whole Department? And what about

Drew's reaction? I know I can trust Diane, but Drew won't know that. I decide a one-way correspondence is better than nothing.

"You can seal the letters and I won't open them. I don't know the game plan and I don't want to know. I just want to help."

I nod. I scribble a note of warning. I make it sound like I'm mad, in case it should fall into the wrong hands. *Drew—we've been over this, and I thought we agreed that you wouldn't try to reach me anymore. DO NOT CALL ME.*

I can't figure out how to tell him that I have information for him, maybe the key to the case, without jeopardizing him. And besides, Bobbie is back, holding Diane's pager.

I fold the note and hand it to Diane, who rocks back and forth on the balls of her feet like she has a secret. Well, I suppose that now she does.

CHAPTER 12

Some houses lend themselves to entertaining better than others. If yours doesn't, it's often a matter of less being more. Take out any piece of furniture that can't be used as a seat, then add small tables next to the seating. Make sure, too, that the music doesn't drown out conversation.

TipsFromTeddi.com

After a second party in as many nights, Dana comes down to the kitchen bleary-eyed and casually tells me that I managed to erase all her music from both her iTunes and her iPod. She reassures me that it's no big deal, since she'd just duplicated it for Kimmie and now Kimmie can do it for her.

This is not the girl who leaps on my every mistake with relish. "Who are you, and what have you done with my daughter?" I ask her.

And she laughs. Now I know she's been abducted and replaced by an alien replica.

"You got in pretty late last night," I say. "It must have been a great party."

Her cheeks turn pink. "Oh, Mom, it was so great," she says. "Roger and I are like going out."

I tell her she and Roger have been going out for over a month.

"No," she says and that *you're so stupid* voice sneaks in for a second before she controls it. "We're, you know, *going out*." She puts little quotes around the words.

"Like going steady?"

She tells me no one calls it that anymore, but yeah, if by that I mean they are seeing each other exclusively. Okay, she doesn't use those exact words, but between the *likes* and the *you knows* and the *kindas*, I take it that's what she means.

"Can Roger come over this afternoon?" she asks me, but I feel like there's some hidden question lurking behind her words. "We have to study for a big test on Monday."

"I thought you were going to watch Lys for me today," I say. "I really have to get some stuff done, honey."

She's a little too eager to say sure, a little too willing to be helpful. I tell her I'll try to be home early in the afternoon, to which she replies that I don't have to.

Now nothing could stop me from getting home before Roger shows up.

Jesse straggles down the stairs. He's still mad at me and I'm still worried about his...*situation*.

"Everything okay?" I ask him.

I get something akin to a sarcastic *like you care*, for an answer.

Oh, yeah, I am definitely going to be home this afternoon.

Alyssa dances down the steps and twirls around in the kitchen. "I am the most beautiful girl in the second grade," she announces.

I ask her if she's planning on studying her spelling words today.

"I don't have to. I am the prettiest girl in the class," she says, taking her seat at the table.

Dana pours milk into Lys's cereal bowl. "Can we spell *conceited?*"

"Grandma June says that men like women who are pretty and not so smart," Lys informs us. She looks at me accusingly. "She says you were too smart for Drew and he felt threaded."

"*Threatened,*" Jesse corrects. He glares at me like Grandma June is right.

"Smart men like smart women," I tell all three of my children. "*Like seeks out like.* Only stupid men are interested in stupid women."

"What about opposites attracting?" Jesse asks me.

"And the stupidest of women decide that they should place their fate, their lives, their self-worth and self-esteem in some man's hands instead of keeping their destiny in their own hands."

"Now she's gonna tell you that a woman needs a man like a fish needs a bicycle," Dana warns Lys.

"What I'm going to tell you, Alyssa," I say, "is that if you do not get at least a ninety on that spelling test Monday, there will be no TV until the next spelling test. And if you don't get a ninety-five on that one…"

"But I'm the prettiest one in my class," Lys complains, "and Grandma June says—"

"Try buying groceries with that distinction," I tell her. "Try climbing the corporate ladder."

"Anna Nicole Smith did okay on just her looks," Jesse points out.

"Anna Nicole Smith is dead," I say.

"Yeah, but," Jesse says. His new mission in life is to disagree with me, it seems.

"Beauty is transient," Dana tells Lys. I need a scorecard to know who's on my side these days. "Which means it doesn't last, and if you get smart, you'll learn words like that."

I look at Jess, hoping we've proven our point. "Use it while you've got it," Jess says, heading for the stairs. "Use it or lose it."

"Yeah, we all know that's your philosophy," Dana says, chuckling. "More like *use it up, wear it out…*"

Jesse glares at her over his shoulder and takes the steps two at a time.

"So, anyway, you don't have to rush home," Dana assures me, getting up and stretching like she has no agenda herself. "Roger and I can handle everything."

I don't want to say that Dana's allowing Roger to "*handle* everything" is just what I'm worried about. She offers to help Lys study later, but Lys isn't biting.

"Well, I am the prettiest," Alyssa tells me, clearly frustrated that no one has reassured her she is.

I look critically at my youngest daughter. She may be right, but I'm not going there.

"So what?" I ask her, leaving her speechless.

ON MONDAY MORNING, after I've grilled Lys about what Dana and Roger did and didn't do to my satisfaction and relief, I stand on the corner with her long enough to get frostbite before putting her on the school bus. I wave goodbye to her just as I see the UPS truck stop in front of my house. I call out to the driver and he meets me in the street with a small package I don't remember ordering.

Inside the box is one of those little webcams. I check the address on the box and they've delivered it to the right address, but I can't figure out where it came from. And then a thought occurs to me.

I install the software and hook up the camera on my laptop, because, if I'm right, I don't want the kids accidentally coming across this. Shortly after I choose my free carrier, the "phone" rings. I click on answer and there is a fire-breathing dragon on my screen. I've used webcams before and know that you can add mustaches, hide behind avatars, disguise yourself a million ways. And I'm pretty sure who is behind the dragon, and why he's breathing fire.

"I got your note," the dragon says.

I tell him that Rio pulled a bug out of my landline and now I'm pretty certain someone is on to the Bat Phone.

The dragon morphs into Drew and he assures me that he's got it under control. "So? Did I light your fire?" he asks, referring to the dragon, I suppose. He's sitting at his dining room table. I recognize the shelf on the wall behind him, since I was the one who suggested putting it up so he'd have a kind of makeshift bar in the dining room. "You hot for me?" he says, shifting slightly in his seat.

"Is this secure? Can I talk freely?" I ask coyly. I mean, besides the more important information I have for him, I wouldn't want some tape of me salivating over him showing nightly on the Internet.

"As long as you haven't selected Record, our conversation will disappear when we're done," he says. "Click on Start Video, so I can see you."

I am tempted to say that I don't know how to work the program because the truth is that I'm a mess, and all those things that people used to say about how video phones would never catch on because who wants to be seen doing what we do when we're on the phone, come to mind. I choose, instead, to just ignore him.

"Drew, I have information for you," I say. "But first, I assume you know I got a phone call the other night before yours, right?"

"Got your not-so-subtle message. What information?"

"I got into the Love Nest," I say and he responds with an enormous smile.

"I knew you could do it," he says. "Which is why—" He stops midsentence and complains that he still can't see me.

"Why what?" I ask. Why he loves me? Why he agreed to my investigating for him?

Or why he asked me to marry him and is allowing me to keep it a secret?

He asks me to turn on the video feed. "Please?" His eyebrows go up and I have to stop myself from touching the screen.

I turn the picture on and see myself in a corner of the screen, seeing what he sees. I look like poop on a Popsicle.

"You look beautiful," he says, and laughs when he sees me

squinting at the screen trying to see what he sees. "What's your information?"

I ask why he said "that's why," but he doesn't answer me. Instead he looks over his shoulder and tells me he's pressed for time.

"I have a list of Peaches' clients," I tell him.

He gives me a patronizing grimace. "You and every cop on the force, kiddo," he says. "We got it off the computer from the Love Nest."

I smile at him, kind of a wicked, I-know-something-you-don't-know kind of smile.

"What?" He looks over his shoulder again.

"Is someone else there?" I ask. I lean to my right a little, but it doesn't change the picture on the screen. I could swear that when he turned around I saw… No, I couldn't have. "Did you drop something?" I ask.

Drew looks down, dipping his head for a second and there they are. Two wineglasses on the bar behind him.

"I'll be talking to you, Drew," I say, though what I'm thinking is, *or maybe I won't.*

Drew looks behind him. I know, because I can see him. He gives me the old *It's not what you think* line.

"Maybe I should have gotten in on that office pool," I say.

"I said—" He starts, but I assure him that I heard him the first time. "Believe what you want," he says, like two wineglasses behind him could mean anything else.

"Seeing is believing," I say. "Great little devices, these webcams."

He glances over his shoulder again.

"Expecting someone?" I ask.

"In fact, I am," he says. "O'Hanlon. So if you haven't got anything better than the list we already have, I better go."

"Fine," I say. "I don't suppose there could be any discrepancies between the list you got from her computer and the one I got off her iPod." And then I click on the end call icon.

I watch the call icon flash and let the phone ring.

And ring.

And ring.

I HATE HORSES, I think, traipsing out to the stables behind Susan Michaels' house. I hate stables, I hate being a decorator, I hate that my partner isn't here although she promised to be, I hate winter, and I hate Drew Scoones.

And I couldn't care less if his partner gets the chair, even though they don't have a chair in New York, do they?

I feel used.

I feel manipulated.

"Hello, Zorro," I say, holding out some carrots in my gloved hand. "Remember me? I'm the idiot with the Kick Me sign."

Zorro rubs his muzzle gently against my hand, urging me to pet him.

"Nice boy," I tell him. I think he makes a point of not scaring me.

I move on to the other two horses. They seem happy to see me, too.

Okay, maybe I don't hate horses, but everything else stays on the list.

Especially Drew Scoones.

"THESE WERE ON THE PORCH when we got home," Jesse says, showing me an enormous bouquet of tulips. Springtime in a vase. Jess is so hopeful I could weep. "There's no card. Do you think they're from Drew? Maybe he wants to make up. Do you think?"

I tell him it's not likely, and that they're probably from a satisfied client. I wonder how I'm going to get his ring back to him. Waltz into the precinct and throw it at him?

"Maybe you should have tried to satisfy Drew," Jesse says, and it's surprising my jaw doesn't break when it hits the floor.

I almost tell him that someone else seems to be satisfying Drew these days, but the kid's eleven.

And Drew's the only hero he's got.

I'm tempted to throw the flowers out, but who will that spite, really? So I take them to the sink and pull them out to cut their stems. Attached to the bottom of the flowers is a ziplock bag with a note. ANSWER THE DAMN PHONE. Now how could anyone resist that?

If I didn't have pertinent information, I'd never do it. And because I'm still angry, I take my sweet time about it. First I see how Alyssa is doing, ask about her spelling test, forbid her from watching TV all week, drift into Dana's room to see how miserable I can make her, too, and then lock myself in my bathroom with my laptop.

I have a stall shower in here, an old-fashioned one with those inch-by-inch tiles lining the whole thing and a heavy glass shower door. I sit on the floor of the shower, the laptop propped in front of me, attach the eyeball, and fire the baby up.

I click on the only contact I have. Drew answers.

"Don't hang up," is the first thing he says. It's not fair that he always looks so good.

"If you give me the list, I'll compare it," I say.

He squints at the screen. "Are you in the shower?"

I nod, and realize that I don't have to speak. How funny that seems.

"Are you naked?" He smiles at me.

I stretch up a little so he can see I'm dressed. "I don't want to play with you," I say.

"I can explain," he says.

"I don't think so. I think you left those glasses out knowing I'd see them, *meaning* for me to see them," I say.

"Teddi, why would I do that? You know I need your help on this."

No *why would I do that when I love you? When I want you to be my wife?*

I tell him that he has my help, but only because I care about the truth.

"And not about me," he says, being sure we're clear.

I nod again.

"And you don't want to hear my explanation," he says flatly.

I tell him I don't.

"You're wrong," he says. "I know exactly what you've figured out, and you are wrong."

He always does this. Now he'll make some totally idiotic guess. I'll have to tell him the truth or he'll never stop guessing.

"You want those names, or not?" I ask.

I see him glance at his watch. He's in his bedroom. At least he's alone there.

"Some other time?" I offer.

"I'm just wondering how long it will take. How about we cut to the chase, shall we? You're thinking I let you see those two wineglasses on purpose because it would be easier than coming out and saying that I'm not in it for the long haul, that I don't want the baggage you come with, don't want the kids and the lawn and the PTFuckingA."

Okay, so this is a different game, a game where he guesses right the first time. I'm trying not to let my face show how deep into my gut that blow came. I look away from the screen, bite the inside of my cheek, try to find something to say and a voice to say it with.

"It so happens I have all night tonight, so take your time," he says. "But it would really help to move this along if you could be half this conversation. Or even a quarter."

"It doesn't seem to require my input," I say.

"It damn well does," he says. "Am I supposed to argue with myself?"

I stare at the shampoo bottles in the caddy that hangs from the shower head. I count them. Once. Twice. Who needs so many kinds of shampoo?

"Fine," he says. He looks to his left. "That's what you think, Teddi, don't you? That I'm sending you some 'I want out' message."

He turns to his right. "Yes," he says in a high voice that's hard not to laugh at, "I do."

"Well—" to the left "—you're wrong. Wrong on every level."

"No, no—" high voice "—I'm not. I know men, Drew Scoones. I've been burned before and I'll walk away first before I get burned again."

"I won't burn you." He looks directly at the screen. "I'm not your ex-husband. I won't hurt you, Teddi. I promise."

"I said I'd give you the list," I say. It's not what I mean to say, but it's what comes out.

Drew's mouth is a taught straight line. He says he wants more than the list.

I tell him I managed to get the calendar off, too. "I have when she was with who."

He says that isn't what he meant, and then what I've said hits him. "On the day of the murder?"

I nod. "Wasn't that in the computer?"

CHAPTER 13

Rooms should be decorated with their purpose in mind. It sounds obvious, but not all bedrooms are restful, not all living rooms invite living in them. Don't use bold, exciting colors or patterns in your bedroom unless you enjoy insomnia. Don't make living spaces so minimal that simply being there appears to disrupt the serenity.

TipsFromTeddi.com

I've agreed to meet Drew in a motel not far from the house, which is good because the rain has turned to snow. I've made it clear that it's only to go over the lists with him.

"Damned if I do, and damned if I don't," he said to me before we hung up. When I asked what he meant, he said that if he made a move on me I'd accuse him of using me, and if he didn't, I'd assume he was getting it elsewhere. "I'm tired of playing this game, Teddi, and it can't go on. The minute we wrap up this case we're going to have to—"

I didn't let him finish. Talk about damned either way.

Now I've donned my armor and, knocking on the door of room 218 at some No Tell Motel that I've slunk into like a cheating spouse, I take a deep breath. How long do old wounds take to heal? And how long before you can't hide behind them anymore and you have to damn the sharks and jump into the ocean again?

Drew lets me in. The man gets handsomer every time I see him. Handsome didn't work out well for me the first time, but I remind myself that not every handsome man is Rio Gallo.

Drew is awkward. He's nervous about coming on, I think. He offers to take my jacket. I shrug out of it without his help.

"I printed the list out," I tell him, pulling a folded-up piece of paper from one of my pockets before tossing the jacket—with the ring in the other pocket—on the bed. He picks a folder up off a slab of wood that is supposed to be a desk. Or maybe it's a luggage rack. From the folder he pulls several sheets of paper.

"I have the iPod, too, so we can look at the calendar."

He tells me that's great, nods, smiles. Quietly he tells me he appreciates it all—getting the iPod, getting the information, giving it to him. I tell him no problem, nod, smile.

It's as if we are standing there naked and pretending not to notice.

"Well," he says after an interminable pregnant pause that I can't even manage to fill with a comment on the weather, which is freezing. In fact, the snow is now coming down pretty hard and I could say that I think we should hurry because I'm worried about driving home. Only, I can't seem to push words out. "Guess we should get to it before the wrong man gets sentenced."

I mumble something like *guess so,* but tears are beginning

to clog my nose and close my throat. He asks me if I want to talk about it.

"No."

"Am I just not supposed to notice?" he asks and I nod.

"Alphabetical order, then?" he says. I put bonus points in his column when he offers to read the names and I can just stop him if there's a discrepancy.

I'm thinking if he just doesn't touch me, I'll be fine. I'll hold it together.

The list is not that long. It takes us only a few minutes to get through most of it. Some of the names mean something to Drew. Most are unfamiliar to either of us.

"Saunders," Drew says. "Sanderson. Smith."

"No Schultz?" I ask. "I have a…John Schultz." We look at each other.

Drew asks to see my list. I don't know what he expects to see.

"It doesn't necessarily mean—" I start to say.

"No, no," he agrees. "Even if he was a client—"

"He could have simply not wanted anyone to know that," I say.

"Or anyone in the Department could have seen the name and deleted it."

I ask if that wouldn't be tampering with evidence. Drew's look confirms it, but also concedes it happens.

"So then," I say. "Do we know if Captain Schultz has an alibi for the time of the murder?"

Drew asks to see the calendar on the iPod. I hand it over to him, telling him Alyssa got it to work. "Smart and beautiful," he says. "Just like her mom."

His thumbs dance across the iPod, knowing what to touch to bring up what he wants. I'm impressed, but I don't say so. While he skims the week before Peaches was murdered, his eyes glued to the little screen, he asks me, "Feeling any better?"

I tell him I'm fine.

His "Good," says he doesn't believe me for a minute, but won't press it. More points in his column, damn it.

"She had this guy Richards for lunch," Drew says.

"I'll bet she did," I say and he looks up, surprised that my sense of humor seems unscathed.

"And lookie, lookie, who was supposed to be there at midnight." He turns the iPod so that I can read the screen. Occupying the midnight slot is John Schultz's name.

I tell him to look at every Wednesday night and see who had an appointment. "And I'd guess he stayed over on those nights," I say.

He looks at me with furrowed brows. "How'd you get that?"

"Remember the night of the murder? Well, the table was set for two for breakfast in the dining room."

He admits remembering it was set for two, but why breakfast?

"Juice glasses. And there was a muffin mix out on the counter, the timer was set on the coffeemaker. Every man's dream wife. Even I was wishing Peaches was my wife, that night."

"They have hot coffee and bagels at Dunkin' Donuts," Drew says. "I wouldn't know a juice glass from a shot glass, and I don't mind my juice straight from the carton. It's not every man's dream wife, Ted."

I pull back the curtain and glance outside. "Look at that snow! I better get home, don't you think?"

Drew says if that's what I want, and I explain about the snow and the kids and make excuses until he's helping me on with my jacket and putting a finger against my lips.

"Start thinking about a date, Teddi. Because when this is over…"

He lets the rest dangle in the air, twisting in the wind, but I know the rest of the thought. When this is over, we could be, too. My choice. The idea makes me dizzy, makes my head spin.

"I'll follow you home," he says, putting on the same leather jacket he wore all fall, though it's thirty degrees colder.

I tell him he doesn't have to, that I'll be fine, that someone may be watching. We both look out at the deserted parking lot. The snow is now blinding and no one could see us from more than ten feet away.

"You're not driving in this," he says, pulling out his cell phone and flipping it open.

I protest, telling him I have to get back to the kids, only now I'm not simply using them as an excuse.

"Jo Jo," he says into the phone. "You out plowin'? I got a mother here with young kids at home who got caught in the storm. Can you run her back to her place?"

He smiles that crooked smile at me and gives me a thumbs-up.

"Thirty minutes is fine. Forty-five is even better. She'll be in the diner by Picquets Lane. You know the one? You're the best, Joe. I owe you one."

Flipping the phone closed, he takes my chin in his hand. "I can take care of anything," he says, slipping my jacket off and running his hands down my arms, sending chills where heat should be. "You need anything else?"

I let him twirl me around until I'm facing away from him and he puts his arms around me so that we can watch the snow together.

He nuzzles my ear, blows on it softly. "Forty-five minutes to kill…and we don't even have a deck of cards," he says.

"Captain Schultz wasn't the only one with a standing appointment with Peaches, you realize," I say softly, trying not to break the mood. I'm lying. That is exactly what I'm trying to do. I'm trying to avoid seduction. I'm trying to keep two feet on the ground, literally.

Drew says he assumes John Schultz wasn't the only one, and did I have a particular client in mind?

We both know I mean Hal Nelson.

"Peaches had a standing ten o'clock appointment on Wednesdays with Hal. Only it wasn't filled in for the night of the murder."

He asks if I have any guesses why not. And while he's asking, he's slipping his hands under my sweater, warm hands that unhook my bra effortlessly and then come around to cup my breasts. I shut my eyes and ask myself why I'm fighting it. What is it going to take for me to step off the precipice and trust that he'll catch me?

"I'm waiting," he says. "But not patiently."

"Could be that the client cancelled," I say, leaning my head back against him to keep the room from swaying. "Could be she didn't bother writing him in because he always came, but that's not likely."

"Always coming isn't likely?" His hips press against my bottom, his hands are everywhere and I think I could drown in his arms. I think I *want* to drown in his arms.

Only now my breath starts coming in deep gulps. So deep that I think the room begins to spin.

"Teddi? Are you all right?" Drew guides me to the bed and pushes on my shoulders until I'm sitting. He tries to lower my head between my knees, but I fight him.

"I'm scared," I tell him. "Scared of depending on you, counting on you, melding into you. I'm scared of losing me."

"So scared it makes you physically ill?" he asks, touching my forehead. "You've got a fever, Teddi."

"Thank God," I say wobbly. "I was beginning to think the idea of spending the rest of my life with you made me sick."

He pulls the covers back on the bed, muttering about how he should have picked a better place for our rendezvous, and gets a wet washcloth from the bathroom for my head. I tell him I'm perfectly fine, but the truth is I feel like someone's using a Mixmaster inside my head. I'm Sydelle Silverberg's kitchen and she's rushing around in me making horrible combinations that turn my stomach.

Drew helps me to the bathroom where I lose the contents of my stomach and apologize over and over again on my way back to the bed.

I hear him call Bobbie and ask her to round up my kids and

take them over to her house, explaining that he ran into me in the storm and I've taken ill. I can hear her doubting his veracity, claiming we're shacked up somewhere having the time of our lives while she's stuck with five kids.

Bobbie says she'll just come and get me if I'm really so sick.

"You can't just come get her," he says into the phone, exasperation dripping from each word. "The roads are impassable and you're going to have enough to deal with what with five kids in your house."

Bobbie shouts something, but I can't make it out. The buzz in my head is deafening.

"I am not keeping her prisoner." Drew pushes the words out between gritted teeth. "Sex slave? Yeah, that's it. You found me out. I've got this kinky thing for women who can't keep a glass of water down."

There's a pause and then he adds, and he sounds like he's begging here, "Just get the kids, Bobbie. And remember that Alyssa has this thing about closets, so if your husband could maybe take the door off…"

I don't remember telling him about Lys and the closet doors.

"Christ! Because in addition to the roads, your best friend is puking her guts out here, and unless you want it all over your car—"

He doesn't only know my daughter well, he knows my partner well, too. She stops insisting she can get me.

I try to sit up and reach for the phone, but a wave of nausea hits me right between the eyes. Drew manages not to drop the phone as he grabs the wastebasket and positions it just where I need it.

Drew says he's got to go, eliciting a promise from Bobbie that she'll keep the kids with her until she hears from me. He holds the pail until I nod at him that I'm done. He eases me back down on the pillows, and then whisks away the wastebasket.

"You okay?"

I nod, which initiates a new round of nausea.

I hear him calling off Jo Jo, the man with the plow.

Time passes, I think. CNN plays very quietly on the small TV. The washcloth on my head is cool. I swear Drew takes my pulse. I sleep. Larry King is on. He's interviewing Peaches Lipschitz. She's selling iPod players that look like old radios. She's saying she knows what men want—apple pie and Chevrolet trucks. I sleep again. Nancy Grace is shouting and Drew is shouting back.

"What?" I ask and he's immediately at my side, solicitous. "Is she talking about Hal?" I ask. "Or am I still dreaming?"

"I wish," he says. "She seems to have the case all wrapped up for the prosecution."

Maybe it's the fever. Maybe it's Drew hovering over me and wiping what I hope is drool from the corner of my mouth. All I know is that if Nancy Grace is working for the prosecution, I'm all in for the defense.

Drew clicks off the TV with the remote.

"Don't you want to see that?" I ask. He shakes his head and looks at the TV like he'd like to kick it out into the snow. He shrugs into his coat and I think that maybe he's going to do just that.

"I'm going to get you soup," he says, tucking the blankets in around me. "I'll be back in ten minutes." He puts my phone next to my head on the pillow and tells me if I need anything to just call him.

I accuse him of trying to prove he can take care of all my needs and he smiles.

"Thanks for the opportunity," he says, dabbing with a washcloth at something I suspect may be vomit on his sweater.

"I'M SICK," I hear him say, and I come out of my haze to see him standing by the window on the phone, looking as hale and hearty as ever. It's bright behind him, so I figure it's morning. I've been throwing up forever. "I'll be out a few days." He sees me open my eyes and smiles at me, indicating with a finger to his lips that I should be silent. "Stomach flu. Nothing to worry about. Just barfing my guts out."

He hangs up the phone without saying goodbye and comes to sit beside me on the bed.

"You're getting some color back," he says. "A little pink in your cheeks."

"That's embarrassment," I say.

"Did I ever tell you about the time I went camping with my uncle and my cousins?" he asks. I shake my head and this time when the room sways, it rights itself without flipping my stomach. "Tom and Glenn were about nine and eleven, I think. I know I was nearly eight and I'd never been camping before. I mean, I'd peed in the woods, but that was in the daytime, with my father around, or a bunch of kids comparing—"

I suppose I snicker, because he looks up from the spot he's been studying on the blanket and tells me they were comparing *distances*, not…

"Exactly as I thought," I say, "since this is about embarrassment."

He feigns insult and threatens not to tell me the rest of the story unless I promise to behave myself and be properly sympathetic.

"It was the middle of the night," he says, not waiting for my agreement, "when nature called. I mean boomed in my ear that there'd be no ignoring it."

Nature is actually beginning its siren song for me, and I'm just praying that this stomach virus stays above my belly button.

"You with me?"

More than you know.

"So I get up and open the tent flap and it's dark as pitch. I mean, no moon, no stars, no campfire glow in the distance. Tommy asks if I'm going or not. If I'm scared."

"But brave Drew said, 'No, I'm not scared,'" I pipe up.

"It was a taunt, not an offer to help," he tells me. "So I go out deep into the forest, or what I think is deep into the forest, and I pull down my pants. And then I hear it. A bear, clomping in the woods. Growling, coming to get me and my little wienie, which is out in the cold air shrinking to the size of a peanut. Shelled."

"And then?"

"Clomp, clomp, clomp, coming closer and closer. I'm running with my pants down around my ankles, when the bear calls me by name!"

"The bear called your name?"

"Hey, I was eight years old. Raised on Disney. I didn't stop to think 'if a bear calls your name in the woods, is Little Red Riding Hood with him?' I started running. At least, I tried to run…"

"But your pants—"

"They framed the photo. Put it up on the mantel every time I visited until I was tall enough to take it down and stamp on it. First thing I did as a cop? Got Hal to pretend he had a warrant for their arrest."

I don't want to talk about Hal, so I shut my eyes. Drew feels my forehead.

"Think you could hold down some aspirin?" he asks me. From nowhere, in the middle of a snowstorm, he produces a bottle of aspirin and shakes out two, helps me sit up and hands me a glass of water.

He climbs up on the bed and nestles me in the crook of his arm. Just before I fall asleep again he leans down and whispers that he loves me. "But if you want to stop working on Hal's case, I guess I can live with that."

I could be a cynic. I could doubt he means it. I could interpret it as a sophisticated attempt at manipulation. Instead, I accept it as a gift, and I snuggle down against his hard body and try to imagine the kid he was with his pants around his ankles, running from a bear calling his name.

CHAPTER 14

Your bedroom is your refuge, and should contain those things which give you comfort—piles of soft pillows, both a down comforter and a chenille throw for napping under. Room-darkening shades can make Sunday mornings last almost forever.

TipsFromTeddi.com

"**I** don't need rescuing," I tell Bobbie the next day when she calls.

"Ohhh," she says, the word loaded with innuendo. "So I was right. You aren't even sick?"

I tell her how I had a fever and threw up all over Drew, and how I think I'm in deeper than I'd planned.

"So, is it Drew Scoones raising your temperature," she asks me, "or the flu?"

"You know how you're always making bargains with God? Like if there are black Jimmy Choos on sale you'll promise to visit Mike's mother and not complain about how she favors Kristin over Kimmie?"

Bobbie tells me the fever has affected my brain. "I would

never do that. Not for black Jimmy Choos. Now if they were red…"

"If Hal Nelson gets off, I think I might, maybe, possibly go through with marrying Drew."

I hear something fall in the bathroom while Bobbie asks if he wouldn't need me more if Hal got convicted. And she reminds me that I have already accepted his ring.

"Not accepted," I say. "I'm holding it. That's different. And I'm not a consolation prize if Hal's convicted," I say, more quietly in case Drew is actually hearing me. He opens the bathroom door, a towel tied around his waist, and smiles at me. He's holding up a toothbrush and toothpaste in my direction. I tell Bobbie that I've checked messages and Susan Michaels wants a progress report. I ask if she can take care of it for me.

"I'm taking care of five kids here, Teddi," she says. "And you're tucked away somewhere with Detective Dreamy, bargaining with God about getting married again. I don't know squat about how far you've gotten on the Michaels place, and even if I did, it's you she hired and you she trusts and—"

"What's really going on?" I ask, watching as Drew dries himself with a towel that doesn't hide much. Through the open bathroom door I see our undies over the shower bar. I don't remember taking mine off. Drew winks at me and slides into his jeans sans briefs.

"Hungry?" he asks me.

Not for food, I want to tell him, but I'm barely sitting up in the bed. Of course, sitting up isn't required for what I have in mind.

"I'm stuck in with five obnoxious kids," Bobbie reminds me.

Watching Drew I forgot she was on the phone altogether. I am definitely feeling better.

I suggest that Mike, her chiropractic husband, bring all the kids downstairs to his office and give them each a treatment. It'll take up a bunch of time and in the end she'll have five well-adjusted kids.

There is dead silence on the other end of the line.

"He's not home?"

More silence.

"Please don't tell me he's with his hypnotherapist friend," I say, referring to the woman he left her for a few years ago, the woman he claimed to know from a previous life. We thought that was over, behind us.

She tells me that the official word is that he is stuck at his office in Farmingdale.

I don't bother telling her that he always goes to the Farmingdale office on Tuesdays to see the patients that live out that way, and that it's merely coincidence that the hypnotherapist's office is next door. And that the snow was really bad and roads are closed. Bobbie always assumes the worst. Sadly, she's often right.

Drew takes the phone away from me. "Listen," he tells Bobbie. "We don't have a charger here, so if you need Teddi, if the kids need her, I mean, call us at this number." And he reads the number off the motel room phone. "Room 218."

Bobbie says something mean to him. I can tell from the expression on his face. But he is polite to her, for my sake, and when he's hung up with her he asks if it would be all right if he took off for a few hours.

"Where are you going?" I ask him.

He looks deep into my eyes, searching for something without asking. "To make sure Hal is found not guilty," he says, shrugging into his jacket. He stops at the door. "And then maybe, possibly, I might think about, perhaps, pressing you for a wedding date."

It's probably a good thing that he shuts the door before I reach for the wastebasket and heave.

I SLEEP ON AND OFF for the next few hours, vaguely aware that the snow has ended and the sun has come out, dust-filled rays of light streaming through the slit in the window curtains. Like the great outdoors, I have weathered the storm and my fever is gone, my nausea abated. I can hear the trickle of snow melting off the gutters and dripping on the cement below and marvel at how much faster the world seems to be recuperating than I am.

Okay, I'm not really marveling. I'm putting the pillow over my head so that I don't have to hear the uneven drip, drip, drip that won't let me fall back to sleep. I'm just beginning to wonder where Drew is when the phone on the nightstand rings and I toss the pillow aside and reach for it.

"Sorry to interrupt your little lovefest," Bobbie says, "but I thought you'd want to know your son's been picked up for shoplifting."

All I can think to say is that she's got the wrong number. I mean, it sounds like Bobbie, but my son wouldn't even go out in the snow, never mind forge his way through a storm to commit robbery.

"Teddi? Are you there?" Okay, so it's not the wrong number. It's a joke.

"Not funny," I tell her. "You're too old for phony phone calls."

Bobbie tells me that you're never too old for phony phone calls, but that, unfortunately, this isn't one. "I didn't even know he was gone," she tells me. "I thought he was playing video games in the basement."

"I ask you to watch my children for a matter of hours and you lose one? What if he'd died in the snowstorm? Would you have noticed that?"

"If I'd had to step over his body to get to my car to go out in the midst of this to pick up another one of your kids at the police station, then maybe," she shoots back.

I ask her if that's where she is now.

"They're processing him, whatever that means," she says. "But they don't want to release him to me because I'm not his parent."

I hope it's the fact that I've been sick for the last two days that makes me incoherent. I seem to need to have everything spelled out for me. And repeated.

Ten minutes later Bobbie is losing patience with me. "As I said, the snow stopped. The sun came out. I suggested the girls take Lys out to make a snowman, because I am a good friend and neighbor and I wanted the kids to enjoy the gift of a snow day appropriately."

"Yeah," I say. "I get that you were sick of them and wanted them out of the house."

Bobbie ignores this comment and relates that the girls

declined the opportunity and suggested that Jesse take Lys out, since he was just playing with himself in the basement.

"By himself," I correct, though I'm guessing he was more likely doing the former.

"And I sent the girls down to ask him and they came back up to report that there was no sign of Jess, that his boots and coat were gone, and that there were footsteps in the snow leading out from the back door."

I suggest that maybe he just went home. Bobbie reminds me that she is at the police station picking him up. I ask what they are claiming he's done—besides take years off my life and earn himself grounding on top of his detention.

"He apparently walked to CVS and tried to buy cigarettes," Bobbie says.

"Cigarettes?" What's next? I wonder. Have we started down the slippery slope to marijuana and crack and cocaine? Is crack cocaine? "He's too young to buy cigarettes. Didn't they just refuse him? They didn't arrest him for that, did they?"

Bobbie tells me that no, they didn't. "It gets better. When they refused to sell him the cigarettes, he stomped off and went up and down the aisles looking for something. What with the storm, he and some random guy picking up baby aspirin were the only two people in the store, so there wasn't much for the clerk to do but watch him put three jars of Vaseline into his pocket and head for the door."

"Vaseline?" I don't even want to go there. I'm praying Bobbie doesn't ask me what I suppose they were for.

She glosses right over it and suggests Drew tear himself away from me and come down to get my son. I tell her I'll be there as soon as I'm dressed. I could straighten her out about Drew's whereabouts, but I know Bobbie. She's simply not in the mood to be straightened.

I've got on my bra and sweater, my socks and sheepskin boots, and I'm desperately trying to dry my underpants with the hotel hair dryer when Drew comes in on a blast of cold air.

"Aren't those supposed to be black leather? With high heels, *kitten?*" he asks me, gesturing toward my getup. "And I'd be interested to know where you think you're going, anyway? Get back into the bed. I've got some news."

I tell him I've got news, too. Jesse's been arrested.

Drew flinches as if dealt a physical blow. I add insult to injury. "Remember how I told you about his obsession? Well, he apparently forged his way through the snow to the drugstore for several jars of Vaseline. Wanna guess what he wanted that for?"

Drew says he doesn't have to guess. "I suppose it's time for my little talk with our boy, huh?" he says, like Jesse's having been arrested doesn't even play into it.

And no, I didn't miss the fact that he referred to him as "our boy." Funny, because this is the point at which most couples start referring to their mutual child as belonging to their spouse—as in *your* son, *your* daughter.

"Drew, there are always two twenty-dollar bills in my desk drawer in case the kids need something and I'm not around," I tell him, slipping into my nearly-dry panties and reaching for my jeans. "And Jesse knows that. He was sending me a message—"

Drew tells me to get back into bed. He tells me that this

little trick of Jesse's wasn't about Vaseline, or money, or me. "The message was meant for me," he says, looking chastened. "And I get it."

I tell Drew how upset Jesse's been about our breakup. Drew holds up the covers and gestures for me to scoot under them and tells me not to worry about it. I zip up my jeans and pick up my jacket, not looking at him as I tell him that Jesse thinks his equipment is not working properly.

The covers drop.

"What, exactly, does that mean?" he asks.

"Damned if I know," I admit. I ask if he really thinks Jesse would tell his mother more than that.

He says that it says a lot about our relationship that he told *me* that much.

I suppose it does.

He tells me again to get into bed. He'll go collect Jesse and have a talk with him. If necessary, and he's sure it's not, he'll make arrangements for him to see someone about the problem.

"Don't you think I should be there?" I ask. "I mean, how are you going to explain to Jesse, or to the Department, what your interest in all this is?"

He tells me that as far as the Department goes, he'll say that his problems with me have nothing to do with Jesse, and that he and the kid are pals.

"And as for Jesse?" I ask.

He looks at me with that half smile that's so Drew. He points to the bed and I climb in, because the truth is that I'm done in and if I didn't feel crappy enough, this business has finished me off. "I think it's time for the jig to be up, as far as the boy is concerned. He's old enough to understand the importance of our secret—"

"Then he's older than I am," I mumble.

"A few more days," he says. But he says he can't ask Jesse to wait any longer.

And out it pops, unbidden, uncensored, unplanned. "I love you," I say, as if it's the most natural thing in the world.

Drew tucks me in without saying a word. He kisses my forehead and touches my cheek. "I know," he finally says. "It's a bitch, isn't it?"

He's out the door before I can answer him.

CHAPTER 15

*If your budget permits, replace hollow core doors with solid
wood ones. You'd be amazed at the difference that one change
can make. It gives your house substance, helps with sound-
proofing, and, should you need to slam one for effect, you'll
find them quite satisfying.*

TipsFromTeddi.com

An hour later I hear Drew outside the door, talking to someone I suppose is Jesse. Except, while Jesse's voice is admittedly
high since it hasn't changed yet, it's never sounded sexy before.

He murmurs something to the woman he's with, and then
I hear the key in the door. They slip in and he shuts it behind
them. "Teddi?" he calls softly in the dim light. "You awake?"

"Where's Jesse?" I ask him. Not hello, not thank you, not
why the hell is O'Hanlon with you?—so, not terribly polite,
but not rude, either.

Drew and his new partner stay glued to the door, exchang-
ing looks while he tells me not to worry. Only now, of course,
I've got two worries.

Jesse, he says, is at my house, with my parents. Seems my

son called them when he couldn't reach me and the police wouldn't release him to Bobbie.

"So here we all are," Drew says, rocking on his heels and looking at O'Hanlon and at me.

I am speechless. And not just because I'm shocked, but because I have no idea how I'm supposed to react. Am I supposed to be mad at Drew? I mean, am I supposed to pretend that I am? He's brought his partner, looking like that blonde on *Gray's Anatomy*, with no warning. Of course, I have no change of clothes, in a room which smells vaguely of vomit…

They both tiptoe farther into the room. O'Hanlon mumbles something about how sorry she is that I'm sick. "And that you got the wrong impression," she adds.

I say something coy and vague, like *oh, did I?*

Drew raises an eyebrow as if to ask if I really don't remember. I want to get out of bed and go rescue my son from the lecture my mother is no doubt giving him, but I wiggled out of my jeans and damp undies after I got back into bed, and so I'm stuck where I am.

Which means that I'm reduced to having to ask, in front of Detective O'Hanlon, what happened with Jesse. "Are they going to press charges?"

Drew shakes his head. "They wanted to scare the bejesus out of him, I think. When your mother showed up and started in on him, I think they felt he was going to be punished enough."

"Or that the embarrassment would kill him," O'Hanlon adds. Then she seems to catch herself, as if she isn't supposed to know as much as she does.

I ask if Drew got a chance to talk to him. Privately.

He nods, and it appears to be all he can do to keep a straight face.

I ask him if he'd like to share the joke. I could use some amusement about now.

"It seems," Drew says, and now his shoulders are shaking, "that your son and his friend got hold of some X-rated videos, and—"

"Where would he...?" I start to say, but there's only one place I can think of. "I'll kill him." Modesty be damned, I'm ready to fling back the covers and go after my ex-husband with the sharpest object I can find, which may well be my tongue.

Drew tells me that Jesse took them out of the garbage, along with a broken VCR.

"This just gets better and better," I say. "Rio's garbage?"

Drew shrugs. O'Hanlon busies herself with a speck of lint on her black, un-dog-haired trousers. "It does get better," Drew says. "He and Danny watched the tapes and Jesse decided that he was...inadequate."

"My laundry says otherwise," I say, embarrassed on Jesse's behalf with the Izzy Stevens look-alike privy to this conversation. Jess would just die on the spot. And I still can't figure out why Drew brought her here, but I figure as long as we keep talking about Jesse, I'm safe.

Drew tells me that in the movie, "when the star...ejaculated—" and now no one is looking at anyone and we're all finding lint on our clothes, or our blankets, or floating in the air "—it traveled a great distance, shall we say?" He makes a motion with his hand to indicate a long arc, headed for the wall and beyond.

Detective O'Hanlon is laughing behind her hand, doing her best to hide it.

"What you're saying," I ask, just to make sure, "is that Jesse felt that he should be shooting across the room?" I admit a bit of incredulousness creeps into my voice. And I feel my own lips begin to twitch.

"Across the state," Drew says, the arc he draws this time greater still. "Across the continent."

I picture Jesse in his room, the poster of Natalie Portman, former Syosset High School student, now movie star, with the target drawn on it and feel my face flush. "Poor Jess!"

"Oh, it doesn't…?" Detective O'Hanlon asks with a straight face. "I mean, not an eleven-year-old's, but surely…" She opens her palm at Drew, then laughs.

Of course, she laughs alone, as I remember the pair of wine-glasses on the webcam.

"What?" she asks, looking from me to Drew and back again.

"Teddi thinks that you and I…" Drew starts, and knowledge blooms on O'Hanlon's gorgeous face.

"For God's sake, Scoones. And you didn't straighten her out? Why not?"

Drew says nothing, and O'Hanlon rushes to tell me that there is nothing going on between the two of them.

Drew tells her that there's no point hiding it, that I saw the wineglasses and have figured out the truth.

"I'm confused," she says. "You mean that she knew that was all a set up for Williams to see? Then why would she think that you and I had anything going?"

"Williams?" I ask, looking from one of them to the other.

"You may not have been exactly convincing when you met with Lynette," O'Hanlon says, almost apologetically. "When Ron started implying the whole breakup was a ruse, Scoones let me in on it. Didn't he tell you?"

I don't say that I didn't let him. I'm grateful he doesn't say so, either.

He does say, "Teddi has some trust issues."

"Doesn't every ex-wife?" O'Hanlon asks. "And don't we all have our reasons?"

"Someone cheated on *you*?" I ask, and my voice cracks comically.

O'Hanlon says that not only did the man cheat on her, but she gave him a second chance and he did it again.

Drew tells her that my husband tried to drive me crazy. I wait for him to say it was a short trip, or that he was too late, or that Rio was too stupid to realize I was already there. He just leaves that information hanging out in the air.

"Listen," she says. "I should go. I think I've been here long enough for a quicky, don't you?" She winks at me and Drew sees her to the door.

"A quickie?" I ask. "Is someone following you two?"

"Me, you, who knows?" he says.

Somehow, I think he does.

CHAPTER 16

*If you truly want to feel on top of your life, clean out those
neglected spaces that you encounter every day. An organized
garage can make coming home a much more serene experience, as can a pared-down front hall closet. Really, do you
need your sun hat in there in December? Your mittens in there
in June?*

TipsFromTeddi.com

One thing about twenty-four-hour viruses. They sound in-
nocuous, but it seems to me they always take forty-eight hours
to go away and even then they leave you feeling like you've
been run over by a Mack truck. As I drive to the hospital to
see Hallie again, I think about my last conversation with Drew
and am surprised to find myself smiling. The man really wants
the whole package—me, the kids, even my mother, who he
views as the greatest challenge ever to his charm. I assured him
there would be no winning her over, but he just winked and
said, "Watch me."

If I had any doubts about whether he was just leading me
on to get me to investigate for him, the fact that he told Jesse
the truth has evaporated them. Even if I doubted how he feels

about *me*, I've never questioned how he feels about Jess, who can't stop grinning from ear to ear. The kid's even begun cleaning out the basement in case Drew wants to store any "stuff" down there. He owes Drew big-time for getting him out of trouble with the drugstore and the police.

I sat down with Dana and explained the situation to her, the need to keep it a secret, and the ramifications of our plans. I can't say she was jumping for joy, but she was accepting, mature, understanding. Which is to say that she gave me the *I'm not stupid, Mom* look. Her only comment, "Whatever," seemed to imply agreement to both the marriage and to keeping it a secret for now.

Her reaction to my assurance that Rio would always be her father and a part of her life and that Drew would *supplement* rather than *replace* her dad in that role was met with her patented, "Duh." I don't know when I got so stupid, but I've heard that when she gets older I'll get smarter again.

"So he's a supplement?" she asks. "Which one? Vitamin Sex?"

We haven't told Lys because telling her is the same as telling my mother, which is the same as telling the world.

Okay, so that's an excuse. I don't want the confrontation with my mother just yet. I want to enjoy the feeling of being loved for five minutes before she ruins it for me.

Bobbie is throwing herself into this marriage thing with everything she's got. It turned out that Mike really was stuck at the office, that his old flame wasn't even in town, never mind in her office, and Bobbie's so happy to have him home that she doesn't know what to do with herself.

So she's driving me crazy with wedding ideas and plans.

Which I can't think about now. I have to concentrate on why I'm going to see Hallie again and what I need to get from this little visit. As Drew and I have pieced it together, John Schultz must have been one of Peaches Lipschitz's clients. That or he was taking bribes to have the Department look the other way. Did John's wife know? Grace Schultz is one cool customer, but I don't think she'd close her eyes to her husband fooling around, especially with a hooker. Hallie spent the night that Peaches was killed with Grace Schultz. And shortly after that, Hallie tried to kill herself.

So…

So…

So I have no idea where that leaves us, but with a little more information…

I park the car and go into the hospital, asking for Hallie at the desk and finding that she is in the solarium. Having been a patient at South Winds I know that "being in the solarium" means that she is no longer a PSI, or *Possible Self Injury*, patient. This is good news for both of us. We can talk more freely in the solarium with no one listening in.

Pale and wan, all she wants to know is if I've seen Hal again and how he is.

"I haven't seen him," I admit, but promise that I will.

"Now?" She's nearly frantic, her eyes searching mine, her hands wringing each other. "I can't understand why he confessed. I mean, I know he didn't do it. Can you ask him for me? Will you go see him now and then come back? I have to know what's going to come out of all this."

Now, I could go on with the charade that I'm just her friend and I don't know anything about Peaches' murder, or I could believe that she is truly worried about Hal and wants to help him. I'm choosing to trust in the inherent goodness of man (or woman) and the power of love.

Okay, yeah, I'm still high from the touchdown dance in the end zone Drew did when I agreed on a date for our wedding, so I decide to tell her what's going on and why I can't go see Hal.

"So you and Drew are just pretending to be split up when you're actually planning on getting married?" she asks me when I've finished explaining the bare outline of our stupid plan. I nod, feel my cheeks redden, and crack a smile.

"When?" It seems like an odd question, but maybe she just wants reassurance that we won't abandon Hal and head off for a honeymoon in Hawaii. In my head I hear a Spalding ball bouncing and little girls' voices chanting, *Hi, my name is Hallie and my husband's name is Hal. We come from Hawaii and we hack housewives. Hate hookers? Hack housewife hookers?* It takes me a minute to come back to the present and answer her question.

"Two weeks after Hal's case is settled," I say. I don't mention that we decided whatever happens, we will go forward with the wedding. It'll be a small affair. Just the five of us—Drew, me and the kids—at a judge's office, then a nice catered reception at the house. I think that Drew is a little disappointed, but a big wedding would take lots of planning (which would involve my mother, who you might notice won't even be at the ceremony) and would put off the marriage by months, at least.

Hallie doesn't say anything.

"So it's important to us that Hal is cleared," I say. "It wouldn't be much of a celebration, and I'm not sure Drew would even feel it's official, without Hal there."

Hallie brightens some. "You didn't come here just to tell me that," she says, proving that she isn't crazy.

I admit that I didn't intend to tell her at all, but that I need her help. "Tell me about John and Grace Schultz's marriage."

Instead of answering, Hallie picks at a piece of lint on her sweat suit. I can't understand why people in hospitals wear sweat suits. It's not like she's going out for a jog. She'd feel so much better dressed up and with a bit of makeup on.

Oh… My… God. I sound like my mother!

"You were pretty friendly with them, right?" I ask, digging for I don't know what.

"I guess," she says with a shrug. "Grace came to visit me yesterday, so she seems to think we're friends."

"That was nice of her," I say, wondering what Grace wanted. Probably to be sure that any information Hallie has goes straight to John. "Did she ask you about the night of the murder?"

Hallie tells me they talked about that night, but she really couldn't remember as much as Grace did about it. "The doctor says it's probably trauma, and that the memories may never come back."

Great. That's a big help.

I go back to how friendly she and Grace were. "Good friends?" I ask.

"Not really. I mean, we went out with them once or twice

a few months ago." She pauses to think about it. At least, I think that's what she's doing. She suddenly seems evasive.

"Oh, that must have been nice," I say, inanely. "I mean, I met Grace the other day and she seems…elegant." Hey, that sounds a lot nicer than *pretentious*.

"I guess," Hallie says. "She sure didn't fit in at the firing range."

I must look as surprised as I feel, because Hallie laughs.

"She wasn't shooting or anything," Hallie says. "She was just waiting for John and Hal and I to finish. It was when I got that gun and Hal was teaching me how to shoot it."

Clue! Clue! my brain is shouting.

Yeah? Clue to what? I'm answering.

"I wish I'd never agreed to getting that damn gun in the first place. It's funny. If Grace hadn't been robbed, I never would have gotten it and Hal wouldn't be in jail now."

"So John Schultz knew you had a gun?" I ask.

Hallie tells me that he was the one who put the bug in Hal's ear that she ought to have one. "'If someone was brazen enough to hold up my wife,' he said, and the next thing I knew I was the proud owner of a .38 Snubnose."

I ask if they all went to dinner after the firing range. Hallie says they did. I ask how John and Grace seemed to get along.

"She was her usual cold self," Hallie says. "He was pretty jovial, considering he had to go back to work after the dinner was over."

I ask if it was a Wednesday night, and when it turns out it was, I have a pretty good idea of why he was jovial. I'm just surprised that Hal made it there.

"So the night of the murder you and Grace were at a party at the Inn Between," I start. "You were both drinking a lot and one of you got sick."

"Who said I was drinking?" she asks, apparently angry. "I wasn't drinking. I wouldn't have." She places her hands protectively on her stomach. Her womb.

"Oh my God! Are you pregnant?" I ask, grabbing her hands and squeezing them.

She shakes her head sadly. "No, but I don't drink because it would be bad for the baby and since we are trying...*were* trying...I'd never have risked the health of my baby for some stupid drink with an umbrella in it."

"And yet you swallowed a whole bottle of Valium?" I say.

The look she gives me reminds me of one of Dana's. It says I'm not listening, not following along, not... "Oh. I see. You took the pills because it turned out you *weren't* pregnant. It had nothing to do with Hal's being arrested."

She looks away.

"Did he know?" I ask.

"Not that night. We were still hoping then. I was a day late, but those EPT tests aren't a hundred percent accurate and I thought... That's why I was so mad about Peaches. Every time he went to her, he wasted sperm. Sperm that belonged to me that should have been making babies in me."

"So you went to the party, angry about Hal seeing Peaches again, and Grace was there, talking about how husbands always cheat. And then what?" That didn't sound good, did it? It sounded almost accusatory.

"And then Grace got sick and I took her back to my house

o she could sober up before she went home. Apparently John loesn't like her to drink." Which explains why she told me that t was Hallie who was drunk.

"She claimed you guys took a cab," I say and Hallie thinks minute and then nods.

"I'd gotten a ride there from Nancy and so I didn't have my ar."

Good save, I think. Which makes me wonder what it is I'm hinking. That Hallie did it? That she and Grace did it? That ohn did it? That Hal really did it, after all?

"And a few hours later, Grace called a cab and went home." say it like it's fact, though it seems to me that the ladies have lifferent versions of the story.

Hallie says she has no idea how long Grace stayed. "We had ome coffee—I wanted to help her sober up, I suppose. I set ner up to rest in the guest room and then lied down myself. Grace says she called the cab around eleven-ish. I was already asleep, I guess," she says. In the morning, Grace was gone and Hal was in jail.

"The worst part," she says in a very quiet voice, "is that I never slept better."

I make a mental note to tell Drew to check with the cab company to see what time Grace left Hallie's place. And in the meantime, I cut to the heart of what's been really eating at me.

"You do know Andy Lipschitz, right?" I ask.

Hallie does the guilty hem-haw.

"Okay," I say. "I showed his picture and yours to the bartender at the Inn Between and he said you were both there together. So now, you do know Andy Lipschitz, don't you How?"

She tells me she doesn't see what difference it makes.

"Look at it this way. If you were with Grace and then asleep you didn't kill Peaches. You're sure Hal didn't kill Peaches Grace was with you, so she didn't kill Peaches. John wa working on paperwork at the precinct that night, so he didn' kill Peaches. So maybe Andy killed Peaches?"

Hallie tells me that's the most ridiculous thing she's ever heard. Of course, the most ridiculous suspect almost alway turns out to be the murderer, doesn't he? "He and Peaches were a team. I mean, if the couple wanted them to be…"

"Excuse me?" Curiouser and curiouser, no?

Hallie says that when she found out about Peaches she con fronted Hal, who said that Peaches was a therapist of some sor and that she was helping restore his macho. She was trying to convince him that he was still king of the castle. "Even though I was making him feel like the Duke of the Dung Heap. He swore he wasn't even sleeping with her, and like an idiot, I bought it. Can you believe that? Only after a while he couldn't…you know, perform. I wasn't too impressed with her therapy, if you know what I mean."

I never thought I'd feel like I didn't want all the informa tion I could get in an investigation, but this was clearly TMI

"I tried everything. Dirty movies. Raunchy magazines. It jus kept getting worse. Then I got a call from Andy. He said that he thought I might be feeling a little lonely and neglected and he'd like to meet me somewhere and talk about it."

Jeesh. Even I'm not that naïve.

"Of course, I told him no, but he swore it was on the up-and-up, and asked me to meet him at the Inn Between. 'You'll be comfortable there,' he said, and he was right."

I'm glad someone was comfortable, because I'm squirming in my chair about now.

"He told me that he could help me satisfy Hal, that it was easy, that he knew what Hal wanted. And he took me to the house where, you know, Hal and Peaches met. And he showed me the underwear she wore and all that King of the Castle stuff. And—"

And here she stops and I can't really ask just how far the tutoring session went, can I?

"And did the instructions go beyond show-and-tell?" Oh. I guess I can just ask, after all.

"You mean, did we have sex?" Hallie asks.

What else could I mean? At least I now know why her fingerprints were at the scene.

"Well, Hal swore that he hadn't had sex with Peaches, and I told Andy that, but he showed me what Hal was paying Peaches and it was pretty hard to believe that he'd pay that just for some pillow talk. And Andy said that I could kind of even the score, if I wanted to, with him."

This is killing me. Did she?

"He convinced me to just try on the bra and undies that Hal liked Peaches to wear. She was a lot bigger than me, you know, upstairs, and I had to stuff the bra with tissues. It was one of those old Maidenform ones that look like ice cream cones or something. Like Madonna wore in that video? Only it was white. And the undies were white cotton."

I tell her I know just what she means and she looks at me as though I've said I wear them.

"I showed Andy and I could see he really liked me in them. He was, you know, aroused."

"I bet he was," I say. What else could I say? *This is kinky, Hallie?*

"I hadn't turned anyone on in a long time, Teddi," she says.

I'm thinking that if Hal knew, Mrs. Lipschitz wouldn't be lying alone in her grave. "So you—"

"There was a chance that it was Hal's fault I wasn't getting pregnant. I mean, on the rare occasions he shot, he could have been shooting blanks, couldn't he?"

"I…I…" I got nothing. I make some sort of noise, but Hallie isn't really waiting for my response.

"Hal knew I spoke to Andy. He said lots of the wives did. Andy would contact those that he and Peaches thought they could help."

"Regular philanthropists," I say. Hallie doesn't realize I'm being sarcastic and assures me that they charged for the help. Man, but I'd like to get back into Peaches' house and see if that second bedroom didn't have Beauty on one pillow and Beast on the other. I can't bear to ask.

"Their method works very well," Hallie tells me. "It's like Hal said—they're really just therapists."

"Without the license, the education," I say.

Defensively she insists that they helped her and Hal.

"Right into jail," I say.

"Hal didn't kill Peaches," Hallie tells me. "I know that for a fact because we had an appointment for the day after Peaches was killed."

No, I didn't miss that pronoun. "We?" I ask.

"Andy and Peaches and me and Hal."

"All of you?"

It's as if suddenly she realizes she should be embarrassed.

"It's not what you're thinking," she says. "It was going to be like an instructional video, only you can ask questions and they can see if you're doing it exactly right so that it'll, you know, *take*."

I ask if she's talking about conceiving.

"They've had six kids," she tells me, though I don't remember reading about more than two in the newspaper. "And if I didn't get pregnant—"

Oh my God. "She'd get pregnant for you? She told you she'd give you her baby?" My voice is squeaking now. I'm so angry I could spit.

"Hal's baby," Hallie corrects.

"But Hal confessed," I say. "Why would he say he did it?"

She shakes her head, bewildered, and says she just doesn't know. Neither do I. Why would someone confess to something they didn't actually do? And if he didn't do it, who's making it look as though he did?

"And what about that knock-down, drag-out fight you had on the night that Peaches was murdered? You told me you threw him out and told him it was over between you."

Her eyes widen. "Oh, I did. Really. Only Hal knew it was just a hormonal thing. He'd been through a million of them before. Moved down onto the couch, wooed me back. I know he didn't think I meant it this time because the last thing he said to me was, 'You'll come around, Hallie. You always do. And we'll get our baby.'"

"And you didn't tell the police any of this because?" I ask, though it's a stupid question.

"I knew that Hal wasn't guilty, that innocent people don't go to jail. So I wasn't worried. Only now I am."

I shake my head and blow out air between my closed lips. "You should be," is all I can say.

On the way out, with that little phrase echoing around in my head, I pass Lynette Chapelle-Williams in the hospital entrance. Hallie was particularly loose-lipped today. What if she thinks it's all right to tell Lynette the truth about Drew and me? "I'm worried," I mumble to myself.

You should be.

CHAPTER 17

White is my favorite accent color. It compliments pastels, brights and deep colors, as well. But alone, white is stark, boring and impersonal. A white wall suggests not only that anyone could live there, but that someone else might be moving in at any moment.

TipsFromTeddi.com

I'm waiting for Drew to call and tell me to meet him somewhere. I'm embarrassed to say that the conversation with Hallie has left me…keyed up, shall we say? Okay, fine. It's left me horny. Is that better? I've convinced myself this is merely a test—this being the white undies and a cotton bra I bought at the dollar store on my way home.

Will they turn Drew on? I wondered as I followed up with the painters on Susan Michaels' media room, aware of what I was wearing as I made my phone calls. *Did it work for Hallie?* I mused as I called the cab company whose card I picked up at the Inn Between to follow up on Grace Schultz's story.

Does this stuff really work? I ponder now as I give Maggie May a treat and throw a lick and a promise at my house, starting in the living room, which looks like someone not only lived, but died, in it. Three of Dana's *InStyle* magazines are on the floor, and she's not going to appreciate the crayon marks that Lys apparently thought enhanced the covers. I think my youngest may have been giving the models tattoos.

The couch cushions are scattered and the remote is wedged in between two of them. *The next couch I get,* I think as I pull out the remote, a candy bar wrapper, two crayons and a condom, *is not going to have cush—*

I stare at the turquoise foil packet in my hand. Trojan. The brand that Rio used to carry in his wallet when we first met.

I am not hysterical. I will not be hysterical. I will not act hysterical.

"Dana!" I scream, scaring poor Maggie May within an inch of her life. "In the living room! Now!"

Dana, wearing a blouse that makes her look pregnant already—oh my God, could she be?—saunters down the steps and gives me that *you're overreacting* look without even knowing why I called her. I see Lys standing by her bedroom door, ready to eavesdrop and report to Grandma. I tell her to go into her room and shut the door.

"What did *I* do?" Lys whines.

"You colored in your sister's magazines," I say, because I need a reason for her time-out. That one is handy and it works.

Of course, it gets Dana's nose out of joint, but it's not Dana's *nose* I'm worried about. She's still ragging on her sister and complaining when I open my hand and hold out the condom.

"Wanna explain this?" I ask.

Dana stares at it as if she's never seen it before. She reads the label, stalling.

I ask if Roger was here today and get accused of always assuming the worst. I try to keep my voice level, even. I spell out the facts for her. She's dating. The boy she's dating spends a lot of time with her on the couch. I'm not here a lot. She has a lot of freedom, but with freedom comes responsibility. She might see using a condom as responsible behavior. "Is that it?"

"We are not having sex," she says. "If that's what your dirty mind is supposing."

"Oh. So you're planning a surprise party and you wanted to use it as a balloon?" I suggest.

"I wanted to see how it worked," Dana says, chin stuck out, eyes glaring. "For the future. For someday, not today."

"Uh-huh," I say. I am not really calm, but I'm doing a better imitation now.

She points out that it isn't used, a fact that escaped me. Do I feel better now, or worse? What is that stain on the couch? Spilled milk? Or something to cry over?

"I'm still a virgin, Mom," she says, like that could change at any moment. "Roger and I aren't using condoms because we aren't having sex. At least not yet."

Where's the damn *Mother Handbook?* What am I supposed to say here? What am I supposed to do?

I stare.

I seethe.

"Look, Mom," she says calmly. "I like Roger a lot, but I don't think I love him. And I'm only going to have sex with someone I love. Does that make you feel better?"

"Is that the line you're supposed to say? And I'm supposed to accept it and pretend I've done right by you because, after all, we discussed this and you assured me you're not going to screw up your life?"

She shrugs and tells me to believe whatever I want. "But it's mine, not Roger's, and I just wanted to see how they worked."

I point out that the packet is not open.

"Which proves what?" she asks. Sometimes she really is a little snot.

I tell her to get a banana from the kitchen and I rip open the packet. It's the lubricated kind and it oozes at me. Yuck. She looks duly horrified, which reassures me a good deal more than her words did.

"You don't have to—" she starts, but the look I give her sends her, shoulders rolled, steps slow, into the kitchen. A moment later she's back, handing me a banana and looking appropriately red-faced.

"When a man, or a boy," I start, but she assures me she knows all this.

"From health class," she is quick to add.

"And they didn't show you a condom?" I ask, vaguely remembering a fairly hysterical conversation between Dana and her best friend Kimmie about just such a lesson.

"It was a long time ago," she says.

I tell her I would like Roger and Drew to sit down and have a chat.

Soon.

About statutory rape.

"Why don't you ever believe me?" she shouts at me, running

up the stairs, her footfalls shaking the glassware in the kitchen cabinets as she goes.

I'm standing in the living room holding the dripping condom and the banana, wondering how she can ask that, how she managed to turn it around and make me the bad guy, when Bobbie breezes in.

"Talk about desperate," she says. "Can't you even wait until you're upstairs?"

"WELL, CAN YOU GIVE ME the driver's phone number?" I ask the dispatcher at the cab company as I drive up to the Michaelses' place—solo because, once again, Bobbie had something more important to do.

Of course she can't. She can confirm that a driver picked up a fare at the Inn Between the night of the murder and brought it to Hallie's house in Hicksville, and that the same driver picked up a fare at Hallie's several hours later and brought that fare to Grace Schultz's address in Lloyd Harbor. I should just let it go at that, but something is nagging at me.

The dispatcher goes on and on about how they don't allow drivers to take calls while they are driving. I wonder about the last time she was in a cab, since I can't remember a driver *not* being on the phone in the last ten years or so.

"How about if you have the driver call me?" I ask. "Please tell him that I'm willing to pay for the information." Okay, it's Drew that's willing to pay. At least, I'm sure he will be. I give the woman my cell phone number just as I pull up the driveway. I'm pissed at Bobbie, pissed at the dispatcher, and not finding the painters' truck already at the house doesn't put me in a better mood.

Susan Michaels is not going to be happy if I don't get her media room done before she gets home from her trip. And at this rate I have to hope her cruise ship is thrown off course and winds up stuck on a barrier reef in Borneo. If they have barrier reefs in Borneo.

Clutching the code to the alarm in my hand so that there's no repeat of my last mistake at Susan's house, I slip my key into the door and open it. No alarm sounds. Could my crew really have forgotten to turn it on when they left last time? Anything's possible, but I've got an uneasy feeling as I enter the house.

"Hello?" I call out. "Anyone here?"

Silence.

It seems to me that things are moved around a bit, which doesn't make me happy. My painters know better than to move anything other than what's in the room they are working on. I've been working with them for three years and I'd trust my kids to them. Which is more than I can say about the kids' dad.

There was a sculpture in the entryway that isn't there now.

I tiptoe into the dining room. One drawer in the breakfront is open. The silverware drawer. Only there is no silverware.

I'm slinking from room to room when my cell phone goes off. I nearly wet my pants from fright.

"Hello?" I whisper into it.

"Yeah. Dis is de driva. I gots a message to call you. What you need to know about those fares?"

It takes me a minute to remember what I want to know, prowling around Susan's house with my heart pounding.

"You picked up two ladies at the Inn Between back on February 20 and you brought them to Hicksville. Remember?"

He says he does.

"Later you picked up one of the ladies and brought her to Lloyd Harbor. Is that right?"

Standing perfectly still, I can almost hear him shrug. I tell him how important this is, how someone's life depends on it. He doesn't sound impressed. I tell him there's a hundred dollars in it if he comes up with anything useful.

"What's youseful?" he asks as I enter the kitchen, where nothing appears amiss.

"Like did she arrange for you to come back for her when you dropped her off, or did you just happen to take the call later by coincidence?"

"She tooked my card," he says. "She called me especial."

"Okay," I say. "Did she seem nervous or upset or anything?"

"No," he says. "Just cold."

"Cold?" I ask. Did I just hear something down the hall? From Susan's bedroom? I begin to creep down the hallway.

"Yeah," he says. "She is waiting for me out of the side."

There is a pair of feet sticking out from beneath Susan's curtains. It's not my imagination working overtime.

I try backing out of the room, but the feet emerge and a large body is connected to them. Then the large body is connected to me and I hit the wall. A fabulous Boguslaw Lustyk painting obscuring the thief blurs before my eyes and disappears out the patio doors.

"Call the police," I shout toward my phone, which has scooted across the room. I tell them there's a robbery in progress and give them the address. "Tell them to hurry!"

And then, like I'm some sort of policeman myself, I take off after the thief, all the while asking myself what I think I'm doing, hearing Drew's voice asking me what the hell I think I'm doing.

It's cold out, and the ground is covered with snow and patches of ice. It's not that hard to track a man carrying an enormous painting in the snow. There are the footprints, of course, and bright splashes of color appearing here and there. All I have to do is stay far enough back not to be a threat to him while I wait for the police to catch up to me.

"Go back," he yells at me.

"Leave the painting," I yell back. Of course, the man's stolen more than the painting, and I can't just let him disappear into the forest. I hadn't realized just how much land Susan owned. She could afford a lot more than she's paying me, the cheapskate.

She doesn't deserve me slipping and sliding out here, trying to save her Boguslaw Lustyk painting, risking life and limb and—"Ow!"—being pelted with ice balls.

I hear the police sirens with relief, but across the shiny surface stretched between the thief and myself, I see his truck. Another minute or two and he will be gone, along with Susan's treasures.

I'm halfway across the frozen pond when I hear the cracking. I freeze. Only it's not me it's cracking under, it's him.

"Don't move," I tell him. "I'll get help."

Naturally, in his situation, he doesn't want help from the police, and he doesn't hesitate to let me know that, though between all the curse words, the message is nearly lost.

"You wanna die?" I ask. "I think those are your choices." Meanwhile, I'm inching back toward land, praying that all the cookies I've been eating have miraculously not landed on my hips and tipped the scale so far that I, too, will fall through the ice.

Another crack rents the air and I see the man and the painting slip gently into the water. I tell him to let go of the stupid painting (I never really liked Boguslaw Lustyk anyway— too much blue) and to keep his elbows on the ice. "Like you're at the edge of a pool," I say. I tell him that always works because I figure that if he panics he's a goner, and not because I have any knowledge about surviving a fall through the ice. There's only me, so I can't make that human chain like the kids do in *It's a Wonderful Life*, so I do the next best thing.

I scream my freakin' head off.

CHAPTER 18

I've found eBay to be an excellent source for the hard-to-find.
I've replaced missing pieces of china, found the odd accent
piece. But buying over the Internet is tricky because what's
one color on your computer can be a totally different color in
your home. And then there's the matter of condition. In all
things eBay, remember the old adage, buyer beware!

TipsFromTeddi.com

Bobbie is too excited to sit down in my kitchen. Instead she's pacing, Maggie dogging her steps, while I nurse my wounded ankle, sprained on the way back to my car when I tripped over a hidden tree root.

"There's this one," she says, opening up a carton into which yards of cream-colored fabric has been stuffed, which, when she holds it up, turns out to be a satin wedding gown with a train that's long enough to reach from the engine to the caboose, and then some. Maggie takes a whiff and starts to back away, teeth bared. "It's from the early forties. Isn't it divine?"

I demur, which Bobbie takes for agreement. I'll admit that if not for the worm holes, the stains and the fact that it's not 1940, I might actually not be repulsed by it. As it is, I think

Maggie and I are in agreement about it. I remind Bobbie that I am getting married in a judge's chambers, not Saint Patrick's Cathedral, and that we're having a quaint little reception in my living room afterward.

"Ha. Not once your mother finds out," Bobbie says, stuffing the dress back into the carton and pulling out a crocheted two-piece dress that isn't half-bad. In fact, it's got a certain charm to it. "Oh, never mind," she says. "This one is mine."

She's reading the labels on the boxes, sorting them before she opens the next disaster.

The phone rings.

And speaking of disasters, I think, since it's sure to be my mother. After all, the day hasn't been bad enough yet, has it? A sprained ankle, a police interview, a hysterical phone call from Susan Michaels about who will take care of her horses now that her groom has been arrested.

Bobbie glances at the caller ID and hands the phone to me with a grimace. "Guess who," she says.

"Hi, Mom," I say, realizing that my leg hurts more when I'm aggravated. So it's true about muscles actually tensing under emotional stress.

I ask how she is and try to make small talk.

Really, I should know better.

"Why are you limping, and why did you come home in a police cruiser, Teddi? Yet again?" Nothing like cutting straight to the heart of the matter. "What have you gotten yourself into now?"

Bobbie holds up a pink dress with *khazerai* hanging from it. I don't know a good translation for *khazerai.* It's extra added junk that makes something look *ungapatchka*—over the top, too much of everything. Glitter, glitz, lace. Let's just say that no one would mistake it for anything from Talbots.

"Dress-up for Lys," she mouths, and I imagine my mother finding it hanging in her granddaughter's closet and having a heart attack on the spot. Or maybe filing for guardianship on the grounds of bad taste.

I tell my mother it was just a slight accident. The ankle is taped up and it wasn't actually a police escort—it was just Bobbie's sister Diane, who happened to be in the vicinity. My mother knows I'm lying. She has radar for that sort of thing. I wish I had that radar and could tell what Dana is and isn't doing. Yet another thing I didn't inherit from Mom.

Well, you gotta take the bad with the good, I suppose.

Bobbie bounds up the stairs and puts the dress in Lys's room while my mother rants about the mess I continue to make of my life. "I'm just glad that a certain policeman who shall remain nameless is out of your life, Teddi," she says.

I suppose that since he's remaining nameless, I could agree with her, but it makes me feel a tad disloyal, not to mention deceitful. "I wish you wouldn't criticize—" I start to say, but I'm drowned out by a gasp from the other end of the line that sounds like a bull seal is dying a slow and painful death.

"You're seeing him again! I knew it. I knew it was too good to be true. Marty," she yells to my father. "Get the car warmed up. And find my mink."

I'm still telling my mother not to come long after there's only a dial tone on the other end. Then I'm insisting that Bobbie get all the wedding attire she's bought over eBay out of my house. She's halfway through gathering up boxes when we hear Lys at the door.

"My room," I shout at Bobbie. "Just shove them in my closet." I jump up to help her, but my leg refuses to cooperate and I'm sitting on the kitchen floor amid wedding dresses when Lys comes in the door.

"Milk and cookies, honey?" Bobbie asks her is if there's nothing out of the ordinary about Mom sprawled across the kitchen and Maggie pulling wedding gowns out of boxes.

"Grandma called me on my cell phone," she tells me breathlessly. "She's coming over and I'm going to sleep at her house."

"Maybe forever," Bobbie mutters, then tells Lys that there's a present on her bed. Lys goes running up the stairs, never even asking about my situation. Never, I suppose, even noticing it. She is, without question, my mother's heir apparent.

The phone rings again, and it's Drew this time. Delicious, wonderful, Drew.

"What the hell did you think you were doing, chasing someone through the woods? He could have had a gun, a knife, anything. Where's your common sense, woman?" Not even a "hello" in there, never mind a "how're you doing?"

Okay, so it's not delicious, wonderful Drew. It's crabby, cranky Drew.

"It's not broken," I tell him in my *lovely-day-isn't-it?* voice. "Thanks so much for asking. It's just a simple sprain."

"Hurt much?" he asks, his voice only an iota more tender.

I tell him, "Not much," which seems to give him license to yell at me again.

"I can't see where tracking thieves is any part of your job

description. You are not a policewoman, Teddi. You are not Supergirl. You're a freakin' decorator. Just a nice suburban housewife who may be too clever for her own good." I imagine him running his fingers through his hair in exasperation.

"You don't seem to have any trouble with me courting danger in the pursuit of exonerating your partner," I say as calmly as I'm able. "Only in pursuit of my career. Am I only supposed to risk my life for your paycheck and not mine?"

There's dead silence. Okay, maybe I went too far. I mean, he really has never encouraged me to be reckless on his behalf.

"Drew?"

"Don't do it, Ted," he says evenly. "Don't try to alienate me. I'm not calling off this wedding no matter what you throw at me."

"Was I doing that?" I ask.

Was I? I'm sitting on the floor amidst wedding gowns with my mother about to walk in the door. I need to tell Bobbie we can't be partners anymore. I need…Drew.

"You were," he says, still calm. "And I'm sorry I yelled at you. I'm not angry with you, I'm angry that I couldn't prevent your getting hurt."

Why does he find it so simple to say exactly what he feels, and I find it so hard?

"You okay with that?" he asks when I'm silent.

"My mother is on her way over," I say. "She figured out that I'm still…we're still…"

"It's gone far enough," Drew says. "I'm on my way over."

I'VE MANAGED TO GET UP off the floor with an astonishing lack of grace. Bobbie has put up coffee so that my mother will have one less thing to rant about and we've cleared the room of all evidence of tacky wedding paraphernalia.

I've thrown just a shot of Kahlúa into my coffee in an effort to gird my loins for the battle to come. I have the urge to find my gauze pads, Neosporin and ace bandages, but I think I've already used them up today.

Jesse and Dana come in the door together. They are bickering because they are breathing each others' air and find that a good enough reason.

"What?" Dana says, looking around the kitchen. Such a way with words, this child has.

"Grandma coming?" Jesse asks. When Bobbie and I exchange a *how-could-he-know?* look, he smiles smugly. "Elementary, my dear Watson. The kitchen's clean, there's coffee up, the liquor cabinet door isn't quite closed and Mom's leg is shaking."

He stares at my other leg, raised on one of the chairs and asks what happened.

"Save it," Bobbie tells me when I start to explain. "I have a feeling you're going to be telling this story more than once."

"Grandma's here!" Lys yells from the living room couch where she has been watching for my mother. "And Grandpa! And some lady and a man!"

"An intervention, no doubt," Bobbie says, pulling out more coffee cups while I ease my foot to the floor and glance at the back door wondering if I can hobble out before they huddle in.

"Oh my God. Grandma knows about your secret, doesn't she?" Dana says, her eyes lighting up like now it's open season.

She reaches for her purse and roots around, apparently for her cell phone, repeating over and over, "I have to tell Kimmie."

My mother and her entourage enter. Sydelle Silverberg is the woman Lys was referring to. I don't know who the man is and I don't want to guess. Lys is petting my mother's mink. Maggie is barking at it to protect us all from innumerable dead rodents.

"I'm sorry," my father says. He looks bewildered. "I told her it was none of our business…" His voice trails off as he looks at the man behind my mother.

Jesse offers to take my mother's dead pelts. "Someday you should be able to afford for your wife to be so insulted," my mother tells him, shrugging out of her mink coat and letting him catch it as it slides down her back like she's some old movie star.

Maybe Gloria Swanson, ready for her close-up.

All the while, in a hushed voice, Dana is narrating the events to Kimmie. "You should see my grandmother's coat. You'd think it weighed like a hundred pounds the way Jesse's carrying it and trying not to touch it. It's hilarious."

"This," my mother announces, nudging Maggie May out of the way with her foot and pushing forward the gentleman who is pushing sixty, while sixty-five is pushing back at him—hard, "is Harry Jenson. You remember I told you he wanted to meet you. Well, here he is." She folds her arms across her chest and looks expectantly at Paulette's widower, waiting, I suppose, for him to get down on one knee.

He says it's nice to finally meet me. His voice creaks, and I don't know if it's fear or age. In deference to either, or both, I try to stand just as Drew crashes in the front door and orders me to stay off my ankle. My mother fans herself and gropes for a chair.

Bobbie stifles a laugh, but not very well. Dana is covering the action like the Hindenburg is on fire once again.

I start making introductions. "Sydelle Silverberg, this is Detective Swoons…uh, Scoones. Drew, this is—"

Drew nods in her direction just as Sydelle rounds on him. "You're his partner? Well, he did it, he did it, he did it," she shouts, swatting at Drew with what appears to be an apron. "How could you have ever been partners with a murderer? You couldn't tell what kind of man he was, just from the way he treated my Dennis? The man should have his whoozits cut off, fooling around with some hooker when he had a wife at home trying to get pregnant…"

Drew looks at me accusingly, as if I told her about Hallie. I shake my head. Sydelle, like my mother, has her sources. But, more like the *New York Times* and less like my mother, she doesn't reveal them.

Sydelle carefully times her pause for breath to coincide with our shock, so that she remains uninterrupted.

"And you," she says, turning to me and shaking a finger. "*Madela*, you should know better. A man who cheats on his wife? You already went there. You think they don't all think alike, these cops? Ten years in a relationship, you don't think this sort of thing rubs off? Diseases, maybe he didn't catch. But attitude?"

I am about to defend Drew on the basis of having lived with Rio for twelve years and not catching his attitude toward fidelity, or the lack thereof, when who should show up at the door but the devil himself.

"Daddy!" Dana says and Drew's head whips around. Sotto voce, Dana tells Kimmie that the cavalry has arrived.

"What's with all the cars?" Rio asks. "Some sort of party?"

"Nothing like a mistake staring you in the face to prevent you from making another one," my mother says, her work apparently done.

"Bachelor Number One," Bobbie says to Paulette's poor, befuddled widower. "You arrive at your girlfriend's house to find her ankle bandaged, her ex-husband present and the man she's in love with all in her kitchen. You a)make a total fool of yourself—"

"Easy for you to say," my mother barks at her—along with Maggie—while Dana tells Kimmie what her mother's said. "You're married. And to a philanderer, yet."

"Mom!" It's one thing to say this to Bobbie, quite another to say it in front of the kids.

"Well, you were in love with a mafia don," Bobbie shoots back, because my children apparently aren't the only infants in the room. Sydelle's jaw drops. Poor Harry Jenson's standing there with his hat in his hand staring at my taped-up ankle. Bobbie grabs her sweater off the back of her stool. "And you make Teddi crazy," she adds.

"Better than disappointing her all the time," my mother says.

Dana stops relating the conversation. After a brief pause, Rio tells Bobbie my mother got her.

I can't print what Bobbie tells Rio.

"That's it," Drew says. "Everyone out. Bachelor Number One," he says to Mr. Jenson. "Sorry, but you're too late. Dibs are already in. Bachelor Number Two," he says, looking at Rio. "You were an idiot. You didn't know what you had and you pissed it away. I owe you, buddy. Mom, Dad, various friends and family, Teddi's had a hard day. She chased down a thief, cornered him in the woods, nearly fell into a frozen lake and came home to this.

"Enough. Go away. Bother her tomorrow. She and I have things to discuss."

Oh wow. He's right. Like why was Grace Schultz waiting outside for the cab?

"Who the hell do you think you are?" Rio asks. "I'm still the father of the children in this house—"

Jesse humphs. "Some father. You're only around when you want something from Mom."

Instead of letting it pass, Drew takes Jesse's chin in his hand and their eyes connect. "Don't dis your dad," he says.

And, be still my heart, Jesse apologizes.

"Out," Drew says. I can see he wants to lay some claim on me and he's resisting. And I can see it isn't easy. But telling the assembled crowd—read: my mother—will only prolong this agony indefinitely.

And we almost get away with it. If only Lys didn't come tripping down the steps, falling head over heels and landing in a puddle of satin at Grandma's feet…

"A wedding gown?" my mother shouts above Lys's cries. "Call South Winds and tell them I'm on my way."

Yeah, if only!

I remind her that her granddaughter just fell down a flight of stairs, to which she replies that Lys is obviously fine. "How hurt can she be, yelling like that?" my mother wants to know.

Poor Mr. Jenson is shuffling toward the door, looking like a deer who's been caught in a Hummer's high beams. Sydelle is scrounging in my refrigerator, pulling out what appear to be ingredients. I have no idea what she's planning to make, but whatever it is, I bet everyone here is going to stay to eat it.

Lys is being seen to by Rio, Dana, my father and Bobbie. I look longingly at Drew, my expression asking if he really wants to marry into this.

Then, like in an *Officer and a Gentleman*, my own Richard Gere comes over and picks me up and carries me silently out the back door. I'm not sure anyone notices, and that's fine with us.

"I can walk," I tell him. "I just have to lean on you a little." Drew smiles. "Music to my ears," is all he says.

CHAPTER 19

Everyone knows that the best way to keep a room tidy is to hang up your clothes or put them in the hamper after they've been removed. But everyone also knows there are those times when that is impossible, inconvenient or, frankly, inappropriate. Which is why in any bedroom I decorate there is a bench at the end of the bed. It takes up very little room and is so much more preferable to dropping your drawers on the floor.

TipsFromTeddi.com

"Comfy?" Drew asks me after he's carried me into his apartment and tucked me into his bed. "Need anything?" He's already taking off his shirt and unzipping his pants.

"I'm supposed to put ice on my ankle," I tell him. He agrees, but instead of heading for the freezer, he's slipping out of his jeans and taking his shorts with them.

"Now?" he asks, standing stark naked and at attention.

An erection is a terrible thing to waste, so I tell him, "Later," and shimmy over to the side of the bed.

Drew tells me how very brave I was this morning. "Do I have to add *foolish?*"

I explain that I couldn't just let all that artwork disappear. And I didn't seem to be in any danger. At least not at the time. I admit that, in retrospect, I can see it was a pretty stupid thing to do.

Drew lectures me like a child about not entering a house with an alarm system unless the *all clear* sound is blaring. But while he's lecturing me, his hands are dancing over my body, playing a different tune, and any alarms that might be ringing have gotten the *all clear* sign from me.

"You're sure you're up to this?" he asks me.

"I am if you are," I say, my hand reaching out and testing. "Oh, I see you are."

He laughs against my hair, my neck, my breasts. "Mine," he says, his hand possessively stroking the fire between my legs. It's as if he catches himself and hears how that might sound to me. Hurriedly he shifts so that my hand falls in roughly the same place on his body and murmurs, "Yours."

My cell phone rings and both of us ignore it. Okay, he ignores it and I try to. It rings and rings and finally I admit I can't do it and reach for it, claiming it could be the kids, though with all those adults in the house, the only thing they could need is rescuing.

I miss the call, but I recognize the number. Mid-Island Taxi Cab Company. Which reminds me about Grace Schultz. I fill Drew in and he encourages me to call them back. He's had a bit of a breakthrough himself that he's anxious to chew over with me.

I return the call and get the same dispatcher.

"Which fare were you interested in?" she asks me. "The one to that address in Lloyd Harbor, or to the shopping center?"

"Excuse me?" I ask, not quite following, which may be because I'm stark naked and sprawled over Drew, his waning excitement nestled against my belly. "Which fare?"

"We had two pickups from that address on Jacobs Lane in Hicksville you were asking about. One to Broadway Mall and one to that Lloyd Harbor address."

I'm doing that nervous thing with my hands, shaking them like my fingertips are burning and I have to put them out.

"Different driver?" I ask.

She confirms that. I ask if she can give me the times and she does. One cab pickup was at nine-twenty to Broadway Mall, and one was at five after eleven to Lloyd Harbor.

I repeat aloud what she's saying, thank her profusely, take down the number of the other driver and roll off Drew.

"They both went out," I tell him. "Hallie left the house after putting Grace to bed."

Drew's heard my end of the conversation and while I can see the gears moving, nothing is coming out of the spigot, or whatever it is that is at the end of the Rube Goldberg contraption that makes a detective's mind go around.

"Are we finished here?" I ask, groping under the covers to find that Drew's attention in flagging, rather than poling.

He groans.

"I could—"

"No, no," he says. "It's all right. I'll make it up to you to-morrow night."

Oh, exactly what Rio would say in the same situation. *Not.* "Hey, didn't you say you had some information?"

He says it's not exactly information, just a feeling, a hunch that he's got to work out. "The Captain claims he was working late the night of the murder. But there are no calls out of his office. No calls on his cell phone except to Grace's cell phone, which went unanswered. And yet he didn't try her at home. There are three reports from that night with his signature on them, but they were signed by other officers in the afternoon."

"You're saying he wasn't there?" I ask.

Drew hedges. "I'm saying no one saw him. Not exactly the same thing. The most dangerous thing a detective can do— besides pursuing a suspect into the woods in the winter with no backup and no protection—is assume." Especially when it's about his boss.

I know that. And a warning bell goes off in my head. What am I assuming? What have we got wrong?

BOBBIE HAD TAKEN Dana and Jesse overnight, so when I return home in the morning, I limp in to find a stack of nasty notes on the kitchen counter. The first reads like the words should have been cut out a magazine. My parents have taken my youngest. Command performance at my mother's tonight or I don't have any hope of getting my daughter back.

The next one is from Dana. She claims she couldn't ask my permission to go out because I wasn't here (Excuse me? She suddenly is unaware of those little things in our purses that ring and connect us with the rest of the world?), so she's out with

Roger and they'll be in a public place so I shouldn't go off the deep end.

Rio's note asks if he can leave Elisa with me for a few days. He's got a possible job interview upstate. *Right.* What a coincidence, since when we were married he always went upstate with his buddies right around this time. Supposedly they were hunting deer, but my guess it was more likely beaver.

"Not happening," I mutter under my breath as I reach for the phone to answer Bobbie's note, which says simply, "Call me."

"Jess?" I yell before dialing.

No answer. I flip through the notes again and find his on the back of Dana's. *At Danny's building a radio-controlled car. Be back for dinner. Can Dan eat over?—Jess*

I figure I'll call him later to try to pawn him off on Dan's mom, since I've got to reclaim Alyssa.

And I dial Bobbie. "Hey," I say when she picks up. She tells me she'll be over in a flash.

While I wait, I think about what it is I'm assuming in Hal's case. Maybe it doesn't involve the case at all. Maybe it's my kids, or Drew, or Bobbie Lyons, friend and partner, who is, at this moment, slipping in my back door and stamping the snow off her boots.

"Your mother's right," she says. Three words I never expected to hear coming out of her mouth, coming out of any mouth, really, except maybe my dad's, and then only if my mother was standing over him threateningly with a bottle of pills or a noose.

"I realize that Drew seemed high-handed, but he didn't

exactly throw me over his shoulder caveman-style and drag me out of here. If my ankle wasn't—"

She's shaking her head. "This is not about Drew."

"Then what?" I ask.

"I do disappoint you, all the time."

I lie and tell her that it's not all the time, because that's the polite thing to do. She doesn't bother arguing, since we both know it's true.

"I think I should resign," she says.

I am so relieved that I don't have to ask her to, that it must show all over my face. She puts up a finger, indicating that I should wait a minute and runs up to my room. A minute later she comes down with yet another of her stupid boxes. She opens it up and pulls out a winter-white suit. It's silk, has one of those peplums that make my waist look tiny, or at least smaller than it is, and the most gorgeous flowers down one lapel. It takes my breath away.

"I was only kidding about the other ones. I'm using the fabric to make wedding albums. This is my resignation gift. Are we still friends?"

I nod while I'm fingering the fabric, which is as soft as a baby's bottom. I hold the skirt up against my waist and it looks like it was made for me.

"Amazing what you can find on eBay," Bobbie says. "Like your best friend."

We're hugging and sort of teary when Dana storms into the house, rattling the timbers as she slams the door shut.

"Men!" she shouts at us, smacking her books on the table. "Why do we even have them?"

"They're good for—" Bobbie starts, but a look from me stops her in her tracks. "Opening jars," she finishes. She smiles slyly at me. "What did you think I was going to say?"

"They lie every time they open their mouths," Dana says.

"No, no, no, honey. Only when words come out," Bobbie agrees. In deference to my newly engaged state, she qualifies that. "Except the honorable Detective Scoones, of course."

"Well, you can do what you want, Mother," Dana tells me dramatically. "But as for me, I'm never speaking to one again. Do they have Jewish nuns?"

"No," I tell her. "Jewish women just get headaches."

Bobbie chokes on the coffee she's drinking, while I silently thank God that I won't have to ban Roger from the house because my daughter already has. If she weren't so miserable about it, and if my ankle wasn't swollen, I'd be dancing on the ceiling.

She refuses to tell me what it is he's lied about, though high on my guess list is what he intended to use that condom for.

"Men can't be trusted. That's all there is to it," she tells me.

"Don't you think you're tarring a few innocents in there with all the guilty?" I ask, wishing Bobbie wouldn't agree with Dana, which, of course, she already has.

It's a neat trick for me to convince her otherwise. Every tack I try seems to be countered by my own experience. Mine, my mother's, Bobbie's. I can only hope, as I finger the suit Bobbie's gotten for me on eBay, that Drew will restore her faith in men. Hers and mine, both. For now, let her believe she should stay away from all of them.

Maybe I'll encourage her to give them another try when she's somewhere around thirty. Or forty, like her mom.

Dana goes up to her room to call Kimmie, and Bobbie and I adjourn to my bedroom, where I try on the suit and we ooh and aah quietly so as not to piss off Dana. I admit that I feel like a real bride and I'm actually looking forward to the promises. Then Bobbie takes off for home, and I trudge back to my real life of laundry, straightening and limping.

I start in Jesse's room, which smells ripe with teenage boyhood. It's not just his avocation. There are his sneakers, the pajamas he only changes when I steal them and throw them in the wash, the half-finished bottles of Sunny D by the computer with varying degrees of mold in them...

It's a phase, I tell myself, which is, as every wife who has carried down the evidence of late-night snacks knows, a bald-faced lie. Poor Jesse needs a wife to pick up his clothes, bring down his leavings, put his piles of clean laundry into his drawers. The smell reminds me I promised Susan Michaels that I'd feed her horses.

Mental note: go over there first thing in the morning.

I'm not a snooper. Really, I'm not. In fact, there's lots I'd just as soon not know. And I do believe in the right to privacy, even for preteens, which is why I deliver clean laundry to the tops of bureaus and suggest that my children move them from there to their drawers. Well, that and the fact that I firmly believe children ought to pitch in and do some of the work involved in running a household. I'm not asking them to wash the floors, scrub the toilets or defrost the freezer, am I?

But Jesse seems to ignore the piles on his dresser in favor of what's in his bureau, and if there's nothing there, I fear he'll wear the same pair of underpants until he's married. So, I open the drawer to put away his jockeys and find the reason his socks have been matching up for the last little while.

Trojans. The same sort of Trojans that I found in the couch. The one that Dana was so quick to claim.

Never assume. Never assume.

I assumed it was Roger's. Hell, Dana assumed it was Roger's. And so, rather than have me blame him, she confessed to something she didn't do, because...she...believed...he...did... it.

I reach for the Bat Phone and punch in Drew's number. When he answers I tell him why Hal's so sure Hallie did it, though she denies it. "They had a terrible fight about Peaches. Both of them leave the house and when he comes home, he finds Hallie passed out and the gun missing."

"And he did say he found the gun case and an open bottle of Valium on her nightstand when he got home," Drew adds. "All the talk about it being his fault makes sense if you're right. And it explains why he went back there after he'd already been with her that night. When he found Hallie's gun was gone, he was afraid that she'd gone to confront Peaches. But he got there too late."

"It all fits. And now that we know that Hallie went out... she probably gave some of that Valium to Grace after she brought her home so that she'd have an alibi, and once Grace was asleep, she took off and killed Peaches. I knew a woman did it. Shot in the back like that. No cop would do that."

"And arresting Hal would keep him out of the way while the Captain lines up his case against Hallie," Drew figures.

"And it explains the suicide attempt," I continue. "Remorse. And her willingness to commit herself in the psych wing, too. If she's in the hospital it gives her time to make up a story."

"You really think she'd let Hal take the fall for it?" Drew asks.

"She kept telling me that she wasn't worried because since he didn't do it, he'd never be convicted. She was so sure. Maybe it's not just him that thinks it's his fault. Maybe she does, too. Or maybe, like in *Witness for the Prosecution*, she's planning to sweep in at trial and blow the prosecution's case right out of the water."

Something is wrong with it. Drew feels it's too neat.

"Funny you should say that," I tell him. "An attempt to be neat is how I figured it out."

CHAPTER 20

"Different strokes for different folks" doesn't mean simply that George's house should be filled with antiques and Martha's should be Oriental modern. More than one person lives in your house and not all the rooms belong to you. In rooms you share you need consensus, and in rooms that are primarily for others, offer input but try to see those rooms from the inhabitant's point of view.

TipsFromTeddi.com

So, if we really believe that Hallie is the murderer, it should be a pretty simple job to prove it. Drew says he'll go see Hal at the county jail, and I volunteer to meet Andy Lipschitz. I've been kind of itching to do that all along, and now I've got my excuse.

He's completely amenable to meeting me at the Inn Between, which apparently doesn't hold any bad memories for him even though that's where he was the night his wife was killed, maybe by the husband of the very person he was meeting with. Or maybe not. I'm not sure how much I should let on I know, so I just start with how I read about what happened to his wife in the paper and how sorry I am.

He tells me that's not why I asked to meet him. He says this looking so deeply into my eyes, I have to look away. "There's nothing to be ashamed of," he says softly. "You're not the first woman who's needed a little help."

I think about poor Hallie, hormone-crazed under this Svengali's spell. I'm thinking possible defenses here. Drug-induced temporary insanity?

He asks if my husband knows I'm here.

"How did you know I was married?" I ask him. I'm not wearing Rio's old ring, and I'm not wearing Drew's new one, which is hidden in my safe.

He tells me there's only one way I'd know about him, and that was word of mouth. He doesn't, he assures me with a chuckle, exactly advertise. And everyone knows that he only works with married women, though now that Peaches is gone, it's possible that might change.

"Because?" I ask, finding him fascinating in a wrecked-car kind of way.

"I want to help women, not complicate things for them," he says, touching the tip of my nose the way I absolutely hate, as if I'm some dummy who can't understand the big man's concepts and I shouldn't worry because he'll do it for me. "My mission is to make the marital bed blissful, not stressful."

What was it they said in the eighties? *Gag me with a spoon?*

He sighs sadly. "It was so much easier when Peaches was alive and could help me," he says. "She would be able to tell at a glance what was missing in a marriage. You know how there are certain doctors who can tell from looking at your irises what vitamins you lack?"

He tilts my head, ostensibly to see my eyes better, but he holds me in a pre-kiss pose that would be electrifying if he and I were two other people.

"Who did you say referred you?" he asks me.

It doesn't seem to be a good idea to tell him that it was Hallie, since Hal is sitting in prison awaiting trial for murdering this man's wife. I wonder if Lynette used him and figure not. And then an idea comes to me. "I'd rather not use her name, since it would be embarrassing for her and damaging to her husband's career, if you know what I mean."

He says he knows *what* I mean and *who* I mean.

"I know her husband was—" I start, but Andy puts his finger against my lips. Drew is going to so love arresting this man if we can nail him on something.

"Let's just call him Peter, shall we? Peter, Peter the Muffin Eater. That's how Peaches' referred to him."

"So he liked—" I say, feeling my cheeks flame.

"Banana-nut muffins," Andy tells me. "Blueberry in the summer."

I swallow hard. "I didn't realize he'd been seeing Peaches for that long."

"Therapy takes time," Andy says, like he's Freud himself. "I told his wife that, and that I could speed up the process for them, but, it was like Peter Peter Muffin Eater said. She really wasn't interested."

"But a friend of Gr…Peter's wife, was," I say, getting back on track. "I met her at a party here a few weeks ago and she had the nicest things to say about you. How gentle you were, and how caring, and how you were putting her marriage back on track."

He's nodding, not at all surprised. "But I don't think I'd like it if my husband was, you know, seeing Peaches," I say.

GRACE SCHULTZ called this morning and invited me to dinner. She and John, she said, are worried about me. They've heard rumors about Drew and I and they just want to help.

Yeah, right.

I discussed going with Drew and he was dead set against it. Only Hal's sentencing is just a couple of days away and we've got nothing concrete to interfere with that.

"I'm going," I told him, fully expecting him to tell me I wasn't.

"At least let's rehearse what you'll say," he said. When, I wondered, will I fully comprehend that he isn't Rio, isn't other men?

So here I am in the Schultz's dining room in Lloyd Harbor. We've had several before-dinner drinks which I've used to water the plants so that I don't make some idiotic mistake. We've made small talk about my ankle and how heroic I was in the face of danger. We talk about my work and how it's going. I tell them about the kitchen I'm redoing for Sydelle Silverberg and how I'm now responsible for feeding Susan Michaels' horses. I tell them confidentially that I'm afraid of the horses, but even more terrified of losing this job.

Grace says she is going to entertain like Sydelle Silverberg after John gets promoted. Unless he becomes a rabbi, I'm thinking not.

John tells me Grace is always putting the cart before the horse. "There's many a slip twixt the cup and the lip," he says, pulling out my chair for me, his hand resting lightly on my shoulder as I take my seat. He leaves it there a moment longer than I'm comfortable with, a moment longer than Grace is comfortable with, if the fact that her somewhat glassy eyes are glued to his hand is any indication.

"John," she says. "For heaven's sake, let the woman alone. Just sit down before dinner goes cold."

He gives my shoulder a little squeeze and takes his seat, places his napkin on his lap, bows his head and says, "Grace." I don't mean that he prays, unless he's praying to his wife. It sounds more like a curse, actually.

Grace steers the conversation as she gestures for me to enjoy the fruit cup in front of me. Dole fruit cocktail, out of the can. Haven't had this since I was a little girl. Just like when I was young, the peaches slide right down.

"Tonight's dinner is going to be very light, I'm afraid," she says. "We're still so full from last night when we dined with Martin Flint. He's prosecuting the Nelson case, I suppose you know. And he's doing very well in the polls. I think this case is going to win him the election. And then we'll see who's putting the cart before the horse. Or maybe you're not following it?"

Those eyebrows of hers reach for the ceiling. I admit I'm following the case avidly, as she must be. "After all, you were with Hallie Nelson that night."

"Were you, dear?" John asks absentmindedly, his eyes on my

cleavage. Good move, I think, wearing the dress Drew begged me not to.

And, excuse me? What kind of investigation has he conducted that he doesn't know Grace was with Hallie that night?

"I've told you I was several times, John dear," she snaps at him. To me she says, "I swear he doesn't hear a word I say. I don't know why I bother talking to him. Why I bother living with him, for that matter." I see the allure of Peaches clearly as John's wife mumbles something to herself about *eye on the prize*.

"Speaking of that night," I say, my spoon raised and pointed at Grace as I glide over her outburst. "You didn't happen to hear anything when you were resting at Hallie's, did you?"

"No, she didn't," John answers abruptly, his memory apparently kicking in suddenly.

"Hear something? Like what?" Grace asks, almost to spite him.

I suggest maybe someone's voice, a door opening or closing. *Hallie leaving?*

She thinks a minute, her brows knit together.

She says she thinks that she did hear a door open and close, now that I mention it. "The front door."

I think. "Maybe she was letting the cat out?"

Hallie doesn't have a cat.

John casts Grace a warning glance. "I wouldn't want Teddi to get the wrong idea," she says. "I'm not saying anyone went out, or anyone came in."

"But she could have," I say. "Hallie could have left the house?"

"We have the right man," John says firmly.

She agrees, reminds him that he always does, reminding me that his record is why he's the Captain as she gets up and refuses my offer of help as she clears the fruit cups and disappears into the kitchen to bring in the next course, which I suspect will be SPAM. In the can.

"But Captain Schultz," I say when we are alone. "There are so many little details that don't seem to fit."

He smiles patronizingly, gives me the *don't worry your little head about it* spiel, asks me to call him John, and is asking about Drew when Grace returns with Boston Market chicken and mashed potatoes.

"I didn't know John had issued you an invitation until a few hours ago," she says as she pulls the lids off the aluminum trays and I mutter something about loving takeout and being touched at their concern for me. Grace takes a swig of wine, a deep swig, while John clears his throat and says he heard that Drew intervened in the trouble with Jesse.

"I'm really lucky that he didn't hold our situation against my son," I say. "And believe me, Jesse has been straightened out." I realize the double entendre as soon as it's out of my mouth. I'm sure I go three shades of red.

The crack goes right over Grace's head, perhaps because she's imbibing again, but John gets it and guffaws. "I thought *that* was the problem," he says, reaching across the table and taking his wife's wineglass under the pretense of refilling it. I notice he doesn't give it back to her.

"I've been assured that his age is the problem," I say. "And this was simply a bid for attention. I'll tell you, it certainly got mine."

Grace's glass seems to have disappeared, and John now busies himself with his chicken before responding. "So how is it that Detective Scoones knew about the arrest, anyway? You didn't call him. I mean, you wouldn't have. Much too awkward, right?"

Oh, I see. This is a fact-finding dinner on both sides. Interesting. Why would the Captain care about what I know? Is the case against Hal not as iron-clad as the Department is making out?

I tell him that my neighbor, Bobbie Lyons, called Drew when she couldn't reach me.

"So then you and the detective haven't actually been in communication?" he asks. He seems to doubt that strongly.

"We've spoken a few times," I say, covering any tracks we may have inadvertently left. "Things he left at the house, tickets we'd bought for events we won't be attending. At least, not together. That sort of thing."

He's nodding slowly, taking it all in.

"He's still very angry with me," I say. "His pride, you know. But I've learned just what kind of man he is in the last few weeks, and I have to say that I'm comfortable with my decision. Very comfortable."

"Of course you are, dear," Grace says, her words just slightly slurred. "Comfort is important. Paramount. But then, there's moral comforts and there's creature comforts, naturally. And you are so very smart to know beforehand what you're getting into. That way you won't find yourself having sold your soul to the devil for creature comforts at the expense of…any other type of comfort."

"For God's sake," John says, throwing down his napkin and standing up. "You're not making any sense at all. If you can't hold your liquor, you shouldn't drink it."

Well, this is embarrassing. I begin to get up awkwardly from the table. "Actually, I really need to be getting home," I say. "With three kids, one of them is always up to something."

They both beg me to stay and I take my seat again. John apologizes for his outburst. He refuses when Grace asks for her wine back, and she sulks while John pours on the charm.

"I take it you have a theory about this murder case," he says, finally getting to the point. "I'm curious to know if you've discussed it with Detective Scoones."

"*Swoons*, dear," Grace corrects. "All the women call him Swoons because, well, he makes us swoon."

"He's certainly making his new partner swoon," John says, watching me for a reaction.

"And she him, from what I've seen of her," I say. "She's a beautiful woman."

"She doesn't hold a candle to you," John says as if Grace isn't even there.

"So my theory," I say, sitting up and presenting myself as businesslike as I can, pretending the man isn't coming on to me, in front of his wife, yet, "is that Hal came home from seeing Peaches Lipschitz and found her gun missing and assumed that Hallie might have done something foolish. He couldn't wake her because of the Valium she'd taken, so he ran to Peaches' house and found her dead, which is when we showed up and found him over the body."

"Interesting," John says.

"Hallie had motive. Her husband was sleeping with Peaches. She had means. It was her gun that killed Peaches. And she had opportunity. Grace heard her leave the house."

"I did," Grace says. "I heard a car, too. A car door."

John ignores Grace. "Interesting," John says again. "Why not the simple answer, though? Hal was caught red-handed at the scene, the murder weapon was as available to him as to his wife, and his wife had just found out about his mistress. He went to tell her it was over between them and she threatened exposure. He lost his temper—"

"And shot her in the back? No signs of violence? No shaking her, hitting her, trying to get her to be reasonable? And he threw the gun in the sewer and then came back inside the house?"

"You have some points," John says, staring at my breasts. "I'll give you that. But, on the other hand, we have a confession."

I point out that the reason for Hal's confession is his desire to protect his wife.

John is thoughtful for a minute or two. "And what if Hallie's suicide attempt was actually an attempt to prove her mentally unstable enough to plead not guilty by reason of insanity, or for her to be unable to stand trial under diminished capacity?"

I find it hard to believe that these ideas haven't occurred to him before. It's as if he's wanted me to come up with them. Which would fit with my getting away with the search of Hallie's house, now wouldn't it? Do I ask him that, straight out?

I excuse myself to use the restroom and take my purse with me. Once in their guest bathroom, I dial up Drew and explain the situation to him.

"It's too neat, too easy, too obvious," Drew says. "I just can't figure out his angle."

"Why have me show up the Department again? Why make me the heroine? It doesn't make sense," I say.

"Unless we're wrong and this will discredit both of us," Drew says.

I ask if he believes they have some damaging evidence we don't know about. "I'm missing something, Drew. Something big. Something staring me in the face."

"We'll figure it out," he says. "Come on home, Cookie. I think you've gotten all you're gonna get."

"Cookie?" He's called me lots of names, but I think I even prefer *reckless* and *scatterbrained* to *Cookie*.

He tells me it's short for Smart Cookie.

Maybe it's not so bad, after all.

John's waiting for me when I emerge from the bathroom. I don't know what he's overheard, but he has my coat ready for me. He tells me that Grace isn't feeling very well. He cops a free feel as he helps me slip into the coat.

"Sorry," he says into my hair, mumbling something about how Grace is always complaining about his clumsiness.

"It's a shame she makes you feel like that," I say without turning around. I summon all the brazenness I have, which isn't much, and say quietly that some women don't know how lucky they are. "If I had a man like you, I'd be sure he knew he was the king of my castle."

I feel him freeze behind me and I can't help but wonder if I've gone too far. Does he know I know he was a client of Peaches?

I take a deep breath and wait. I mean really, what else can I do?

Well, I can skedaddle, so when he offers to walk me to my car, I decline, telling him it's much too cold and totally unnecessary.

But I feel his lips against the back of my head as I reach for the knob and hurriedly limp out the door.

CHAPTER 21

Accessibility is something healthy, able-bodied people rarely consider when decorating their homes. A ramp can be so much more welcoming than steps at the front of your house to those that have difficulty. And should you sprain your ankle one day, you'll appreciate it, too.

TipsFromTeddi.com

"You told him what?" Drew shouts at me over the Bat Phone.

"I have a plan, I have a plan," I repeat calmly.

He demands to know what it is. I wish I knew.

"Hallie took a cab to the mall," I say, ignoring the plan I don't have. "But according to the dispatcher she was never picked up there. How'd she get home, Drew?"

He asks if I think Hal picked her up, if I think they were somehow in it together.

I admit that I don't think that either of them did it.

"But you said—" Drew starts.

"The Valium!" I shout. "That's what was bothering me. She'd never have taken the Valium that night. She said she didn't even drink that night on the chance that she was pregnant."

"So you're saying that Hal is protecting her and she isn't even guilty. Like Dana," he adds.

I repeat my suspicion that I was being set up tonight to accuse and convict Hallie. We just can't figure out why.

"Okay, I know that the Captain has an interest in seeing Flint get reelected. His own position probably depends on it. If I publicly accuse Hallie and am wrong, the Captain comes off looking twice as smart, right?"

Drew chuckles. He thinks I may be overestimating my prowess. I agree that I am, but that the newspapers love making me seem smarter than the police. "Here's his chance to turn the tables."

"Let's say I buy all this," Drew says, meaning, naturally, that he doesn't. "You think that his case against Hal is so strong that it'll blow the one against Hallie out of the water?"

"No," I say. "I don't think Hal did it, and I don't think the Captain does, either."

Drew wants to know who it is I suspect. I ask who had anything to gain by her death. Who benefitted?

"Mr. Lipschitz?" Drew proposes. "Why kill the Golden Goose?"

I say that the Golden Goose wasn't getting any younger, that no man likes the idea of his wife sleeping around even if it keeps them in the black, that their children were getting old enough to put two and two together, that the insurance policy was for a good sum of money.

Drew wants to know what makes me think Andy minded

his wife's business endeavors, the kids were on to her or any other of my suppositions. He gives me the insurance, though. "Do you have a shred of evidence on any of this?" he asks me like the detective he is.

I admit I don't. But I intend to.

THE FOLLOWING afternoon I meet Andy at the Inn Between again. He's eager to meet me since I've kind of implied that I'd like to perhaps try some therapy of a…*therapeutic* nature.

"I don't know how you can think of others at such a difficult time," I tell him, sipping my wine as if I'm nervous about our meeting. Oh, wait. I *am* nervous about our meeting. First off, this man could be a killer—a shooter-in-the-backer of his own wife. Or he could be innocent of that and just a gigolo. Is that what they call men who make love to women for money? Or, in his case, would *con artist* do?

He tells me it helps to keep his mind off his own troubles. "There's nothing that gets you out of the dumps faster," he tells me, "than helping someone else."

I ask after his children.

"Thank God they are really too young to understand all this," he says. "We've been able to shelter them. I'm even thinking about moving away and changing our name so that when they grow up they won't know what was said about their mother."

Put a check next to the children getting old enough to put two and two together.

"We?" pops out of my mouth without my even processing it.

"Lorelei," he says, almost reverentially. "My sister-in-law. Peaches' younger sister. She's been a godsend with the children."

His nostrils flare when I ask if Lorelei was part of the therapy business. Oh goody. So he did think his wife was a slut (check off #2, old goose, and #3, slut wife, on the list), and as soon as he has the insurance money, he won't need her income anymore.

I've about got the case sewn up when I notice a cab pull up outside with Woodbury Cab Company printed on the side. The missing cab ride could surely have been in another company's cab. Why didn't I think of that?

I scribble down the number while Andy tells me what therapy costs.

"I think we can fix your problem more quickly if I see you more often," he says, making me wonder when the insurance money is due to come through. "Say three times a week?"

"Only three?" I say, since I have no intention of even once, why not make him feel inadequate? "Are you…unable…?"

He reminds me I'm not the only client he has. "But I can understand why you and your husband are experiencing difficulties," he says, taking my hand. "And I sympathize. I can cure you, but this therapy is extremely expensive."

"Really?" I say, feeling sorry for the little Lipschitzes who will have no mother and a father rotting in jail.

My cell phone rings and I see it's Drew. "My husband," I explain to Andy. "I better take this." I promise to be right back and leave the restaurant, picking up the stack of taxi cab cards as I limp out, noticing that there are several different companies in the pile.

I tell Drew everything I've found out. He tells me that the Captain has sent two detectives to talk to Hallie at the hospital. And they have a warrant for her arrest.

"She didn't do it," I tell him.

"I know that," he agrees. "I've called a lawyer and he's going to meet me there. In the meantime, I'm going down there to make sure she doesn't agree to anything she shouldn't."

I ask him what I should do about Andy. He tells me to ditch the guy and get home. "Tomorrow's another day, Scarlett," he says.

"You've been watching movies while we haven't been seeing each other, haven't you?" I ask him.

"Be glad *Debbie Does Dallas* was already rented," he says and tells me he's got to go.

"Will they release Hal if they arrest Hallie?" I ask.

"Not if they think they were in it together," he tells me before saying goodbye.

I'M ON MY WAY to Susan Michaels' place to feed her "boys," feeling as though I ought to do something to get Hallie out of the mess I've gotten her into. It was never my intention to clear Hal by indicting her. I just don't know what I can do about it now.

I pull over onto a side road, dial the precinct and ask to speak to Captain Schultz.

"Teddi," he booms happily into the phone. "How nice to hear from you. And your timing is wonderful." He proceeds to tell me that following up on my good work, he's gotten a warrant for Hallie's arrest.

"I really think I'm wrong about that," I say and I explain about how Hallie would never have taken Valium if there was a possibility she was pregnant.

"There were the remnants of one of those pregnancy tests found in her bathroom garbage," he tells me. He's never going to believe that it was inconclusive. But I've been there and I've held on to hope (okay, hoping that I wasn't pregnant, but it's the same thing, isn't it?). And I'm convinced that Hallie told me the truth.

"And then there's the taxi to the mall," I say. "An enraged woman, furious over her husband's infidelity, disappointed at not being pregnant, reaches for a gun she's never used and is afraid of and goes to the mall? Don't you see something wrong in that?"

John tells me she was covering her tracks. That enraged wives plot out their revenge carefully, over months, and then set up perfect alibis in the hopes of getting away with the crime. "And she'd been drinking," he adds.

There's no point in telling him that she says she wasn't. I asked Lynette and she said she hadn't noticed, that Hallie tended to be discreet about her situation.

"Look, where are you now?" John asks. "I hear traffic."

"Not much," I say. "I'm on my way to feed those horses at my client's house."

"I'll meet you there," he says. "I'm an old hand at horses and I know you're afraid. And we'll talk. I have some information about Hallie you aren't aware of. It'll make you feel better, I promise."

I agree, happy for the help, and give him the address. I try to reach Drew, but he must already be at the hospital because I get his voice mail. I leave him a brief message about our not having all the facts and that I'm off to feed the horses.

I'd feel much better if I could talk to him. I pull into Susan's driveway and see that the painters are gone. I actually think it will get done on schedule, and that Susan will be so grateful that I saved her artwork and fed her "boys" that maybe I'll even get a bonus.

I check my messages at home. Sydelle's okayed all my suggestions and she'd like me to get started ASAP. She's planning a party at her house in six weeks. Will I be done by then?

Is she kidding?

My mother's message is next. I know because there is just heavy breathing, signaling that she isn't talking to me. Finally, my father's voice says I should take care and be well and he hopes Drew and I will be very happy. I get the sense he won't be allowed to talk to me for a while.

Can't worry about it now. Right this moment my job is to figure out how I can prove that Hallie wasn't involved in Peaches' demise.

If I could find the cab company that took her home from the mall, that would take her out of the picture and put the focus back on smarmy Andy. With no sign of the Captain, I pull out the business cards and punch in the numbers. The first two companies have no record of anyone being picked up at the mall and being taken to Hallie's house. The third has a pickup at the mall at around the right time, but the fare was to New Hyde Park, not Hallie's house.

Oh, shit.

"Hello?" the dispatcher says. "Is that what you're looking for?"

"Robby Lane?" I ask. "Is that where the cab went to?"

Of course it is.

"And don't tell me—there was a pickup there back to Hicksville?"

Damn, damn, damn, damn, damn.

There's got to be another answer. Hallie would not have taken the Valium, I know it. Was she just pretending to be so soundly asleep? Could Hal have slipped her the pills? Could Grace have?

Oh, NEVER ASSUME. John was seeing Peaches, too. Grace goes home with Hallie, slips her the Valium, takes the gun, which she knows about, takes the cab to the mall, takes a different cab company to Peaches' place, kills her, leaves Hallie's gun where it's bound to be found, cabs back to Hallie's and then uses the old cab company to go home.

"Can I get that driver's number?" I ask and am given the same party line about drivers not taking calls while on duty. She promises to have the driver call me. That will have to do.

I've got it all worked out, I think, and I throw the car into Reverse to get the hell out of there, only to find John's car coming up behind me in the driveway, blocking my exit.

Think! I order myself. *Stay calm and think.* He might not even know Grace did it.

He gets out of his car and walks toward mine, taking in his surroundings the way I notice Drew always does. I guess a cop is always on duty.

He opens my door for me and offers his hand to help me out.

"I wonder if you could move your car," I say, not taking his hand. "One of the kids just called and I really need to get home."

Hey, it sounds good to me.

He shakes his head. "Come on, we'll talk while we feed the horses. It'll only take a minute. I'd really like to know why you're so sure suddenly it's not Hallie when you were so sure the other night that it was."

"I was probably right the first time," I say as I take his hand and get out of my car. "I should always go with my instincts."

Yeah, and my instincts are shouting to get the hell out of here. How fast can I run on a sprained ankle while a man with a gun chases after me? Faster than a speeding bullet? I think not.

Didn't Drew tell me I wasn't Supergirl?

"So, I thought it was Andy Lipschitz," I say as we walk toward the barn. "But I just learned that Hallie took a cab from the mall to Peaches' place that night, so that does it. Case closed."

"The Valium doesn't bother you anymore?" he asks.

I tell him, "Nope, nope, it doesn't." I'm having some trouble keeping my balance on the slippery path to the barn, and John has an arm around me, helping me maneuver—and helping himself to the outside of my left breast.

"You're a beautiful woman," he says. *And you're blind.* My nose is red and running, I'm wearing an old ski jacket that's ripped under the arm, my hair hasn't been washed since I hurt my ankle and any makeup I started the day with has been rubbed off in an attempt to catch said runny nose.

"Thank you," I say, snuggling closer because I'm not above using any damn trick in the book to survive. "You're pretty easy on the eyes yourself."

"What about Scoones?" he asks. "Your fiancé?"

I start to deny it, but John says he's no fool. He knows we're engaged, knows why we were pretending, even admires Drew for sticking by his partner.

"What stymies me," he says, openly fondling my breast, "is why you're coming on to me. Why you're allowing me to touch you like this."

I try to pull away, but he doesn't allow it.

"You're afraid of me," he says.

"You're Drew's boss," I offer lamely, like I'd let him touch me because of that.

"Your phone's ringing," he says.

I hadn't even heard it over the pounding of my heart. "Probably the kids again," I say cheerily. "I really should be—"

"Answer it," he says in a tone I can't argue with as he pulls me into the barn where Zorro bares his teeth and whinnies loudly at the sight of me, like he thinks I'm lunch.

I dig in my purse slowly, hoping it will stop ringing, but he yanks on my arm impatiently. I find it and pull it out.

The readout says Northside Cab Co. We both see it. I open the phone.

"Hello?"

The dispatcher says she's patching me through before I can tell her I've already got the information and it isn't necessary.

"Yeah," a woman's voice says. "I took the mall fare to New Hyde Park. Whaddya wanna know?"

"I don't suppose you remember anything about her…or him, do you?" I say. *Please don't, please don't, please don't,* I think while Tonto shuffles in his stall.

"Like I told the police," she says, "middle-aged woman, early fifties, maybe. Blond. Uppity type—"

John takes my phone from my hand and closes it.

"You just couldn't leave well enough alone, could you?" he asks, backing me up against Zorro's stall. I'm still terrified of horses, despite having fulfilled my promise to Susan and taken them carrots and sugar cubes and tried to make friends.

I try my patented babbling routine, which I'm hoping will distract him from hearing Drew, should the man decide to make an appearance while I'm still alive. I'm rambling about how there's no evidence against anyone but Hallie, and how it's possible that she and Hal were in cahoots and I start on my theory about how she and Andy were fooling around, too, and maybe they killed Peaches to get her out of the way so that they could be together.

"Andy was doing Hallie?" he says. "While Nelson was sticking it to his wife?"

I sense some prurient interest here and since I think there are now two stiff instruments in John's pants, and only one is a gun, I decide to run with it. "They actually had a foursome planned," I say and let my jacket slip off my shoulder.

"You are a beautiful woman," he says again, reaching out with one hand to touch my cheek while the other reaches behind him and I shut my eyes, thinking this is the last moment of my life, he's going to take a gun from his waistband and waste me.

Only instead of a boom, I hear a metallic click and open my eyes to find one of my wrists now handcuffed. I think he's looking around for what to attach it to when he fingers a riding crop and flexes it. Great. I'm not only going to die, but I am going to get beaten and screwed first.

Seductively, I lean back against the paddock as though I can't wait for him to ravage me. Behind me, I undo the latch on Zorro's stall while I open my top button. If he buys this, I'm going to offer him beachfront property in Arizona when we're done.

If I'm still alive.

I tell him there's this fantasy women have… Everyone knows about it… Doing it with a horse. Is he as big as a horse? I look at his trousers and confirm that he is. I think about the fact that he was a Peaches regular.

"You're a king," I say as I sidle my way to the next stall, undo Tonto's latch and another button. "And your wish is my command."

It's demeaning, it's pathetic, but I simply don't want to die, and if I can just babble long enough, or just get my hands on his weapon—the real one—maybe I'll live to tell this story at my wedding.

He pulls the gun out of his belt and tells me to put the handcuffs on myself. I think, *maybe not*.

I try babbling again, but he raises the gun butt like he's going to whack me with it.

CHAPTER 22

*An intercom system can be a godsend if you live in a big house
or have outbuildings.*

TipsFromTeddi.com

I shriek, not from pain, because he hasn't made contact yet,
but from sheer terror.

I don't know if it's my shout, my peril, or just because he
can, but Zorro, who has been snorting and pawing the ground,
appears to have had it with John Schultz. The mighty horse
pushes his way out of the stall, which gives me a moment to
hide myself in the back of Tonto's stall, putting the huge animal
between myself and John. Whether this will be a smart move
remains to be seen, as Tonto is not happy to see me without
my carrots. Putting my fingers to my lips to quiet him doesn't
help. My only option, when John sees me, is to smack the
horse's hind quarter as hard as I can with the nearest object, a
leather strap.

Furious, Tonto lunges from the gate, smacks into John, and
knocks him off his feet. There is the loud crack of John's gun
and the crash of the chandelier as it is freed from its chain and
careens to the barn floor.

John is underneath it.

I'm not sure if he's dead.

A better woman would do more than scream her bloody head off, but with two loose horses knocking into the walls, the stalls, the feed bins, rearing, snorting, it's all I can do to shut the gate of Tonto's stall and flatten myself to the wall inside it. And scream.

After an eternity, which Drew swears couldn't have been more than two minutes since I still had enough voice left to scream at him, Detective Drew Scoones crashes open the barn door and herds the horses out.

I wish I could say I saunter out from the stall, dust off my hands and present the accomplice-after-the-fact, but I don't. I cower there until Drew says that John isn't dead, just unconscious, and that he's coming to.

DREW DOES THE press release, explaining how Hal's confession was coerced by circumstances that they are choosing not to release for security reasons (which sounds so much better than that he thought his wife did it and he deserved to be the one punished). And that the real murderer of Peaches Lipschitz was Grace Schultz, wife of Captain John Schultz, who was a client of Peaches'. Grace was apparently afraid that if Peaches was arrested, as she was about to be, she might name names. John Schultz, who was arrested as an accessory after the fact, evidently felt that in addition to getting rid of Peaches, he could "nail a dirty cop who was cheating on his wife" for the crime, thus assuring the election of his friend, Martin Flint, and the continuation of his position as Captain of the precinct.

Drew credits the help of citizens, noting, especially, "Teddi Bayer, who has helped the police several times before and who is about to join the force in an 'auxiliary capacity'—as Detective Andrew Scoones' wife."

Sometimes the best thing you can do to get a fresh eye is to steal away for a little R & R… Which is what I'm doing. I'll be back with more tips, but for now, Happy Decorating!
                                                    TipsFromTeddi.com

"Ready?" Drew asks me two weeks later as we're about to leave the house for the last time as single people. The suitcases for our honeymoon trip to the Bahamas are already in the back of his car. "Got everything?"

"I think so." It's not like we aren't coming back here for the reception, but Drew keeps imagining hitches that prevent us from getting to the judge's chambers, and to the airport after that.

He glances at his watch. "We're running late, Cookie," he says, holding my coat for me.

"*Cookie? As in Smart Cookie?* What have I figured out now?" I ask, slipping my winter-white-silk-suited arms into my coat.

"You're marrying me, aren't you?" he asks, turning me in his arms and kissing me.

I pick up the flowers that Bobbie has left for me on the hall table. She is bringing the kids to the courthouse, and Hal and

Hallie will be waiting there. My mother, after threatening not to come, is showing up after all. She says she plans to trip Drew as he's coming down the aisle.

Drew tucks me into the car, reaches in and does my seat belt for me since I'm holding my bouquet, and steals another kiss. "Soon I'll only be allowed to kiss my wife," he tells me. "And everyone knows how sexy divorcées are."

I tell him to get in the car and I switch on his police scanner once he's started the engine.

He switches it off.

I switch it back on.

"Teddi," he warns.

I tell him we have to know which streets to avoid, but he's on to me.

"Nothing is going to interfere with this wedding, Ted."

I agree. I'm ready. I'm sure. I've got Drew's diamond on my finger and his name on my heart as he pulls out of my driveway and nearly hits Rio's truck.

"What the—" Drew starts.

"Go around it," I tell him, watching Rio leap from his truck in a tuxedo, a dozen yellow roses in his hand. "Or better still, hit him."

Drew throws the car into Park and lowers my window. Rio drops to his knees beside my door. I glance at Drew, who tries not to smirk, but doesn't quite succeed.

"I made a mistake, Teddi, but I've learned my lesson. I want you back."

Now *I'm* trying not to smirk as I tell him, "I made a mistake marrying you. You made a mistake trying to drive me crazy. I made a mistake not prosecuting you. You made a mistake having an affair with Marion. I made a mistake insisting you marry Marion. You made a mistake trying to sell nude pictures of me to a girly magazine. We aren't good for each other, Rio. We made good kids, but those years are behind us. Go away."

"What do you want this guy for?" he says, gesturing toward Drew. "He's gonna get killed and you'll be a widow and you'll be sorry you didn't choose me 'cause I'll still be alive."

Well, that cut to the bone. "Not if you don't get out of the way and we run you over," I warn him.

I raise my window and Drew puts the car in gear. "Now we're really late," he says. "How did you ever marry that guy?"

I have this horrible premonition, years down the line, of someone asking the same question about Drew.

Ridiculous.

Never.

I mean, except my mother. She'll ask it tomorrow, if she's speaking to me.

"You're making a big mistake," Rio shouts, pounding on the back window of the car where Jesse has written "Just Marred" in white paint and Dana has tried unsuccessfully to add an "I" with Wite-Out. "A huge mistake!"

I open my window and stick my head out, ruining the hairdo it took Bobbie nearly an hour to perfect. "That'll make us even," I shout into the wind.

When I pull my head back in, I see Drew's knuckles turning white around the steering wheel.

"Not that I agree with him," I say. "I mean, I don't think

this is a—" We're stopped at the light which has turned green and red again without the car in front of us moving.

Drew honks his horn. The driver doesn't respond.

Drew honks again. Still no response. He maneuvers around the car and pulls even with it. The driver's head is lolled back, his mouth open. I start to open my door.

"Don't you dare," Drew says. "I'll take care of it. The guy's probably asleep."

"Or dead," I mumble under my breath as Drew gets out of the car.

Drew knocks on the man's window. Nothing. He opens the door and the man falls halfway out.

I see Drew's shoulders slump, watch as he removes his gloves and touches the man's carotid artery. He shakes his head at me.

I come out of the car and hand him his cell phone to call it in. As he takes it, he tells me to get back into the car. "It's cold and you only have stockings on. Go."

What he really means is, "Don't stick your nose in here, Teddi. Don't start sniffing around and *detecting*."

I walk to the back of the man's car. As I do, a police cruiser pulls up and Drew crosses to it, filling the officers in.

"We got it," the patrolman says. "Don't you two have a wedding to get to?"

"Drew, look at this," I say, calling him to the back of the car.

"No," he tells me. "Get in the car. The man had a heart attack. Simple as that. Let's go, Teddi."

"But look," I say, pointing to the exhaust pipe where a rag is hanging. "I think this pipe was stuffed up."

"Teddi, a car won't run if the muffler is stuffed. Get in the car."

I suggest it was partially stuffed, just enough to cause carbon monoxide to build up…

"In a closed environment," he says. "Doesn't work in the open air."

"And yet—" I start, as he all but carries me to the car. "We're just gonna leave?" I ask, shocked. "There's a dead man, a possible murder—"

He puts the car in gear.

"We're not even going to point out the rag in the pipe?"

He guns the engine and we burn rubber as we take off. "You trying to make us late?" he asks, throwing a glance my way.

I ask how I could possibly do that. I didn't kill the man in the car in front of us. "But someone did, I'll bet you," I say.

"Do you want me to turn around?" he asks me. "Because if I do, the wedding is off. The whole marriage thing, the honeymoon, everything but the sneakers for Jesse."

It's the sneakers that get me. "Drive," I say. "To the court-house."

I figure I can call the police from the bathroom there.

Really, Drew need never know.

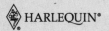

HARLEQUIN®

INTRIGUE®

BREATHTAKING ROMANTIC SUSPENSE

Look for

UNDER HIS SKIN

BY RITA HERRON

Nurse Grace Gardener brought
Detective Parker Kilpatrick back from
the brink of death, only to seek his
protection. On a collision course with
two killers who want to keep their
secrets, she's recruited the one detective
with the brass to stop them.

Available February wherever you buy books.

BECAUSE THE BEST PART
OF A GREAT ROMANCE
IS THE MYSTERY.

www.eHarlequin.com   HI69310

Inside ROMANCE

Stay up-to-date on all your romance reading news!

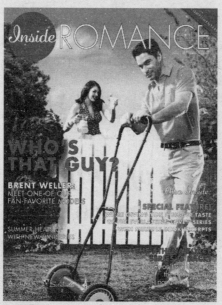

Inside Romance is a FREE quarterly newsletter highlighting our upcoming series releases and promotions.

Visit

www.eHarlequin.com/InsideRomance

to sign up to receive our complimentary newsletter today!

IRNJ07

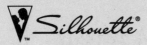

Silhouette®

Romantic
SUSPENSE

**Sparked by Danger,
Fueled by Passion.**

When Tech Sergeant Jacob "Mako" Stone opens
his door to a mysterious woman without a past,
he knows his time off is over. As threats to Dee's
life bring her and Jacob together, she must set
aside her pride and accept the help of the military
hero with too many secrets of his own.

Out of Uniform
by Catherine Mann

Available February wherever you buy books.

Texas Hold 'Em

When it comes to love, the stakes are high

Sixteen years ago, Luke Chisum dated
Becky Parker on a dare...before going
on to break her heart. Now the former
River Bluff daredevil is back, rekindling
desire and tempting Becky to pick up
where they left off. But this time she has
to resist or Luke could discover the secret
she's kept locked away all these years....

Look for

TEXAS BLUFF

by *Linda Warren*

#1470

Available February 2008
wherever you buy books.

www.eHarlequin.com

HSR71470

Silhouette®
Desire

NEW YORK TIMES BESTSELLING AUTHOR

DIANA PALMER

A brand-new Long, Tall Texans novel
IRON COWBOY

*Available March 2008
wherever you buy books.*

Visit Silhouette Books at www.eHarlequin.com SD76856IBC